Tennessee Peaches

By Kelly Killian

~ This book is dedicated to my husband, Brian, who put the Tennessee in my peaches. ~

Also available by this author:

The Jessica Summer Series –

Love, Emily – A Love Story from the Files of Jessica Summer

Love, Rachel – A Love Story from the Files of Jessica Summer

Love, Amber – A Christmas Love Story from the Files of Jessica Summer

Love, Lauren – A Love Story from the Files of Jessica Summer

Chapter 1

Mila stepped out of the pub and into the streets of London. She had just spent the evening celebrating with her friends despite the fact that she wasn't exactly feeling festive. She knew she should be happy – excited even – to go home and spend time with her family in Tennessee. She was sure those feelings would come eventually, but it didn't make her feel any better about leaving. And it didn't make her feel any better about Gabe.

Gabe. Her heart did a tumble. For the past five hours, she had been trying to push down the definitive ache in her chest. Gabe knew they were spending the evening at Trolley's. He knew that after tonight, he wouldn't see her for six weeks. And now it was obvious that he just didn't care.

And if he didn't care, she wasn't going to care, either. It might take her a while to figure out how to do that, be she would find a way.

Ignoring the empty feeling inside of her, she stood on the sidewalk and hailed a cab. It was a cold night in January, snow pushed aside from the storm that had come through earlier in the week. The familiar hustle of the city she had grown to love surrounded her: a playful group of lads who were hardly dressed for the weather throwing snowballs at each other; a proper-looking man escorting his love down the sidewalk; three young girls giggling as they passed by a handsome businessman; that London accent she first fell in love with as a little girl when her friend's cousin came to visit from England. Mila sighed. She was going to miss this.

A cab stopped for her, and she took one last look around, then reached for the handle, opened the door and slid inside.

"Where to, Love?"

"The 300 block of Portobello Road," Mila said quietly, fiddling with her phone in an attempt to signal that she was in no mood to talk. Two things she had learned about cabbies in the time she lived in London: they go through years of extensive training to learn every street in the complex city and the best way to get there and, well, they liked to talk.

"Right." He looked at her in his rearview mirror. "Beautiful night, isn't it?"

Mila forced some semblance of a smile. "I suppose it is."

She stared blankly out the window as she thought about her upcoming trip. In the two years since she had moved to London, this was the first time she was returning home. She had never intended for it to take so long, but life had quickly become a whirlwind with her job and her new friends and living in the city. She had meant to come home for Christmas. But when her best friend, Isabel, announced that she was getting married in January and she wanted Mila to be her maid of honor, everything seemed to fall into place. She would be home for the wedding, but it also worked out that she was between contracts at the advertising agency, so she was able to take an extended holiday.

She barely paid attention to the small talk the cabbie made the whole way to her flat. When they reached Portobello Road, she wished him a good night, paid her fare and stepped out into the snow-lined sidewalk that led to her apartment complex. She walked slowly to the front door of the building, then dashed up the stairs to the second floor.

She hesitated at the landing. She was not going to so much as look in the direction of Gabe's door across the hallway from hers. She would enter the hallway, walk straight into her flat and find a way to leave her feelings for him behind. Drawing a deep breath,

2

she pulled the door open. And there he was, sitting on the floor outside the door of his flat, his back against the wall and his knees bent in front of him.

His eyes met hers.

"What are you doing?" she asked, rather annoyed to think she was about to learn that he had spent the evening locked out of his flat and waiting for someone to bring him a key rather than joining them at Trolley's.

"Waiting to see you."

"I was at Trolley's," she snapped. "You know that."

He nodded, and then he stood. "I suppose I did know that. But I didn't want to see you at Trolley's. I waited for you all night so I could see you here instead." He gestured to the pile of magazines on the floor next to him that she hadn't noticed until now. "Also, I can tell you anything you want to know from the last three months' worth of *ShortList, Time Out* or *Saga.*"

Mila pulled a face. "*Saga*?"

He shrugged. "My grandfather's been giving me copies of that magazine for years. I don't think he fully understands that I take no interest in a publication meant for senior citizens. Anyway, it helped me pass the time." He cocked his head. "I know it's getting late. But I needed to see you before you left. Do you have a few moments to spare?"

Of course she did. He knew she would. Even though she never admitted it, he knew how she felt about him. "Well, you waited this long. I suppose I can spare a little bit of time."

He grinned and turned to pick up the stack of magazines, pushing his door open and standing aside so she could come through. On her way past him, she took a closer glance. There had to have been ten magazines in his arms. "How long were you planning on sitting out there reading literature for geriatrics?"

"As long as it took to see you." He pushed the door closed.

She turned to him. "You could have called."

"I didn't want to spoil your evening."

She wanted to tell him that he *did* spoil her evening by not showing up, but she sensed that something important was about to happen, so she didn't want to waste time squabbling about that. "So, what is it, Gabe? What did you need to see me about?"

"I just…I'm going to miss you is all."

3

Her eyes narrowed. "Then why didn't you come to the pub?" She shook her head, anger beginning to take hold. It had been almost two years since she had developed feelings for him, and in that time all she ever did was hope that someday he would see what she saw. It was stupid. She should have said something to him a long time ago, taken the situation head-on like she did everything else in life.

"You know what, Gabe? You don't have to answer that. I just spent an entire evening watching the door of the pub hoping that every time it opened, I would see your face. But you didn't show up. Instead, you sat in the hallway reading magazines. You could have been with me. It makes no sense at all."

"I know. I should have come." He looked to the ground, kicking his foot against the floor. "I'm really bad at this." His eyes met hers again. "Mila, I don't know why it took you leaving to make me realize this, but I think I'm in love with you."

Her jaw dropped, and for a moment she stood in stunned silence. "You think?" she finally asked quietly. "Or you know?"

He took a step closer. "I know I don't want you to leave. And I know I keep smiling every time I think about your American accent and the sound of your laughter." He reached up and touched her hair. "And I know that I just spent two hours sitting in the hallway waiting for you to come home so I could talk to you." He inched forward. "And I know that more than anything, I want to kiss you."

Mila stood dumbfounded as he bent his head and kissed her. Too shocked to immediately kiss him back, she just stood there, looking into his big brown eyes when he pulled back for just a moment before he kissed her again. The second time, she responded.

It felt poetic somehow, being with him like this. It was the kind of kiss that made her want to call off her upcoming trip and spend the next six weeks holed up with him in his flat instead. Not that it was an option. But for a moment, nothing in the world seemed to matter except for her and Gabe.

He pulled away again, ever so slightly, and looked into her eyes. She returned his gaze, her eyes intense.

"I know my timing is about as bad as it gets," he said, regret etched in his voice. "I know it's late and you can't stay, but I'll be

4

here when you get back. And Mila, I can't wait until you get back." His hand was on her cheek as he leaned in and kissed her again.

When he pulled away and looked into those soulful eyes, he couldn't fathom for the life of him how it was that he had never before seen what he saw in her now.

"Gabe," she whispered, her hands in his hair and those luscious lips falling against his cheek.

He nodded. "I know. You have to go." He reached out to take her hand, then walked her across the hallway to the door of her flat.

She opened her door and turned to face him again.

"I'll be thinking of you every second." He gripped the collar of her coat, his forehead touching hers.

She touched his face, and he bent his neck and kissed her again. He would have kissed her all night long if he thought she would let him.

Finally, she broke the kiss. Slowly, he let go of her coat collar and took a step back. "I'm going to miss you so much," he breathed. "I hope you have a great time in America."

She nodded, catching her breath, thinking about all the reasons that she couldn't prolong the night with him for one more second. And she realized there were none.

"Gabe," she called as he began crossing the hallway to go back to his flat. She leapt into his arms and kissed him with all the excitement she felt as everything he said finally started to sink in. Never breaking the kiss, she pulled him by the shirt back across the hallway and into her flat, closing the door behind them.

Chapter 2

It had been two years since she had ridden in a beat-up old pick-up truck on the streets of Honeybee with her brother Colt. She never quite understood the affinity for trucks every boy in this town seemed to share, but Colt seemed quite at home behind the wheel. The landscape of the town was different, yet the same. New buildings had cropped up here and there, but the streets remained familiar.

As they turned down the road that led to their childhood home, several layers of the disappointment of missing Gabe seemed to fade away, replaced by a genuine excitement to see her family again.

"Listen, Mila," Colt said in a tone that made her feel wary. "There's something you should know before we get there."

She sat up straighter, turning to look at him. "What?"

"Mom and Dad...they were having a time a little while back."

"A time? What's that supposed to mean?"

He glanced at her. "They weren't getting along very well. They almost split."

"What?" she asked, a combination of fury and panic rising in her chest. "When? Why are you just telling me this now?"

6

He shrugged, focusing his attention back on the road. "*I* didn't even know until Dad showed up at my house one night and said he needed a place to stay for a little while. No one knows about it except for me and them and Luke."

"You told your best friend, but you didn't tell your sister?" She studied him and waited for an answer, but Colt didn't appear very apologetic. "Are they doing OK now?"

"I think so, but I don't know for sure." He glanced at her. "Don't go making a big deal about this, either. I just wanted you to know. You don't have to try and fix it."

"Why didn't you tell me about this sooner? You should have told me when it was happening."

"All right." If he was agreeing that he was wrong in any way, she would never know it due to his decidedly self-assured ways. "I knew they were bickering a lot, but who doesn't bicker after 35 years of marriage? You know Dad, he doesn't say much about anything. He was spending all his time at work or in the bowling league, and they started growing apart. When she asked him to spend more time with her, he didn't want to give in to her demands and the whole thing just blew up."

"I hardly think Mom was being demanding."

"Yeah, well, he's not one to take suggestions very well."

"So what happened?"

"He came to my place, and we had it out a few times and he decided to go back home and try to make it work. So that's what they're doing. I'm sure neither one of them will let on about anything, and I've been keeping an eye on it. I think it's OK. I just don't *know* that it is."

She was still trying to wrap her head around it when they pulled into the driveway.

"Here we are," Colt said, breaking into her thoughts. "Home, sweet home."

He shut off the engine and walked to the back of the truck to retrieve her luggage as Mila stepped out onto the sidewalk. "What do you need two full-size suitcases and a carry-on for anyway?" Colt asked, setting her luggage down.

Mila gave him a look. "I need outfits. I need options. Shoes, boots, hats, coats, layers. Accessories. Things you would never even begin to understand."

Actually, he understood all too well. Dating a model for the past few years had taught him everything he needed to know about a woman's need to have options and accessories. But before he could make a valid point about it, he heard his mother calling from the front porch.

"Mila!" Colt picked up the carry-on bag and pulled the other two suitcases behind him down the sidewalk while Mila ran in front of him to give their mom and dad a hug. He had to admit it was good to have most of the family back together like this. He watched as his mother fussed over Mila's appearance – how beautiful she was, how long her hair had grown – and then as his dad pulled her into a protective hug. He'd never before thought about what it must have been like from a father's perspective, watching his daughter move thousands of miles away to a foreign land. The only real experience his dad had with foreign land involved wartime activities, so he guessed his impression of Mila's travels wasn't exactly favorable.

But John had never been as vocal about things as Mary Beth was. Mary Beth had clearly not wanted Mila to leave but after the initial protest had decided there was nothing to do to make her stay, so she offered Mila her full support. When she thought of it as an adventure that would someday come to an end with her daughter returning home, it really wasn't so bad.

Stepping inside the house she grew up in for the first time in two years, Mila recognized the familiarity in the depths of her soul. Oddly it didn't feel like home anymore. Just familiar, from the smell of baking bread in the kitchen to the collages of family memories that hung in the hallways.

"I can't believe how much I missed this place," Mila said, taking it all in. In truth, it wasn't the place at all. It was the feeling of being surrounded by the people who loved her the most.

During dinner, she watched for any indication one way or another about the stability of her parents' marriage. She noticed nothing unusual about either of them, but she wasn't sure what that meant. Colt had barely given her a chance to digest the news, let alone know what she was looking for or figure out what she could do to save them.

When they finished with dinner, they sat in the living room, and it immediately felt like old times, only better. When they were younger, Mila always felt like she had to prove something to Colt, like she was under his scrutiny every day of her life, and he was just waiting for her to screw something up so he could jump in and correct her. All of that seemed to be gone now, and he was genuinely as happy as she was to have the opportunity to spend an evening together like this.

It was well into the night when Colt announced that he was going to go home since they had an early start the next morning on a house they were working on. Colt worked with his dad and Luke in the family business, Wilson Construction. In recent years, they had expanded into a few side projects involving flipping houses, one of which had been taking up the majority of their time for the past several weeks.

"Good night, Mom. See you tomorrow, Dad." He gave his mom and then Mila a hug. "Good to have you back," he told her, and she smiled up at him.

"Good to be back." It was true. She had realized it the minute she walked through her parents' front door. It was her first night in Tennessee and she already knew that she wasn't going to have enough time with everyone in the next six weeks.

She turned to her mom and dad after they saw Colt off. "I'm awfully tired," she said. "Mind if I turn in? It's been a long day."

"Of course not," Mary Beth said. She wanted to tell her mother that she knew, and that it was going to be OK. Mila could sense that she needed her, as a daughter who could understand her problems and not a son who was trying to protect her from them. But she wasn't about to bring it up tonight.

"Good night, Mom," she said, her gaze fixed on her just a moment longer than necessary before she looked at her dad. "Good night, Dad."

As she started down the hallway toward her old bedroom, she knew that even the issues that her parents were having in their marriage were not going to keep her awake. She would fall asleep quite literally as soon as her head hit the pillow.

***

Colt blinked, forcing his eyes to focus on the clock. Then he blinked again. For the love of Pete. Who would be calling him at 2 in the morning? He didn't recognize the number that came up on his phone but took the call anyway, answering with a curt hello.

"Colt?"

"Richie?"

"Hey, bro," Richie said, his voice etched with relief and a very irritating tinge of amusement.

"Richie." Colt's voice was deep with slumber. "It's 2 in the morning."

"I'm sorry, man." It almost sounded sincere, like Richie knew he was a pain in everyone's backside. "Look, there was a little misunderstanding. I'm in the county jail."

Colt's eyes popped open. "What? Why?"

"I told you. It's a misunderstanding."

He doubted that. Richie had been a problem since the first time Colt met him, before his parents decided to adopt him and raise him in a good Christian home. All in all, he had fared better living out his teen years with the Wilsons than he would have if he'd continued to be bounced between foster homes. But that didn't mean he ever learned how to stay out of trouble and become a productive member of society. Not even fatherhood taught him that.

Colt sat up, and the covers fell from his chest, leaving only the unwelcome coolness of the air around him. "Where are the girls?" He gripped the phone, waiting impatiently for a response.

"Well, they're at the house. And I don't know how long it's going to take to get this sorted out."

Standing, Colt pulled on a pair of jeans. "What did you do, Richie?" he demanded.

"Misunderstanding," Richie said in his typical smart-alec way. Most people outgrew that tone of voice somewhere in their teen years. Richie carried it on indefinitely, using it as a mechanism to make people feel uncomfortable and not ask too many questions.

He could have been in jail for any number of things. Richie had been known to run into trouble with the law from time to time, mostly because of drug and alcohol related offenses. Several times Mary Beth had considered staging an intervention, fearing that something was going to happen to Richie's daughters ever since their mother abandoned the family and took off for Oregon.

"Richie. When are you going to learn how to be a man for those girls?"

"Spare me the lecture, dude." Colt shook his head. It was like they were sitting around a campfire, Richie high on weed like he often was, and Colt was giving him advice on something trivial. "I have bigger problems right now. Can you just go get the girls and take them to your house for the night? I should be out of here by tomorrow."

"Fine." There was no point in arguing with him anyway. What was it they said about arguing with idiots? Whatever it was, the point was that it was unwinnable. "I'll take care of the girls."

"Thanks, bro."

"Don't thank me. You disgust me, 'bro.' I'm not doing it for you. I'm doing it for them." He hung up before Richie could respond and pulled on several layers of clothes before he drove off into the night to pick up Peyton and Hallie.

***

Peyton was none too happy to see him. Or, more accurately, to be dragged out of her house at this hour of the night because her father had screwed up - again.

"This is ridiculous," she said for at least the fifth time. "We have school tomorrow. We shouldn't even be awake right now let alone be made to go anywhere. Why can't you just stay here?"

Colt put up a hand. "Peyton, stop. You're coming with me. End of discussion."

She rolled her eyes and stormed down the hallway. Colt stood in the living room by the door and waited. When she wasn't in opposition with him, he admired the fire inside of Peyton. She had a lot of fight in her. He was sure she would make more of her life than Richie ever could.

He crossed his arms in front of his chest and leaned against the door, looking at the time. It was almost three o'clock. He was giving them five minutes. Five minutes, and they better be out there with their bags packed.

Hallie was first, still in her nightgown, hair sticking up on one side, lugging a gym bag behind her. She blinked up at him with the sleepy eyes of an innocent six-year-old. Colt sat on his heels and offered her a reassuring smile. "I'm sorry about this, Hallie," he said softly. "But on the bright side, you don't have to go to school tomorrow."

11

Hallie scratched her head, an adorably puzzled look on her face. "I don't?"

Colt shook his head. "Uh-uh. You get to go visit grandma tomorrow."

Hallie's face lit up, and behind her, Peyton rolled her eyes.

Colt stood. "Ready?" he asked both girls.

"Yeah!" Hallie said, as if they were off on an adventure.

Peyton scowled. "As ready as one can be at 3 in the morning."

Colt paused to look at Peyton. The two sisters were nothing alike. Peyton was a rebel from the day she was born. She was picking the lock to her mom and dad's bedroom door by the time she was Hallie's age and racking up endless hours of detention her first year out of elementary school. Today, at 16, she stood before her uncle almost a woman, her long honey blonde hair flowing over her leather jacket, the attitude in her eyes only serving to make her look tougher.

He regarded her carefully, weighing his next move. Telling her this wasn't his fault would only send her on a tirade about Richie, which would draw this out considerably. So instead, he picked up Hallie's bag and then Hallie and opened the front door.

He turned to Peyton. "I can take your bag, too."

Again she rolled her eyes. "Don't be ridiculous," she muttered and followed him out the door, locking it behind them. "We'll be back by Sunday night, right?" Peyton asked as they approached the truck. "So we can go to school on Monday?"

"I hope so," Colt said, lowering Hallie into the back seat. He watched to make sure she fastened her seatbelt correctly, then closed the door and looked over the hood at Peyton. "I don't know. I don't know why he's there. He says it's a misunderstanding, and he won't be there long."

Peyton scoffed. "And you believed that?"

Colt grinned, silently pleading the fifth. "Just get in the truck, Peyton." Thankfully, she did as he asked. She sat in silence the whole way to Colt's house, staring out the window and wishing for the hundredth time that her mother would have taken her with her when she left.

Chapter 3

Colt stood in his kitchen, facing off against Peyton for the second time in 12 hours. Coffee in one hand, he ran his fingers through his hair with the other. She was unbreakable. He knew that. But he was still going to win.

He put the cup down, squaring up and looking her in the eyes. In return, he saw nothing but resolve.

"Who was that on the phone?" she asked again.

"That was your dad," Colt said. "Listen, he's not getting out of jail anytime soon."

Peyton crossed her arms in front of her. "Go on."

"I can't keep you here. You're going to your grandma's to stay."

"Like hell I am."

Colt cocked his head. "Do you know that if I would have talked to my uncle that way, your grandfather would have cracked me right across the mouth?"

"I'm not interested in how my grandfather raised you or how it makes you a better person than I am," Peyton said coolly. "The only thing I'm interested in is going home."

"You're not going home."

"I am."

Sweet peaches, he believed her. He knew the girl. She would find a way.

He shrugged. "Go home, then. I'll report you as a missing person." He leaned forward, his palms on the countertop. "As soon as you show up at school, they'll bring you back to your grandmother's house. If you keep doing it, you'll go to some juvenile hall. Then you'll end up in foster care. And I think you know where the story goes from there."

Tears stung her eyes. Colt knew she would never admit defeat, but the tears were a good indication.

"I want to go live with my mother, then," she said.

"No, you don't. If you go live with your mother, you'll never see your boyfriend. And we both know that all you really want is to not be separated from Trevor. Isn't it?"

She glared at him. The accusatory tone he took with her wasn't helping. "I don't want to talk to you about Trevor."

Colt threw his hands up. "That's fine. You don't have to talk to me about Trevor. But you do have to get your things together and go to your grandma's house. And Peyton? It would be in your best interest to not give them any trouble. I don't care if you direct your anger at me. But you cause any grief for my mom and dad, and it won't be so easy."

"Whatever." She walked down the hallway to get her things, quickly deciding that a brief stay with them would be better than any kind of a stay with Colt.

***

Peyton stood on the porch of her grandparents' house scowling.

Colt gave her a sidelong glance. "You best put a smile on your face and act like you're happy to see them," he said quietly just before his mother came to the door.

"Mom," Colt said.

"Grandma!" Hallie's eyes lit up. It was as if her father being hauled away to prison was of no consequence to her.

Mary Beth stooped down to give her a hug and fuss about how big she was getting before she looked over at Peyton. Colt followed his mother's gaze. She wasn't smiling but she wasn't scowling anymore, either.

"Hi, grandma." She gave Mary Beth a brief hug before they all went inside.

"Let's get you two settled," Mary Beth said, grabbing Hallie's bag and leading the girls down the hallway.

Colt looked at Mila. "I guess this means you'll need a place to stay."

She pointed over her shoulder with her thumb. "Couch?"

Colt shook his head. "You can't sleep on the couch for the next six weeks. You can stay at my house. I have room for you."

"I forgot my leather boots," Peyton announced from the hallway, and then appeared in the kitchen.

Colt's eyes narrowed. "You can do without them."

"No, I can't." She looked at Mila. "I can't."

"I'll take you to get them." Mila cast Colt a look that stopped him short of making any kind of argument.

"Thank you," Peyton said, visibly relaxing.

"Go get your coat. I'll take you right now."

As soon as she was out of earshot, Colt spoke to her in a hushed tone. "She's just playing you."

"No, she's not," Mila retorted without considering it. "And even if she is, so what? Her life has just been turned upside down. How would you have liked it if you were torn away from your friends and your girlfriend in eleventh grade?"

Colt shrugged.

"Who were you dating junior year, Colt?" she whispered in a scolding tone. "Carolina Gentry? Do you think you would have walked away from her without a fight? You two were practically surgically connected to each other. It was disgusting!"

"Nice. Thanks for the unsolicited feedback."

They heard Peyton coming down the hallway again.

"I could go on," Mila said quietly, then turned to look at Peyton. "All set?"

Peyton nodded. "I asked Hallie if she needed anything and she said no. So it's just you and me." She gave Colt a less than thrilled look and then looked back at Mila. "Right?"

"Yeah," Mila said. "Let's go." Peyton walked out to the porch, and Mila turned back to look at her brother. "Colt?"

He looked up, his hand on the back of his neck as he tried in vain to rub out some of the tension. "Yeah?"

15

"I'll see you tonight."

"I'll get a room ready for you."

She thanked him and walked out the door.

***

Mila opened the door to Colt's house without knocking. She stepped inside and saw him in the kitchen stirring a pot of something on the stove.

"Hey," he said. "How'd it go with Peyton?"

"OK, I guess." She crossed the floor into the kitchen and sat down at one of the bar stools in front of the countertop. "You don't need to be so hard on her, Colt."

He turned to face her. "Yes, I do."

"She's going through a tough time. She needs understanding. Friendship, even. Not an overbearing uncle who can't remember what it was like to be her age."

"If I don't make her feel a little uncomfortable, she's going to give Mom and Dad all kinds of trouble, sneaking out of the house, stealing cars, trying to get to that boyfriend of hers."

"Stealing cars? Really, Colt?"

He leaned against the counter, raising his brows and gesturing in an indication that he thought that was entirely possible. "Someone has to make her feel like she should think twice before she does all the stupid things she's going to do. Mom and Dad don't need the kind of grief she can dish out."

Mila looked over at the stove. "What are you cooking?"

Colt crossed the floor and stirred the pot. "Ramen noodles."

"Are you a college student?"

He shrugged. "I don't cook."

Mila got up and opened the fridge, taking inventory: a couple bottles of beer, a pizza box, soda, a carton of milk and various condiments. She closed the door, returning her attention to him. "What do you eat?"

"Take-out mostly." He gestured to the pot. "And Ramen noodles."

"How are you in such good shape with a diet like that?"

"First of all, I don't have a desk job," Colt said. "Secondly, I go to the gym, like, all the time." He popped a handful of cashews in his mouth. "All the time," he emphasized, as if trying to convince her.

16

"I can't live like this." She chose to ignore the smirk on Colt's face. "I'm going to the grocery store to get some real food in this house."

"Suit yourself. Go grocery shopping tonight." He pulled the pot of noodles from the stove and poured some into a bowl. "I'm going out."

"Alaina coming to town?" It had been a long time since she'd seen Alaina, and although Colt had yet to mention anything about her, she assumed they were still together. It was something of a mystery that they had lasted this long given the circumstances of their relationship. They met when he was on vacation at South Beach in Florida. Having just returned a rented jet ski, Colt was walking along the beach when he heard a woman calling for help and saw her struggling to hold onto her little girl and swim back to shore. He raced into the water and swam out to them, bringing them both back to safety on the beach. Once in the sand, the mother frantically explained that the tide had carried her daughter out and she was trying to save her while someone administered CPR on the little girl. Everything turned out OK, but the rescue effort had attracted a crowd, and one of those people in the crowd was Alaina.

"No," he said. "Alaina's not coming into town. I'm just going to Cobra's."

Ever since Mila could remember, that was the place Colt and Luke hung out. Even before they were 21, they were drinking at the bar and flirting with older women. It was a rough place, as she recalled, one that Colt didn't want her anywhere near when she was younger.

She cocked her head. "Isn't Cobra's still a place you wouldn't want to catch your baby sister at?"

Colt grinned. "Yes. But if you're going with me, you'll be fine."

"Right." She had to admit she was more than a little curious about the company her brother was keeping these days. "I'm in."

***

Cobra's had all the appeal of a dead possum. It was nothing like the pubs Mila went to in London. It was hard to believe that this was the place her brother frequented when Alaina wasn't around. The lighting, for one, was horrible. The bar, slightly to the

17

left of the door wasn't exactly dirty, but it looked run down. The tables and booths were old and dingy looking.

"Can't you find a nicer place to hang out?" Mila asked as she followed Colt to a table and pulled out a chair. She looked at the chair and frowned. They were rickety old things covered with fake leather, and hers had a hole in it with stuffing spilling out. She looked at him. "I'm not sitting in this chair."

He rolled his eyes and walked around the table to find her a more suitable chair, pulling one out where the seat cover was still intact. "Will this one do?"

She had the same feeling toward it as she had toward slimy eels slinking around in fish tanks: not really capable of doing her any harm, but they made her uncomfortable nonetheless. Reluctantly, she took the chair from him and watched as he slid the other one out of her way. "Honest to Pete," he mumbled, as he walked back to the other side of the table and took his seat again.

Mila sat down across from him and eyed the crowd.

"Will you stop?"

"What? I'm not doing anything." He gave her a look, and she relented. "OK. There are just some rough looking people here. That's all."

He turned to see the group of young punks she was staring at. "Those guys? Please." Colt smirked and then focused his attention back on Mila. "Anyway, it's been a long time since there were any brawls at this place."

"What's a long time? Two weeks?"

He ignored her in favor of looking at the menu. Mila picked up her own menu, trying to ignore the fact that it was covered by some dirty, sticky film, and glanced over her options. Bar food. Not much better than Ramen noodles. He could have taken her someplace nicer. She was about to tell him that when he appeared to become distracted by something on the other side of the bar.

"Luke's at the pool table." Colt slid out his chair. "Want to go say hello?"

Mila shrugged indifferently. "Yeah, I guess."

It was an irritating remark, bordering on snobby as far as he was concerned. Why she wouldn't want to see his best friend, who had been a friend of the family since they were kids, was beyond him. But he ignored it and got up, and Mila followed.

18

They crossed the floor, and Colt leaned against the bar, watching Luke in the dimly lit pool area as he focused on sinking the last solid on the table before the eight ball. It was somewhat fascinating watching Luke play pool, the way he was able to shut everything else off and just focus on what was on the table in front of him. Colt had watched him go from a casual player to someone who could beat just about anyone. He was challenged by someone a couple times a week, and tonight he was playing Walter Dasano for at least the third rematch.

Colt wasn't at the bar for more than a minute before the barmaid had a beer in his hand. He turned to her. "Thanks, Chrissy."

"You betcha," she said. "What'll it be for the lady?"

Mila thought for a second. "How about a vintage cabernet? Something imported from France or Italy. I don't like American wines."

Chrissy looked her up and down, taking in the designer clothes, the high-heeled boots and the handbag that probably cost the same as a semester's worth of tuition at her daughter's college. Her smile faded quickly. Where did this woman come from? What was she doing in a place like Cobra's anyway?

"She'll have the same thing I'm having," Colt said as if he were covering for her.

Chrissy popped open a beer and leaned over the bar to whisper to Colt. "You dating some snob from out of town these days? What happened to Alaina? She was sweet."

Colt smiled. "I'm still with Alaina." He nodded his head toward Mila. "That snob is my sister."

"Oh!" Chrissy's eyes widened. "I'm so sorry."

"It's OK," Colt said. "No offense taken." He winked and took her beer, walking away from the bar and handing it to Mila.

"What'd I miss?" he asked sitting at the high table across from her.

"Luke sank the last solid. He just needs to sink the eight ball now. And why the beer? I don't want beer."

"Stop being a snob. If you don't want it, I'll drink it."

"Fine," Mila turned her attention back to the game. "Who are the promiscuous girls hanging all over Luke?"

Colt shrugged. "I guess they're girls who like guys who win pool games."

"Right, OK," Mila said, noting that Luke was fully focused on the game and not the girls. He lowered himself to the table and eyed the cue ball, the eight ball and then the cue ball again. Mila casually assessed him, but quickly decided she didn't need a lot of time to notice how good he looked. It was no surprise. Luke always looked good, and girls always swooned over him. It was clear that nothing had changed.

"Hey, how's he been doing since...?"

Colt put up a hand. It was then that she noticed the entire area surrounding the pool table had gone silent waiting for Luke to make his shot. Mila turned to look at Luke, hoping he hadn't been distracted by her, only to find his baby blues staring up at her. A moment of uncomfortable silence passed where he didn't remove his eyes from her. They were guarded. Weary. Kind of sad. But still beautiful.

Mila reached across the table. "On second thought, I think I will have that beer," she murmured to Colt, then took a chug and waited. Luke was no longer looking at her, but the three girls were. She took another drink. And finally everyone turned their attention back to the game.

Mila held her breath as Luke drew the cue stick back, then waited as he hit the cue ball, skillfully sending it in the direction of the eight ball, where it seemed to take a majestic roll to the corner pocket Luke had pointed to before he took the shot. He laid his stick on the table and looked at his opponent with a grin.

"That's the game, Walt." Luke appeared casual and triumphant at the same time.

"Dammit, man," Walt said, reaching into this pocket to pull out a wad of cash and hand it to Luke.

"Thank you." Luke took the money and shook Walt's hand, then turned to the three girls who were fawning all over him. "Round of drinks, girls?" He handed them a few bills, and they walked off to the bar as Luke crossed the floor to Colt and Mila's table.

"Hey, Mila." Luke put his hand on the back of her chair, and she repositioned herself to engage with him. "Good to see you. I heard you were coming back for Isabel's wedding. How's London?"

"London's good. Sorry about that...distraction." Mila still felt foolish for just about asking Colt in front of everyone how Luke had been since Scarlett died.

"No problem," he said. "It didn't stop me from winning a hundred bucks tonight." He sat down next to Colt. "What will I do with all this extra money? Corvette? Vacation in Hawaii?" He put his head on his hand and looked wistfully at the bar. "Round of drinks for every girl in this place tonight?" He winked at Mila.

Still a cutie. Too damn cute for his own good. She turned away, taking a drink of her beer.

Luke slid off his seat and leaned against the table. "I'm not sure how they say hello in all the fancy places you've been to, but here in your hometown, we still say it with a big old hug. How about a proper hello?"

There was something about him that irritated her. Or would have if he weren't so magnetic. If a woman wasn't charmed by his physical appearance, the light eyes and the darkish hair, all she had to do was give it a second. The southern drawl and the mischief in his eyes would surely claim her within minutes of talking to him.

Mila stood, and Luke pulled her into his arms. "Welcome back." He said it quietly, as if there were something intimate between them, and then he hugged her like he meant it.

She was kind of appalled at the way her body responded to him, as if it would welcome some kind of intimacy with Luke. It was a good thing her mind was in control. Clearly she couldn't listen to her body.

She pulled back and, despite herself, smiled up at him in a flirty way. "Thank you. It's good to be home."

For the first time since she stepped into this place, she felt like she meant it. But before she could fully enjoy the feeling of belonging that only old friends could give you, his attention was back on the three girls who had been plaguing the evening as far as she was concerned.

"Let it go, Mila," Colt said quietly as they watched them walk away.

"What? I didn't say anything." She turned her back on Luke and the girls, taking her seat at the table again.

"You don't have to. Anyway, don't they kiss each other on the cheeks to say hello over in London?"

21

"Only if you like a person."

"So you're saying you don't like my friends."

Mila stared across the table at him. "I'm saying I don't approve of your friends. There's a difference."

Colt took another slug of beer. "Walk a mile in his shoes," he said. "Or don't. Either way, stop being so damn condescending."

"I'm not being condescending."

"You're *always* being condescending. He nodded toward Luke. "He's been through a lot. He's finally starting to live again. Maybe you could be supportive of that."

He had a point, but she wasn't about to acknowledge that. Instead, she leaned closer, glancing around to make sure no one was paying attention to them. "What happened that day anyway?" she asked. She knew that Luke lost his girlfriend in a car accident, but that was all she knew about it.

"She was on her way to work. A truck driver fell asleep at the wheel and crossed the center line and hit her."

Mila's eyes widened. "An 18-wheeler?"

"No. It was a commercial vehicle, though, and he was driving too long without any sleep. So there was a lawsuit. And that was ugly, too. You weren't here to see it and you should probably be thankful for that. But I'm telling you, there were times when I thought he would never come back." He took another gulp of beer and looked across the room at him. "He's still not himself. But at least he's having some kind of fun."

Mila watched as one of the girls shrieked, throwing her hand up in the air and laughing. "Yeah," she said. "Some kind of fun." She couldn't help it. Places like this and girls like that were exactly the reason she made up her mind to leave a long time ago.

Chapter 4

This was ridiculous. By no stretch should Peyton be forced to enroll in a new school because her dad was a criminal. She should look into getting emancipated or something. She was 16; surely that was old enough to do *something*. She could make her own decisions. She could probably even stay with Trevor until her dad came back.

She walked into her new homeroom and looked around. A cluster of girls stared at her unwelcomingly. Peyton widened her eyes at them to show that she would not be intimidated, grabbed a seat and blew a bubble.

"Excuse me, miss?" It was the homeroom teacher, and she didn't appear to like Peyton very much either.

Peyton nodded. "Peyton Wilson."

"Peyton, you can throw your gum in the trash and take a seat in the third row, second chair."

Peyton rolled her eyes but did as she was told, taking a seat behind a boy who looked like a typical jock. Two girls who were undoubtedly on the cheerleading squad whispered and giggled to one another as Peyton sat down. She ignored them and tapped her pencil eraser on the desk, reviewing her schedule and waiting for the morning announcements to be over so they could start their day. One day down would be another day closer to seeing Trevor at the winter dance on Friday.

She and Trevor had been together for more than a year now. It might have never happened had the bus not broken down on the way home from a basketball game one day. Trevor was on the team, and Peyton kept their stats. That fateful day, they had been sitting on the side of the road for more than an hour, and Trevor started crunching Fritos in the seat behind her so loudly she wanted to strangle him. When she peeked her head over the seat to give him a death stare, he grinned at her. And her heart flopped. The rest was history.

When the bell finally rang to start the day, Peyton walked out of homeroom, steering clear of any friendly conversation on her way to her first class. Not that it was difficult. The student body wasn't exactly welcoming her with open arms.

She sat down in English class and opened her book, pretending to be very interested in the chapter she happened to flip the book open to. The late bell sounded and the teacher started class.

"Today we will start our journey into understanding Dickenson," she announced as if this were a topic they were privileged to hear about.

"Fascinating." Peyton looked with amusement at the blond boy who was sitting across from her. He smiled when he saw that she noticed him, but the smile immediately faded when he caught a look from a girl who was presumably his girlfriend.

"You don't like Dickenson?" Peyton whispered.

"Miss Wilson," the teacher said. "Welcome to Henderson High. Is there something you would like to share with the class about Dickenson?"

Peyton looked around the class, then looked at the teacher and answered the question honestly. "No. But since you asked, I'm not a fan of her work."

The teacher raised her brows. "Really?" she asked, her tone both challenging and curious. "Care to share with us why?"

Peyton shrugged. "I don't like reading about death and dying, which is what the vast majority of her poetry is about. She basically lived her life as a recluse and most of what she wrote, while quite cinematic, is also dark and depressing. I prefer Frost, even though he had to go to England in order for people to give proper attention to his talents."

The teacher looked slightly taken aback while several of Peyton's classmates quietly chuckled. "I see," she said, and then focused her attention back to the class. "Does anyone else have an opinion on Dickenson that they'd like to share?"

Peyton tried her best to give the appearance of being interested. All she could do for now was just keep counting the days until she would be back in Trevor's arms, if not for good, at least temporarily at the dance. Maybe there they could plan some kind of escape.

***

Colt slowed his truck to a stop, pulling over to the side of the road. He did not have time for this kind of thing, ever. But he couldn't just ignore the fact that a black lab was running freely along this well-traveled road with no owner in sight.

He got out of the truck as cars whizzed by without even slowing down. The dog hadn't noticed him yet. It was still too busy running through the field, getting dirtier by the second.

"Hey!" he called, and the dog spun around in his direction. "Where's your owner? Anybody out here?" He waited for a response and got none. It was no surprise. People let their dogs run freely in this town all the time and nothing was ever done about it. He didn't care about that. He was just afraid this one was going to get hurt. "Get over here, dog," he said, and the dog barked. Colt crouched down and called for her again. It wasn't until the dog got closer that he noticed just how dirty she was. Mud was caked all over her feet and halfway up her legs. Dried thistle clung to her in various spots near her shoulders and down her back. Her face was wet. Her big bubble-gum pink tongue hung out to the side. She looked like she was ready to pounce and give him big wet kisses.

"*Stay.* You stay right there."

The dog got down on her front legs and wagged her tail playfully. She barked just before she launched herself at him, nearly knocking him over in her attempt to lick his face. Mud streaked all over his pants and jacket as he pushed her away.

"Dammit, dog, I didn't want you to do that," he muttered. "Why did you have to go and jump on me?" He let her run for a few seconds and then spoke to her in a commanding tone. "Settle

25

down! Sit!" Eventually, she did, and this time when he approached her, her furiously thumping tail was the only indication that she was still highly excitable.

"You stay!" Colt told her in no uncertain terms. The dog wore a collar but no tags. Still crouching down near her, he looked around to see how many houses he would have to visit to see if anyone was missing their dog. He decided instead to keep an eye out for missing dog signs on the way to the shelter.

"All right," he said. "You're coming with me. Come on, girl."

The dog quickly jumped up and bounded over to the truck. He looked down at her. "In the back. You're not getting into my truck like that." He lowered the tailgate. "Come on, girl."

The dog ran to the back of the truck, her front paws landing on his tailgate, and barked. Colt grunted and grabbed her around the belly, lifting her into the truck and closing the tailgate. The dog did a few circles and looked at him happily.

"You smell bad, do you know that?" Colt asked the dopey looking dog. "Don't be trying to get out of the truck when it's moving. Just hang tight and I'll get you to the shelter. Hopefully someone's looking for you."

***

There was no such luck. No one had been looking for a dog that matched this one's description, and beyond that, the clerk at the shelter in town had just informed Colt that they were full and they couldn't accept any more dogs at this time.

Colt leaned against the counter, trying to figure a way to bargain with her. "Look, I understand your position. Really, I do. But look at me. I'm a filthy mess. My hands smell, my clothes smell." He shook his head, smiling. "I can't go to work like this. I need to get home and start my day all over again. What if you just kept her for the day and I'll come back and get her after work?"

The woman looked at him over the top of her glasses. "No," she said firmly.

Colt lowered his head, trying to think of another strategy. Normally, he was a pretty successful sweet talker, but this woman was a rock, and she had no interest in impressing a guy like him.

He rubbed his chin. "Come on," he said quietly, grinning at her again. "What would you have me do here? I saved the dog from being hit by a car. I can't take her home with me. I'm just trying to be a responsible citizen."

"Tell you what," she said. "There's a shelter just outside of town that might be able to take her. I'll give them a call and see if they have any room." Her mouth twitched upwards in what could have been interpreted as a smile. "Be back in a second."

"Great." Colt walked to the door to make sure the dog was still in the truck. Thankfully or unthankfully, she was. He watched her out the window for a few minutes until the woman returned to the counter.

"Good news," she said. "You're in luck. They do have room for the dog at the other shelter." She grabbed a pen and paper and wrote something down. "Here's the address and phone number in case you get lost."

Colt approached the counter and took the paper from her. "Bridgetown? I've never heard of it. How far away is this place?"

The woman smiled and shrugged. "Never been there. But I don't imagine it would be more than twenty minutes or so."

Colt eyed her suspiciously. "Right," he said finally, nodding as if he didn't believe her for a second. "Well, thanks."

She smiled at him triumphantly. "You have a good day."

"You, too." He turned and walked out the door.

***

The drive was closer to thirty minutes out of town than twenty. But the woman he talked to on the phone had given him good directions, so he had no trouble finding the place, even though it was tucked back in the middle of nowhere and well off the beaten path.

He pulled into the parking lot, put the truck in park and looked at the time. By now his dad would be wondering where he was. He made a quick call to let him know he would be late and jumped out of the truck to get the dog. He pulled a rope out of the back seat to use as a leash and tied it to her collar, then opened the tailgate to let her out.

They stood before the shelter, a small wooden building with a red roof that sloped downward from left to right. The front porch was a long cement slab with wooden pillars holding up the roof. The red shutters surrounding the windows gave the place kind of a cute look. In front of the door was a mat that said "Wipe Your

Paws." Colt found himself wiping his feet on the mat, even though that seemed silly considering the rest of him was covered with mud.

He opened the door, and a cow bell announced his presence. Across the room, he saw a young petite blonde behind the counter. She looked up from the clipboard she was writing on and smiled. Colt immediately felt a hundred times better than he had at the previous shelter.

"You must be Colt," the girl said, coming out from behind the counter. "And this must be the dog you rescued." She bent down toward the dog, who was sitting obediently next to Colt and wagging her tail.

"Be careful," Colt murmured. "She's most likely fixing to jump all over you and try to lick you to death."

The girl smiled up at him, scratching the dog behind her ears. "Looks like you were under attack."

"Yeah." He laughed. "She doesn't listen real well."

"That's OK," the girl said. "I'm used to dog attacks." She stood and the dog barked, seeking more attention. The girl held out her hand. "I'm Lizzy."

Colt shook her hand, noting how tiny it was. She could have only been a couple inches over five feet tall, and she was so cute he found himself trying not to stare at her. It was the eyes that had him. They were so blue they looked like crystals.

He blinked, bringing himself back to the moment. "Nice to meet you," he said. "Look, I don't mean to dump her off like this. I can't keep her. I just didn't want her to get hurt out there."

She nodded. "I understand." He felt like she did. Like he wasn't being judged at all. Nothing at all like the animal shelter in town.

"I was looking for missing dog signs all the way through town, but I didn't see any. Is there a website or anything like that I could check?"

"I'll take care of that," she said.

"How about bathing her? Can you use help with that?"

Lizzy shook her head. "I have it all under control." She reached to pet the dog again. "She's going to get the royal treatment. The works. Lizzy's spa services at her service."

Colt looked around, noticing that there was no one there to help her.

"If it's all the same to you, I'd like to stay and help you get her cleaned up." His dad was not going to be happy, but he couldn't just dump the dog on her and leave.

Lizzy cocked her head, smiling up at him. "OK," she said. "That would be nice."

"Great," Colt said, shrugging out of his muddy jacket and following Lizzy to the bathing area.

Chapter 5

Luke rolled up his sleeves and sat down. The barmaid leaned against the bar, coy grin on her face. She was an older blonde who was probably a knockout in her younger days. Now the make-up she wore was too heavy, and the lines on her face told the story of a hard partying youth.

"What'll it be, kid?" she asked.

Luke looked at the drinks on tap. He shouldn't drink tonight. Not tonight – on what would have been Scarlett's 27th birthday. "Tequila Sunrise," he said, finally. It was her favorite. She never kept the stuff in the house, but when her daughter, Ava, was with her father, and Luke and Scarlett got a night out, she ordered one. Never more than one just in case Ava needed her.

The barmaid returned with his drink and Luke took a sip. "Perfect, thank you," he murmured in a tone that was meant to cue her to walk away. He wasn't looking for company tonight. Every woman in the world couldn't make him forget about Scarlett tonight.

He remembered everything about her like she could have been there tonight, sitting on the barstool beside him, and just excused herself to go to the restroom. Remembered her wavy blonde hair, red lipstick and sparkling green eyes. Remembered the way she smelled and that genuine laugh. Remembered the night he fell in love with her. Everything about the woman was like magic.

Some days she still felt so close. So many nights, he wanted to ask her why she left, why she gave up on him and Ava. He had so many plans for their future. And then, nothing. Gone. Just gone.

He leaned forward in his chair and swirled the ice around in his glass. From a short distance away, he heard the cadence of a woman in high heels walking closer. In his side view he saw her sit down on the barstool next to him.

"Hey," she said quietly.

"Hey," Luke said. "Listen, I'm not in the mood for company right now…" He turned only to realize that he was looking into the deep hazel eyes of Colt's sister.

"It's just me," she said softly.

The relief on his features was apparent. "Hi, just you."

"I just stopped in to pick up my take-out." She held up a white paper bag. "And I saw you at the bar all by yourself." She looked around and smacked her lips together. "Not that you'd be by yourself for long…"

"Yeah," he said vaguely, looking more at the drinks behind the bar than he was at her. He looked uncomfortable, like there was something wrong.

"Rough night?" she asked.

"Yeah." He exhaled and looked up at the ceiling.

She gave him a moment to elaborate, but he didn't. "Care to talk about it?"

"No." He got out of his seat, laying down a tip and pushing in his stool. "But I'm glad you showed up here tonight." He gestured to the door. "I'll walk you to your car."

"Don't you want to finish your drink?" She glanced down at the nearly untouched beverage.

"It's probably better if I don't."

Without asking any more questions she knew he wouldn't answer, Mila got up and walked toward the door.

***

Peyton sat inside the fellowship hall of the church, arms folded in front of her. She had enrolled in the youth group at her grandmother's insistence, but she remained unwilling to talk any more than she had to with the people around her. They had just

31

read several passages in the Bible that talked about forgiveness, and the youth pastor asked them to write down a list of people who had wronged them in their lives.

Peyton uncrossed her arms and put her pencil to the paper. Well, this shouldn't be too hard.

Dad, she wrote first, then without even glancing up, quickly followed that with *Mom*.

"At least three people," the youth pastor said. "You should be able to think of three people pretty quickly, right?"

Peyton thought for another second, then wrote down a third name: *Colt*. She grinned to herself. It wasn't really that Colt had wronged her per se, he just didn't understand her and didn't even try to.

She tapped the eraser of her pencil against the top of the desk, staring down at her paper and waiting for the pastor to talk again.

"How many of you put down your mom and dad on the list?" he asked, and there was laughter throughout the group. Peyton frowned. She would give anything to have parents who had only wronged her in ways that really just showed that they cared – made her abide by a curfew or grounded her for bad grades. But that's not what she had at all. Her mother had left her family in favor of a carefree life far away, and her father was in jail. She would be willing to bet no one in the room could top that.

"I want you to think about forgiveness," the preacher said. "It may be hard at first, but I want you to try to warm up to the idea of forgiving the people on your list. Think about why they did what they did. Try to look at each situation with love and compassion toward that person." The preacher paused before continuing. "I want you to break off into groups of two or three and talk about this. You don't have to talk about who is on your list or what they've done. But I want you to talk about ways to forgive them."

Peyton watched as friends paired up with friends. She would probably be that kid in the class that the leader would have to take under his own wing because no one wanted to talk to her. She was looking down at her paper, contemplating the assignment as it related to her dad when someone came and sat down beside her.

32

Peyton looked up. It was a boy she recognized from school. He was actually kind of a big deal, or at least all the other kids at school made it appear that way, judging by the number of people he constantly had hanging around him.

"Hey." The boy smiled, confidence oozing from every pore. Peyton wished she could feel that way, that it wasn't all just an act. "My name's Dylan. Dylan Showalter."

She didn't return the smile. "I'm Peyton." Her tone was slightly wary. She meant for it to be like that.

He didn't seem to notice. "I know," he said. "I've seen you around."

"Yeah." Peyton looked down at her paper. "Right."

Dylan leaned closer. He had that look that so many girls found appealing. Dark hair cut neatly at the bottom but careless at the top. Dark eyebrows and – the thing that really got your attention – eyes the color of the summer sky. His face was flawless, his skin without a blemish. She had to admit he was pretty damn attractive – if you were into that kind of look. "So do you want to talk about ways to forgive people?"

"Not really."

He laughed. She didn't.

"Well, we still have 45 minutes and we both need a partner, so we may as well make something up together."

She tucked a piece of hair behind her ear and shrugged. "Sure," she said unenthusiastically. She wasn't about to show him what she had on her paper. Nor was she going to launch into her life story and how both of her parents had betrayed her in far worse ways than anyone in this room could ever imagine.

They trudged through the exercise and at the end of class, she tucked her paper into the Bible she brought and headed outside to wait for her grandmother to come pick her up.

She leaned against the cool brick of the church and looked out over the parking lot. It figured her grandmother would be late coming to get her.

She wasn't there by herself, being ignored by all the other students from the class, for more than a minute before Dylan walked up beside her, leaning against the church and looking at her with a grin. Honestly. He would be creepy if he weren't so popular at school. Anyone who was that loved by the student body couldn't be all that bad of a person. Or could they?

"We have lit class together, you know," he said. "I remember you because of the way you shut down Mrs. Bolden with your opinions on Dickenson and Frost." He was looking at her like he admired her. It wasn't a look Peyton was used to, and she surely didn't think it was sincere.

She responded with defiance. "If you're trying to get into my pants, it's not going to work. I have a boyfriend." She licked her lips and continued. "I have a school, and it's not your school. I'm only here temporarily."

She thought for sure he would back off, but he didn't. "Well, we're happy to have you at our school, temporarily." He turned away from her and faced the parking lot, his back against the church. "Good to know about the boyfriend."

She half smiled and looked down at the ground. In spite of herself, she kind of liked him.

Dylan wasn't used to conversation with a girl being anything but easy. Over the years, the school had become his territory, and just about everyone in it seemed to worship him. He didn't necessarily want it that way, but he didn't mind it, either. He always had his pick of the girls, but he never formed a lasting relationship with any of them. He didn't have time for that. He was too busy playing sports and hanging out with his friends, who were willing to follow him wherever he wanted to go.

Peyton seemed to care about none of that. Not his good looks, not his charm, not his popularity or his star football status. She seemed cold and closed off, immune to the seduction that everyone else had fallen prey to. He appraised her out of the corner of his eye. She was beautiful in a tough looking way. She reminded him of a very young looking Alicia Silverstone. Beautiful. Sexy. Smart. Challenge written all over her. All the things he found irresistible.

"There's my ride," she said when she saw her grandmother's station wagon pull into the parking lot. Station wagons. She felt a flush of embarrassment. Cool people didn't ride in station wagons, did they? She glanced at him out of the corner of her eye, assuming that by now he was on his smart phone talking to his friends. "See ya."

He pushed off the church. "I'll walk you to your car."

It wasn't until after she told him good night and got into the car with her grandmother that she realized Dylan had driven himself to youth group, which meant he could have driven off without stopping to talk to her. She wondered why the biggest deal at the school was making a bigger deal out of her. And she could only think of one reason. She had news for him. She meant what she said. He may be able to have his way with every other girl at the school, but he wasn't going to have his way with her.

He would know it in time, and he would eventually walk away, just like most other people in her life did. She had learned some hard lessons in her short life, and the only thing she knew for sure these days was that the only person in the whole world that she could rely on was Trevor. In a million years, she wouldn't betray him. Not for Dylan Showalter or anyone else.

Chapter 6

Mila stared at herself in the three-way mirror, piling her long brown locks atop her head to get a better idea of what she would look like on Isabel's wedding day. The wine colored A-line dresses Isabel picked were elegant and beautiful. This was the first time Mila was seeing it in person, and she immediately fell in love with it.

She turned her attention from her reflection to her best friend, hoping she would approve of the way she looked in the dress.

"Stunning." Isabel was beaming. "You know the bridesmaid isn't supposed to be prettier than the bride."

"Oh, please." Mila rolled her eyes, and Isabel handed her a pearl choker and white satin gloves. Mila smiled. This was going to be one classy wedding, Mila was sure of that. Isabel was a class act and always had been. It was hard to believe how much they had disliked each other when they first met all those years ago on the junior high volleyball team. They were the two top players on the team, which sparked a natural competition on the court that didn't take long to spill over into other aspects of their lives.

The situation continued for the better part of two years, both girls trying to force everyone on the team to pick a side. They imposed an intense amount of stress among the players, and it came to a head when the coach told them she was willing to kick them both off the team if it continued. They were forced to work together on the court, but the competition continued in more subtle ways, like the time Isabel enlisted Colt's help to get her votes when she was running for student council. Despite Mila's unrelenting protests, Colt insisted he was not getting caught up in that kind of drama and agreed to help Isabel. It was a rift she never thought could be fixed between them.

The rivalry persisted until their freshman year when the coach had to pick one of them to be the team captain. When she picked Isabel, Mila considered walking, but eventually decided she wasn't a quitter. And somewhere along the way, the rivalry dissolved into mutual admiration and respect, and eventually the most meaningful friendship either of them ever had.

All the memories today were good ones. They had been through so much together, and there was still so much more to come. Even with the time and distance between them, Mila knew Isabel would always be a part of her.

"I was thinking we should go out to Chubby's when we're done here and get one of those ice creams that we used to love so much," Isabel said with a grin. Chubby's was their guilty pleasure all through their teen years. The place was a dump, and the parking lot smelled like old cigarettes. The cones were always stale and half the time they were out of their favorite ice cream flavors, but they hadn't minded any of that.

Mila's eyes lit up, and she clasped her hands together. "Is Chubby's still open? I would *love* to go to Chubby's."

"Hold still." She had momentarily forgotten where she was, and that the seamstress was pinning the bottom of her dress. "I'll just be another minute here."

"Sorry," Mila said, but she didn't pay much mind to the seamstress. She was too busy beaming at her best friend, and so thankful for the opportunity to be back here and celebrate the big day with her.

***

"Dammit," Luke swore under his breath as the valve seal fell to the cement floor of his garage. Never had he experienced so much trouble replacing an engine valve before. He stepped back from the truck and wiped his hands on a rag, then cocked his head to get a better listen at something he just heard. Footsteps, in the form of high heels, coming closer to the garage.

He exhaled quietly. He didn't want the company of a woman tonight. Didn't feel like putting on the pleasantries, saying or doing something to make someone else feel good about herself. It was a funny thing about women. The most beautiful ones were also the most insecure, unless they had something going for them that was more important to them than their looks. Like Scarlett. Man, he missed Scarlett. Missed her every day of his life and couldn't imagine that it would ever get better.

His little sister Alicia stepped into the garage, and he looked down at his hands. A girl from the bar would have been better. Just about anyone would have been better.

"Alicia." He barely looked her in the eyes when he said her name and then went straight to trying to find the valve seal he just lost.

"Hi, Luke." Alicia sat down on a stool near his toolbox.

"What brings you here tonight?" He said it in a way that there would be no mistaking his disinterest in her or her visit to his house. It wasn't that he didn't like the girl. He was sure she was a nice young lady. He just didn't have time for her in his life. Never did, and didn't have any desire to make time for her now.

She heaved an impatient or perhaps disappointed sigh, but didn't answer him right away.

Luke put both hands on the front of the truck and ducked back under the hood, surveying all the parts of the engine to make sure there was nothing else wrong with it. He had to get this thing running right.

"Car troubles?" Alicia asked.

"Engine valves," Luke said, hoping she wouldn't have anything more to say about it. She was always trying to bridge the gap between them and build some kind of relationship. It didn't seem to matter how obvious it was that he wanted no part of it.

"Good old engine valves," Alicia echoed, nodding her head and feeling defeated. When her brother didn't respond, she continued. "I came to tell you that Dad's not doing very well." He was under the hood of the truck when she said it, and it was so easy to feign interest in the truck, to pretend that what she said didn't matter to him in the slightest. And it shouldn't. Not in the slightest. "He's doing very badly, actually. Downright miserably." He heard her stand and walk to the front of the truck.

Luke continued to survey the engine, his mind racing.

"I guess you're much more interested in the truck than anything I have to tell you," she said quietly. "Dad's dying. They say he has less than a week to live. He wants to see you, Luke."

Luke stood and wiped at his fingers again with the rag. "I have nothing to say to him." Why should he have anything to say to him now? It was his choice to leave Luke and his mom and sister Kim all those years ago. His choice to make his life with Alicia and her family – a family they never knew about until Luke was nine years old. A family they found out about very abruptly the day his father walked out of their lives and never turned back.

Alicia nodded. "I figured you would say that," she said quietly. "I debated about whether or not to tell you. But in the end, I decided it's your decision. And you can only blame yourself when the day comes that you regret not telling him goodbye."

He licked his lips, trying to temper the rage that was bubbling up inside. Years of hurt and neglect, wondering why he wasn't good enough, envying every other kid whose dad was there at their football games. Things Alicia couldn't possibly understand.

He gathered control of himself quickly, shaking off all those feelings like he had done for so many years. "We haven't talked in 20 years, Alicia. No point in starting now." Luke started looking around the truck for the engine seal again. "What would I say to him anyway? Hey, nice knowing you when I was nine, *Dad*. You should have stuck around. You would have seen a hell of a football player in high school." He shook his head. "I've got nothing to say to him."

"Then give him hell," she said. "Tell him how angry you are at him for doing what he did to you and Kim. Tell him about…"

He held up a hand and cut her off. "This isn't a therapy session. I don't want to talk to the man. I'm sorry that he's dying and you're going to miss your father. But he was dead to me a long time ago." His eyes met hers with steely resolve, and he saw her back down.

She reached into her pocket and pulled something out. "I assume you're looking for this," she said, handing him the part he was looking for. "Valve seal. Can't replace an engine valve without one." She handed it to him, and he tried not to look the slightest bit impressed by her apparent knowledge of engines.

She turned on her heel and walked past the truck, stopping at the garage door to turn back in his direction before she left. "I hope you reconsider," she said, only to be met with silence. After a moment, she walked out the door into the chilly night air.

***

Mila sat down across the table from Isabel. Chubby's was exactly the way she remembered it. The windows still looked like they hadn't been washed in years, and the same tiles were still missing from the floor. At the counter, a little boy was seeking comfort in his father's arms after he just found out they didn't have any rocky road today. Mila shook her head and smiled to herself. *Get used to it, kid. Some things never change.*

"Mila," Isabel said with a certain sense of urgency. "Remember Mr. Mueller? He's out there in the parking lot with his grandson."

Mila turned to see a considerably older version of Mr. Mueller than she remembered. He was the high school principal, and Isabel had always had a thing for him. He really was quite handsome, and Mila understood the attraction a lot of women had to men in power positions. More than that, though, was the way he engaged when he was talking to the students. He was one of the few people in the world who stopped what he was doing to listen to people when they were talking. Isabel said he always made her feel like she mattered. And for years, Mila had indulged her when she would stop in the hallway and just stare at Mr. Mueller as he walked by, then ask Mila what she thought the odds were that he would ever consider divorcing his wife for a student.

He walked into Chubby's and nodded in their direction. "Hi, girls," he said, approaching their table with the little boy. He introduced his grandson and engaged in small talk with Isabel while Mila sat back and watched. He was still a good looking man, even with the years that life had added to him.

His grandson could barely stand still long enough for Isabel to tell Mr. Mueller about the upcoming wedding, so they were only able to talk for a moment before he politely excused himself, and Isabel turned her attention back to Mila.

40

She leaned forward, an excitement in her eyes. "Do you remember when we used to think he was in some kind of secret society? And we tried to do secret hand signals to see if he would give us any signals back?"

"And then we came up with the idea to create our own secret society but we couldn't agree on who we would invite into it." It had been long since forgotten, those nights when they stayed up until dawn drawing out all kinds of signals and assigning meaning to them. "Do you still have that booklet we did with all the signals and the rules?"

Isabel nodded. "Of course I do."

She'd *better* have the booklet. She was possessive enough of it when they were writing it. She kept it between her mattresses and never took it out unless Mila was with her. When Mila asked for a copy so she could study the signals, Isabel refused. Eventually, volleyball season had gotten in the way, and they dropped the whole idea.

Mila took a bite of her ice cream cone and made a face. "Were the cones always this bad?"

"Yes," Isabel said, taking a bite of one herself.

Mila missed that glimmer in her friend's eye, and she missed these stupid cones. She took another bite and smiled across the room at Mr. Mueller. Sometimes it was the forgotten things in life and the unexpected reminders that brought back the greatest memories.

***

Peyton slipped into her bedroom and closed the door. When they got back from church, she had told her grandmother she had to study, smiling to herself when she bought the story. Peyton had never studied a day in her life. She just needed some time to herself so she could talk to Trevor for a little while tonight. She missed him to the point of madness sometimes.

She picked up her antiquated cell phone and dialed his number. Disappointment filled her when he didn't answer. Peyton sighed, threw the phone on her bed and turned on the TV. She stared blankly at the screen and tried to figure a way out of her situation. She needed to see Trevor again. Like, now.

She jumped when her phone rang, her heart leaping when she saw that it was Trevor. "Hello?" Her voice rang with excitement. "Trevor?"

"Guess what I'm doing, babe?" He sounded happy, calm, so *cool*, like he didn't have a care in the world.

"What?"

"Look outside your bedroom window."

"What?" she squealed. "Are you *kidding* me?"

"I dunno," he teased. "Come see for yourself."

She walked over to the window and, cradling the phone on her shoulder, unlocked and opened it. The rush of cold air felt good against her flushed cheeks. She looked out into the night. And there he was, like the best kind of hero, standing in the shadows of the moonlight. She squealed again, and he pressed a finger to his lips, grinning up at her the whole time.

She dropped her phone and opened the screen, climbing out the window and running to him, leaping into his arms and wrapping her legs around his waist. He staggered back a few steps under the weight of her enthusiasm and smoothed her hair as she buried her face against his neck.

"I miss you so much." She lifted her head to kiss him on the lips and cheeks. "I can't believe you're here. I was trying to figure a way I could come back to you, but you're here." She slid down his body and glanced around the yard. "How did you get here? Your car's not running."

"I borrowed my brother's car," he said, pointing to a spot beyond the garage where he must have parked it.

Peyton's eyes widened. "He let you borrow his car?"

Trevor smiled. "I didn't say *that*. And I can't stay very long or he'll know it's gone or put out an APB or something. But I had to come by and see you."

She wrapped her arms around him again, laying her head against his chest and wishing she could melt into him. "I'm so happy to see you."

"So are all the guys at your new school going gaga over you yet?" Trevor asked.

Her mind flickered to Dylan but she shook her head. "No. They haven't even noticed me. Basically, I just try not to talk to anyone. I'm not going to be there for very long, so there's no point in trying to make friends."

He nodded. "How's Hallie doing?"

"She's fine."

"Any word from your dad?"

"Not a word."

He sighed. "I better get going, babe. I'll call you tonight. And maybe I'll sneak out later this week to see you again."

"I miss you so much, Trevor."

"I miss you too."

She always felt so happy when she was with him. He was able to fulfill her in a way that no one had ever done in her life, including her own family.

"Talk to you tonight?" he asked, and she nodded. She didn't want to mention that she was going to try to get to the dance this weekend just in case she wasn't able to. She knew he would be there. All the football players would be there.

"I love you, Trevor."

He smiled a crooked smile. "Love you too, Peyton. See ya."

She watched him walk off into the darkness, wishing with all her heart that she could follow him.

Chapter 7

Colt pulled into the parking lot of the animal shelter and grabbed the bags of dog food from the back seat. He was hoping that by now Lizzy would have found the dog's owner but had a feeling that she hadn't. He walked through the door, the cowbell announcing his presence as he glanced around the room.

At first he didn't see anyone, but then he saw it – a big orange pom-pom just behind the window on the other side of the half-wall to the dog room. Lizzy was apparently stooped down tending to one of the dogs. As Colt walked closer, she looked up, smiling when she saw him, once again the most adorable thing he had ever seen – even in a floppy bright orange hat that looked like it was three sizes too big for her head.

He gestured with the bags. "What should I do with these?" he yelled so she could hear him through the window. She stood up when she noticed the bags of dog food. Colt watched her run to the door and swing it open. She pulled one of the bags out of his hands. He tried not to grin upon noticing that the bag was almost as big as she was.

"Thank you so much." Her eyes shined up at him, and he smiled. "That was so thoughtful of you." She placed the bag on the floor beside them, and he put the other one down next to it. "We never can have enough food for the dogs."

"How's the girl I brought in?" Colt asked. "Any luck finding her owner?"

"No luck." There wasn't a trace of cynicism in her voice, which was quite remarkable given her line of work. "I'm calling her Luna. And I was just about ready to take her for a walk around the yard. Care to join us?"

Colt raised a brow. "Are you trying to sucker me into falling in love with this dog so I'll take her home?"

Lizzy smiled. "I wouldn't dream of it, Mr. Wilson."

"Colt."

She nodded. "Colt. Do you want to join us for a walk?"

"OK." Together they stepped outside into the sunshine. It was a feel-good kind of day. Maybe that was because it had been years since he had taken the time to do something like this.

They walked around the perimeter of the yard twice before Lizzy pulled a ball out of her pocket to play fetch.

"She would do this all day if I would let her." Lizzy squatted down to take the ball from Luna's mouth. "That's what labs do, you know." She held the ball up to him. "Want to play fetch?"

Luna barked excitedly. Colt threw the ball to the other side of the yard and she went tearing off. Lizzy stood up. "See that? You're a natural dog owner. You really should have a dog."

He kept his focus on the playful dog running across the lawn. He was beginning to think Lizzy was the kind of girl who could talk him into anything.

***

"Peyton."

Clutching her books, she whirled around to see Dylan leaning against the wall near the school doors, a group of his friends standing nearby. She eyed him impatiently. If she didn't get on the bus before it filled up, she ran the risk of having to sit with someone. She hated sharing a seat on the bus.

Dylan waved her over. She had to admit, he looked kind of awesome standing against that wall in his hunter green sweater over top of a button-down checkered shirt. The look was preppy, yet careless. As she walked over to him, she let out a sigh.

"What do you want?" she asked tersely. "I have a bus to catch."

Dylan smiled slowly, as if there were something amusing about her, which was irritating. Her eyes flickered in a way that told him she was close to getting angry.

"Do you want a ride home instead of taking the bus today?"

Upon hearing those words, a hush fell over the nearby group of girls. Time seemed to stop as two of the girls, Autumn and Bianca, stared her down. She turned away from them and focused her attention back on Dylan. "Sure," she said with a smile. "I would like that."

A confident grin, a look that could assure you that he had it all covered, crossed his features and then he pushed off the wall and started walking with her over toward the student parking lot. She felt daggers on her the whole time, but she didn't care. Peyton was no stranger to female drama, and she could hold her own with those girls.

When they reached his car, some kind of a sporty red number, he unlocked it but stopped short of opening the door for her. The girl had a boyfriend, as she had been so quick to inform him.

Peyton got in and put her books on the floor in front of her. Dylan joined her, turning on the heat and then backing the car out of his space and driving down the road.

As soon as they got out to the street, Peyton began to feel uncomfortable. "Look," she said, trying to sound stern. "If I'm some kind of a conquest to you, you can just end it right now. I'm not going to be your conquest."

"You're not a conquest," he agreed. He had such an easy way about him, like nothing anyone said could throw him off. It was mildly infuriating.

"I'm not going to sleep with you," she reiterated. "I don't care who you are. I don't care who this school thinks you are."

Dylan smiled. "I just offered you a ride home. You said yes. Remember?"

"I just don't want you to think it means anything."

"It means nothing," Dylan said. "Got it. Stop freaking out. Tell me where you live."

"Why are you being so nice to me?"

Dylan shrugged. "I'm a nice guy."

"Somehow I doubt that."

"Your address, please?"

"Fifth Avenue. Behind Aunt Bea's Kitchen & Diner."

Dylan nodded coolly, and they drove in silence for a while. "I'm not trying to get anything out of you, so you can stop being so paranoid about it. I just thought maybe you could use a friend."

Peyton looked down at her fingernails. "You're the most popular guy at school. What do you care about me?"

"I don't know, Peyton. I guess I just didn't want you to have a horrible experience here. It's nothing for me to drive you home from school today. And tomorrow, you'll have people tripping over themselves to be friends with you."

"That's presumptuous of you."

He looked at her. "Not presumptuous if it's a fact."

Peyton stared out the window. "How did you get to be so popular?"

"I'm the quarterback," Dylan said. "Every guy wants to be friends with the quarterback, and every girl wants to date him. That's just the way it is."

Peyton rolled her eyes. "It's a stupid aspect of our culture."

"I didn't say it wasn't stupid," Dylan said. "Just a fact."

"You sure do have a lot of facts."

Dylan turned down the road to her grandmother's house.

"It's the blue house with the Bronco parked in the driveway," Peyton told him, pointing at the house.

Dylan pulled the car alongside the sidewalk and parked it. "See you tomorrow."

Peyton paused to look at him. "Thanks for the ride." She gathered up her books and popped open the door, wishing this nightmare of being at this other school would be over soon. The last thing she wanted was to start feeling like this was home.

She got out of the car and closed the door, not stopping to look back before she dashed up the steps to her grandmother's house.

Chapter 8

Peyton had been waiting all week for this. It was finally Friday night. She had gotten Mila to agree to take her to the dance so she could spend the evening with Trevor. She had to get Mila because no one else would have let her out of the house in the slinky black dress she was wearing. She pulled on a fancy black jacket and applied some lip gloss, then grabbed the little pocketbook Mila loaned her and headed down the hallway.

She had come to Colt's house to get ready so as to not be responsible for any episodes of cardiac arrest. Much to her eternal gratefulness, Colt wasn't home tonight. Peyton pulled her hair out of her jacket, slipped on the expensive super-stylish black boots Mila bought her and appeared in the kitchen.

"Ready to take me to the dance?"

Mila looked at her approvingly. "You look gorgeous!" She moved closer to get a better look at the sparkling earrings and the ruby necklace she had loaned her. Perfect. "Trevor is one lucky guy."

It sounded cliché, like something all mushy couples would say, but in this case it was true: Peyton always felt like she was the lucky one. Sure, they both came from a rough childhood and they connected on so many levels because of that, but Trevor was a football player, which meant he could have a lot of different girls. She didn't know why he picked her, but to this day, she thanked her lucky stars that he did.

She could barely contain her excitement when they pulled up to the school. Her heart was soaring and she would never admit this out loud, but her palms were even sweating. Mila parked the car and Peyton looked at her, eyes shining. "Thank you so much bringing me tonight. Ever since I left, all I want is to see him."

Mila smiled, remembering the all-important high school dances she had attended through the years. Were it not for the Christmas dance in her eighth grade year, she never would have had her first kiss on the dance floor with Eric Dunn. Even though they didn't last more than a couple months, it was still a defining moment in her life.

"Call me when you're ready to come home," Mila said. "Don't be getting on the back of some motorcycle with that bad-boy boyfriend of yours."

Peyton's heart thumped just at the reference of Trevor. "OK. I'll call you!" She jumped out of the car and tried to calm the butterflies as she walked toward the school. She got as far as the sidewalk near the doors of the gym when she saw Rob, one of Trevor's best friends, step out of the shadows near the side of the school where he was no doubt lighting up.

He caught a glimpse of her. And instead of looking excited to see her, calling out her name, rushing over to her and giving her one of his bear hugs, Rob looked nervous. No. He looked panicked. Peyton caught of piece of hair that was blowing across her face in the breeze and gave him a questioning look. Then everything started happening in slow motion. She looked behind Rob into the shadows and saw Trevor, his hands on her best friend's face, her hands at his waist. They were smiling. And then he whispered to her and kissed her…right on the nose…just like he used to do with her.

Her heart slammed against her chest, and a numbness took over her body at the same time an intense heat rolled over her.

"Trevor!" she called out, hoping for a moment that she just imagined it, that it wasn't really him looking at Zoe like that.

49

But he turned at the sound of his name. Turned and looked her dead in the eye. And then she saw it. It was immediate. Guilt. Sorrow. Regret.

"How long has this been going on?" she asked, her voice as shaky as her legs felt.

He let go of Zoe's hands and stepped toward her. His circle of friends – *their* circle of friends – seemed to fade into the background as Trevor approached. "It's not what it looks like."

"Not what it looks like," she echoed, then tossed her hair, looking beyond Trevor at her best friend. Zoe was giving her the most pathetic look she had ever seen. She focused her attention back on Trevor. "What is it then?" She stared at him, her eyes hard, nothing at all like the way she looked at him the other night. He blew it. Lost the love of a good girl over something so stupid, something that meant nothing to him.

Instead of defending himself in front of everyone, he took another step toward her and grabbed her hand, walking her toward his car. They stepped off the sidewalk and she jerked her hand away from his.

"Peyton." He was trying to calm her down, get any kind of a reaction from her at all. She said nothing but continued to walk with him to his car. When they reached the car, he turned and stood before her, looking her up and down. "You look beautiful." His words were so soft, his tone passionate and apologetic.

She looked away, blinking back tears.

"I just...I missed you so much, Peyton." She crossed her arms over her chest, and he looked down to the ground. When he looked back up, he didn't fix his gaze on her, couldn't look at the hurt in her eyes and the mess he created. "I started hanging out with Zoe because somehow it made me feel close to you …"

There were no words. So instead of screaming at him, she raised her hand and cuffed him across the cheek as hard as she could.

Trevor grunted in pain as his hand automatically reached up to cover the bruise that would rapidly be developing on his face. OK. She had done what she needed to do, given him what he deserved. Now they could work on getting past this.

He reached out and touched her arm. "Come with me," he said, still trying to shake off the physical pain. "I'll drive you home. We can talk."

"Like hell we will." She pulled her arm away and looked at him with absolute determination, sucked in a breath and gathered up all her strength. She wasn't going to hit him again. She just wanted to walk away without faltering, without crying. She reached for something deep inside of her, the kind of thing people talk about that you don't know you possess until you need it. The kind of thing that shows you and everyone else what you're made of.

"It's over," she said, her tone leaving no room for doubt. "Don't try to follow me." She turned and started walking.

"Peyton."

She whipped back around, glaring at him. "*Don't.*"

He would let her go. Give her time to cool down. He leaned back against his car and watched her walk away.

Peyton strutted down the parking lot toward the exit sign in front of everyone, carrying herself in a way that would tell them that neither Trevor, nor Zoe, nor anyone at this pathetic school meant a damn thing to her.

They were watching. All of them, watching her walk away. Just like they watched Trevor and Zoe get together as soon as she left. What a fool she had been to think he really loved her. To think that Zoe was her friend. To think that anyone at that school had any kind of decency. And now they stood judging her as she walked away. They would never understand the betrayal and what it did to her heart. They would only judge, like people always did. Trevor was a hero at this school. Somehow this would end up being her fault. He would emerge on top as usual.

She hated people. Hated this school. Hated this town. Hated her best friend. Hated Trevor. What a fool for getting all dressed up tonight, thinking it was going to be something special.

She reached the roadway that led to the elementary school and called Mila.

"Hello?" She sounded hopeful, dreamy even, like she was waiting to hear how amazing it was the moment Peyton was finally reunited with Trevor.

But it hadn't been amazing at all. It had been horrible. One of the most horrible moments of her life.

Peyton closed her eyes, hot tears sliding down her cheeks. "I need you to come get me." Her voice was low, quiet, completely defeated.

"Peyton?" Mila's voice filled with concern. "What happened? Are you OK?"

"No," she said shakily, tears streaming. "I'm not OK. I found Trevor with my best friend. Please come get me."

"Oh, honey…" It wasn't time to sympathize, she realized quickly. She needed to get her out of there, away from Trevor and anyone else that had seen the drama unfold. "I'm on my way." Mila sped up the road, her headlights shining upon Peyton about a half-mile from where she dropped her off. She slowed the car to a stop, and Peyton jerked the door open and fell inside. For several moments, they drove in silence.

"I loved him, Mila," she finally said. "He was the only person in the world who was always there for me. I just can't believe it."

"I'm so sorry," Mila said. "I don't know what to say. He can't possibly be the person you thought he was. I do know that." Peyton nodded, but Mila knew she wasn't processing anything right now. "You're going to be OK, you know. I know it might not feel like it right now, but you will be."

"I know." Peyton shook her head. "I just don't understand." She looked out her window and the tears started to fall freely.

"I'm going to take you back to Colt's so we can regroup."

"I don't want to deal with Colt," Peyton said quickly, wiping the tears from her cheeks and then ripping the earrings out of her ears. All that time she spent trying to look perfect for him tonight. Stupid, stupid, stupid.

"I'll handle him." Mila handed her a stash of tissues she kept in her purse. Peyton took them, all the while willing herself not to shed one more tear over someone who never should have been worth it.

***

Colt put the key in the ignition and started his truck. He had just left the home improvement store with Lizzy, and they were headed to her grandmother's house. His involvement in this project transpired before he could even think about what he was doing. He didn't mind helping, though. Especially not when he was helping a sweetheart like Lizzy.

"I appreciate you doing this." Lizzy was crunched in the passenger seat, a bucket of dry wall mix under her feet. "I don't know how I can repay you."

He looked at her with playful eyes. He was about to tell her there was no need to repay him, but his phone rang before he could respond. He glanced down at it.

"That's my sister. Excuse me for a second." He picked up the phone and said hello.

"Colt, it's me," Mila said urgently. "Listen, Peyton had a bad night. She's OK, but I have her here at the house, and if she's still here when you get here, just don't ask any questions, OK?"

"Questions about what?"

"Why she's here."

"Well, why *is* she there?"

"I don't have a lot of time to get into it right now but she caught her boyfriend with her best friend at the dance tonight."

"Oh. Well, that pretty much sums it up."

"Yeah. I'll talk to you more about it later. I just don't want you going all Magnum P.I. on her if we're still here when you get home."

"Magnum P.I. Right, Mila. Good luck with Peyton. Goodbye." He ended the call.

Lizzy looked at him. "Magnum P.I.?"

Colt shook his head. "Family drama."

Family drama was the reason he was in his truck with Lizzy right now. When he'd stopped by the shelter the day before to check on Luna, Lizzy mentioned to him that her grandmother was living in unsafe conditions. A neighbor had noticed that she had some shingles missing from her roof and was concerned about roof rot. When Lizzy ventured to the attic with the neighbor, they found mold. She didn't know how much damage was done or how they were going to fix it, but Lizzy was going to do whatever it would take to make sure her grandmother was safe.

When she told Colt the story, she hadn't known that he had worked in his father's remodeling and repair business for years. She was just extremely upset about her grandmother's situation, and she needed to fix it for her.

When she jumped at the chance to accept Colt's help, he realized how desperate she was. They talked about how they could fix it, and as soon as they had a plan in place, Lizzy was able to convince her grandmother to move into her small apartment with her temporarily.

She put on a good front, but Lizzy knew that Gran's spirit was broken, and it was devastating to see her like that. The look on Lizzy's face when she talked about it was all Colt needed to see. He would see this project through and get the old lady back in her house, no matter what it took.

He had made a trip over to assess the damage and decided that the work involved would only take a matter of a few weeks at best. The main issue other than the roof was that there was a significant leak in the kitchen that she hadn't noticed, and he was pretty sure it caused some rotting underneath the plaster. They would need to fix that, too. But tonight they were only delivering the materials to the house. They would start the work tomorrow.

When they pulled into the driveway, he parked the truck and assessed the house once again. It was a beautiful thing, really, an underdog of sorts. Based on some of the damage to the roof, there were several places that should have caved in by now, but they were still standing.

"What do you think?" Lizzy asked, standing next to him and staring up at the roof like he was. She had no idea what they were looking for. She only knew that he knew what he was doing, and that was all she needed to know.

"I think it's manageable." He slid his hands into his jacket pockets and glanced at her, an amused look on his face. There was really nothing amusing about her. She just made him feel light-hearted, happy, for no particular reason.

"Manageable. That's what I like to hear." She nodded and then her eyes met his. He saw a certain shine to them, one that should have warned him to not get too personal with her. She knew about Alaina, but she also knew Alaina wasn't around much.

He gestured to the truck. "Let's get this stuff unloaded. We have a lot of work ahead of us."

The materials were stacked on the porch within minutes. Colt paused to look over the receipt from the home improvement store and take inventory of what they had, trying to make sure he didn't forget anything.

Lizzy sat down on the porch swing and looked out at the stars. When he was done going over the receipt, Colt tucked it in his back pocket and sat down next to her. It was so peaceful and quiet there. No other houses for miles. Stars twinkling as far as the eye could see. He took a moment to admire it. The scene before him now was everything he loved about living in the country.

"When I was a little girl, my grandfather used to terrify me with stories about the war in the very spot you're sitting in." She looked over at him playfully. "Do you have any scary war stories for me, Colt?"

He shook his head. "I could tell you stories about growing up with my sister, though. That's kind of scary."

She punched him in the arm. "I'm sure she's not scary."

He looked out into the night. "All women are scary."

"What about me?" she asked.

"You're terrifying," he said, and smiled at her, then stood. "Come on. We should get going. Early start tomorrow."

"Absolutely." She followed him to the truck, lost in thought about what it would be like to be involved in Colt's life. She couldn't say for sure, but something told her it would be pretty spectacular. She tried not to think about it too much as she climbed back into the truck with him.

Chapter 9

Mila walked into Cobra's with an attitude. She knew she shouldn't be there without Colt, but she also knew the odds of Luke not being there were pretty slim. It was Saturday night after all. And anyway, she'd seen a truck that looked just like his out in the parking lot.

She sat down at the bar, and the bartender walked over. At first glance, with his long hair that looked messy despite the fact that he had it pulled back and tattoos all over his arms, he looked rather intimidating. But when he moved closer and smiled at her, she saw a light in his eyes that spoke volumes of kindness to her. "Howdy, ma'am," he said with a drawl that told her his roots were further south than Tennessee. "What can I get for you?"

"Something strong," Mila said contemplatively. "Whiskey on the rocks. I've had a hell of a day."

He nodded once. "Coming right up."

When he walked away, Mila looked around the room for Luke. She figured he couldn't be too difficult to find – she would just need to look for the crowd of bimbos, and he would be in the middle of them. Eventually, she found a guy playing pinball and there was Luke, standing next to the machine, a scantily clad blonde leaning into him, both hands on his shoulder, whispering something in his ear.

He nodded as if he were truly interested in what the girl had to say, which was rather intriguing to Mila. He was Luke Hunter, for heaven's sake. He didn't need to act interested. Girls would still love him. She watched as he took a drink of his beer and caught sight of her, smiled and lowered his head slightly as he kept his eyes on her.

Colt was nowhere to be found. That meant Luke would need to keep an eye on her to make sure no creeps approached her at the bar. A girl like Mila wouldn't be sitting by herself for very long. Despite the fact that some people were put off by her decidedly snobby ways, she carried an innate cuteness about her. It wasn't something he would have been able to put into words, but he noticed it, just like every other guy around her seemed to notice it. That, and the fact that she had one killer of a body. She was always dressed in something fashionable, a cute lace-trimmed shirt or bold yellow heels that no other woman he knew would even try to pull off. But he didn't think it mattered what she wore; he thought she would look good in anything, and downright destructive in nothing at all.

The bartender came back with her drink, and she thanked him and took a sip. When she looked back over in Luke's direction, she saw him backing away from the girl and putting his beer bottle down on a nearby table. The girl's eyes remained on Luke, almost possessively, as he walked down the couple of steps and crossed the room to sit down on the bar stool next to Mila.

Just in time, by his estimation. It was impossible not to notice that Benny, the bartender, was eyeing her up, along with several other people throughout the bar.

"Who's the girl?" Mila asked, and he looked puzzled for a moment. "That girl over there that just watched you walk over here. She didn't look happy. I don't want to be pulled into any cat fights, Luke. I've had enough trouble for one day."

He looked down to the ground, hiding the smile that threatened to surface. She was trying to sound serious. And he should have taken her seriously, but that was hard to do when he looked into those soft hazel eyes. She wanted to come off with an attitude, but those eyes wouldn't allow it. There was something so sweet and sincere about them, something that told him that all hope in humanity was not lost.

"That's Lindy." The smile that didn't surface on his lips was clearly visible in his eyes, and he knew Mila would misinterpret it as an affection toward Lindy and not toward her. He looked over at the pinball machine, where the girl stood now, watching the ball move around on the board.

She had to be feigning interest, Mila decided. There was no way any woman was genuinely fascinated with pinball.

"Impressive." Mila turned her attention back to Luke, an exaggerated look of awe on her face. "You know her name."

He looked beyond her and nodded his head just slightly, a look that said he was used to comments like hers and not at all interested in addressing them. Then his eyes met hers, and he gave her a grin that showed a little more cockiness than amusement. "She was trying to console me."

"Console you," Mila repeated, assessing him. "Over Scarlett?"

His features darkened in a way that might not have been noticeable to someone who didn't know him like she did. "Over my dad."

Benny put a beer in front of Luke, and he looked up and thanked him, but didn't touch the bottle.

"Over your dad leaving you when you were nine?"

Now he picked up his beer, took a drink, and set it back on the bar. "My dad's dying, Mila." He gestured toward Lindy. "She works for hospice, and she knows who he is. So she was just…" He looked to the ground again, his voice trailing off.

Mila swallowed hard, feeling like a complete idiot for making stupid remarks without knowing what was going on. "I – I'm sorry. I had no idea."

He looked back over at her out of the corner of his eyes, a half-hearted smile on his face. "Of course you didn't. How would you know?" He said it quietly, and she could hear the defeat in his voice, like he was ready to give up on anything good in life. She couldn't imagine that his father's death would have much to do with that. She knew they hadn't talked since he was a little boy. This had to be more about Scarlett.

She reached out and touched his arm. "What's wrong with your father?"

He laughed in a cynical way. "What's wrong with my father? I stopped asking myself that question a long time ago. But there's something. There's definitely something wrong with him."

She gave him an impatient look. "You know what I meant."

"Heart failure, I guess." He shrugged. "He's been sick for a while."

"Are you going to see him?"

He glanced away. "I haven't seen him in 20 years. Why would I go see him now?"

Mila leaned closer, forcing him to look at her. "To say goodbye."

He shook his head. "I don't like goodbyes."

"Luke." Her voice was borderline scolding. He took another slug of beer. And for the first time since she'd been home, she realized that maybe he wasn't doing as well as she thought he was. Maybe she should back off. He would probably be thankful for that.

Benny appeared, asking her if she wanted another drink. "Please," she said, and watched as he poured more whiskey into her glass.

"Straight whiskey?" Luke asked after Benny walked away.

"I've had the day from hell," Mila told him in dramatic fashion. "I was driving through Sandy Mills and my mom's car ran out of gas. I called Colt to come get me and he said he couldn't be there right away. I told him I didn't know what was wrong with the car and then he told me that the gas indicator doesn't work. Can you believe that? It was like a set-up from my own family. And the thing stopped in the middle of Sandy Mills, the absolute worst place it could have happened."

Luke grinned. Sandy Mills wasn't so bad. He was sure that nothing would have happened to her there. If she had been in any kind of real danger, Colt would have gotten her out of it immediately. She knew that. She was just looking for a reason to sit at Cobra's and drink whiskey. Why, he didn't know. Cobra's was not a place she should want to be.

She continued. "I ended up having to call Isabel. She had to get Michael and they put enough gas in my car to get me to the station." She looked at him, her eyebrows furrowed in a troublesome way. "I could have died out there."

She studied him. He was clearly amused and not the least bit concerned for her safety. She took another sip of her drink.

"Yeah. Good thing you made it out of that one alive," Luke said finally, and before she could respond, the blonde from the pinball table appeared, sitting on the bar stool next to Luke. He turned to her, and Mila fought the startling urge to scratch her eyes out. Too much whiskey, she decided. Nothing to do with any kind of jealousy. Nothing to do with Luke, that was for sure. She had the man of her dreams waiting for her back in London.

"I have to get going," Lindy said, folding a piece of paper and handing it to him. "Give me a call tonight. I'm serious. You'll never regret it." She shook her head as if to convince him as Mila silently assessed her IQ and decided it was entirely possible that she *was* fascinated with the pinball machine.

"Thank you," he said quietly and smiled. It was the same intimate way he talked to Mila the first time she saw him here. She swallowed down more whiskey along with an even bigger wave of…not jealousy. Irritability. Who wouldn't be irritable with someone like Lindy around?

She watched as he tucked the paper into his jeans pocket, then stood and walked her to the door. Lindy put her arms around his neck and kissed him on the cheek. "I hope I wasn't interrupting something," she said, her hands lingering on his chest as she looked into his eyes. "That girl at the bar doesn't seem to like me very much."

"Oh, that's um…" He looked down at her hands, which were slowly making their way down his chest and onto his stomach, landing at his waist before she pulled them away and gave him another smile. "She's an old friend." He was distracted by her little move and she knew it. He took a breath and continued. "You know Colt? That's his sister."

"Oh." Lindy nodded in recognition, a smug look on her face as she noted Luke's reaction to her. Colt's sister had nothing on her, she was sure of that much. "Call me."

He took a step back. "See you later, Lindy." He watched her leave and then walked back over to the bar taking his seat next to Mila again.

"So, you gonna call her?" Mila asked.

"No." He sat down and tried to get a quick read. There was a look on her face, something that told him a storm was about to erupt if he wasn't careful with what he said. Not that she would go all-out crazy on him. He just didn't want any lectures. "I don't even really know her that well."

"Well, she seemed quite comfortable with you for not knowing you that well."

He felt his mind starting to slip into a dark place, a place he didn't want to go to. He pulled himself back out of it quickly and offered her a smile, bumping his knee against hers. "I told you. She's trying to console me." He took a drink of his beer and put it down on the bar again. "I'm inconsolable."

"Right," Mila said. Too late, she was starting to feel the whiskey go to her head.

***

Day one of the house was mostly demolition. Colt had to show Lizzy how to remove the plaster from the kitchen walls, but once she got the hang of it, she took off, hitting her mark with the back of the shovel, just like he'd shown her.

By early afternoon, they had the plaster cleaned up and put into the dumpster, and Lizzy sucked up the dust with the shop vac while Colt brought in the tools to start on the lath.

"You can take the respirator off now," Colt said from across the kitchen.

She turned. "I can?" The little voice behind the mask sounded so hopeful. Colt dropped his head and smiled. She didn't like the respirator. Didn't want to put it on until he absolutely insisted. He understood. Respirators were a pain in the butt. That and the safety goggles. She'd balked at those, too.

"Yeah, you can." He watched as she took it off and grabbed her ponytail to shake out her hair. She was an adorable mess. He wasn't quite sure how she managed to look so cute covered in dirt like she did. "Keep the goggles on," he said.

"I was going to." She said it in a way that told him that she wasn't.

He held up a crowbar. "Ready to learn how to do the lath?"

She took the crowbar from him. "Ready." She followed him to the wall in the kitchen and listened carefully to his instruction.

61

Who knew there was a right way and a wrong way to demolish part of a house? It was demolition, for crying out loud. It didn't really matter how it went down.

But apparently it did. And apparently it was all about safety and minimizing the clean-up effort.

Removing the lath took them well into the evening. Lizzy was sitting on the plastic cover on the kitchen counter eating the pizza crust she'd rejected earlier that day from the pie they'd ordered at lunch time.

"It's come to this," she said in dramatic fashion. "I'm eating pizza crust." She was starving, and Colt had the entire kitchen sealed up, rendering them completely unable to raid the refrigerator or cupboards.

"We can stop now if you want." He leaned against the counter and crossed his arms, watching her eat the pizza crust. "That crust is good, isn't it?"

"No."

He shook his head. "The crust can be the best part of the pizza."

Her eyes widened in protest. She swallowed the piece of crust she was chewing. "The crust is *never* the best part of the pizza."

"You haven't been eating the right pizzas, then. I'll prove it to you someday."

She liked the sound of someday. Who knew what someday might hold for them?

"Do you want to go grab a bite to eat?" he asked.

"Of course I do. Do you think I would be eating pizza crust if I wasn't starving?"

"What are you in the mood for?"

She grinned. "Something bad."

"Something bad...like Fat Freddie's?"

Her eyes widened in anticipation. "*Just* like Fat Freddie's."

Thank heavens. He was tired of all the healthy meals Mila was always cooking at the house. *So* ready to indulge in greasy burgers and fries after a long day like today. He grabbed the keys to his truck. "After you," he said, and she threw down the pizza crust in a flash.

***

Mila downed a glass of water. Somehow the evening had gotten away from her. She was sitting at the bar talking to Luke and drinking whiskey until he suggested, then insisted, she switch to water.

"What time is it?" she asked him in a sudden panic.

Luke looked at the clock. "7:30. Why? Do you have a date tonight?"

"I do, actually. Isabel's bachelorette party." She stood up, opening her purse to square up her tab. "I should have left by now. I'm going to be late." And now there would be no time to connect with Gabe tonight. Ugh. It had already been days since she had spoken with him, and now she would have to put it off even longer.

Luke stood and threw some money down on the bar, enough to cover his drinks and then some. Mila turned and stepped away from her bar stool. "Nice talking to you tonight. I have to run."

Luke put out an arm to catch her as she tried to walk past him and pulled her to him. "I can't let you drive after all those drinks. Colt would have my head if I did that."

She waved him off. "I can handle Colt."

He loosened his grip and looked down at her. "I'll get you to the party."

"I can't just go to the party," Mila protested. "I have to go home first and change into my bachelorette party clothes. I don't have time to stand here and argue with you."

"Then don't."

She sighed. "Fine," she said. "Fine. Drive me to Colt's."

She tried not to notice the people who were watching them as he followed her out the door. People noticed when girls left bars like Cobra's with guys like Luke. They noticed, and they talked. Her awareness of this should have made her feel awkward, but instead she felt oddly proud of herself. Why, she didn't know, but she quickly decided it must have been the whiskey.

***

She would have been perfectly fine to drive to Colt's herself, she thought for the dozenth time as she slipped into her sparkling red dress. It was a cute little sleeveless thing that fell partway down her thighs. The dress came with a matching red jacket that had made the outfit irresistible. She grabbed a black and white clutch purse and put on a fresh coat of lipstick and smacked her lips together. Pulling on a pair of strappy black diamond-studded heels, she hurried back down the hallway toward Luke.

"I'm ready," she said, pulling her hair aside and putting on a pair of diamond earrings. He looked her up and down. "What?" she asked. "What's wrong?"

"Nothing wrong." His eyes traveled over her again, more slowly this time. "You look…"

"Like one of those girls you would take home from the bar?" She made a face. "Ugh. Maybe I should change. Do I have time to change?"

"Hilarious," Luke said, turning to walk out the door. He helped her into his truck and started driving her toward Baldwin's Bar and Grille.

"Do you have your phone with you?"

"Yes."

"OK, good. Get it out and type this number into it." He waited for her to pull out her phone, then gave her the number. "Got it?"

"Yes."

"Read it back to me."

"Oh, for Pete's sake," Mila said. "I'm not even drunk." She read the number back nonetheless, and Luke confirmed it.

"Call me tonight if you need a ride home."

"Won't you be with *Lindy* tonight?" Her tone was more playful than accusing.

He shook his head. "I already told you, I'm inconsolable. Look at me, Mila. Unhinged with grief."

She turned serious. "Why don't you care that your dad is dying?"

He gave her a puzzled look. "Should I care?" He shook his head. "No. One thing I've learned is that there are two kinds of people in this world: people who matter and people who don't. And we spend way too much time worrying about the people who don't. And the thing is, when you lose someone who matters, it makes it a whole lot clearer who doesn't."

She looked out the window. Those were some cold words. She knew what his dad did to his family, that they had managed a lot of years without him. But this was it. One last chance before forever.

She turned to him. "We're all just trying to do the best we can," she said quietly. "Sometimes you make good decisions and sometimes you make decisions that can destroy another person. I'm sure it wasn't his intention to hurt you and Kim."

He nodded, and she could see that he was getting angry. "What was his intention, then?"

This was going nowhere good. "I don't know," she said quietly.

"I'll tell you what I know." He turned down the street to Baldwin's. "I know that he had 20 years to reach out to either one of us. I know that he missed every big thing that happened in our lives, and all the little things, too. And I know that he never cared enough to swallow his pride and try to make a connection with us. Twenty years, and not one word from him. Now that he's dying, now he wants to see us. You know why? Because a dying man can guilt a person into doing a lot of things." He shook his head. "That might work with Kim, but it won't work with me."

"Maybe he wants to say he's sorry."

Luke pulled up to the bar and put the truck in park, turning to look at her. This conversation about his dad had already gone on long enough. Despite her intentions, which he knew were good, he wasn't going to change his mind.

"I'm not trying to be a jerk about it, Mila," he said softly. "It's just…too late for that."

She looked him up and down, and he saw the compassion in her eyes. She nodded, licking her lips and looking down to the floor of the truck.

"Call me if you need a ride back tonight."

Her eyes met his again. He was so enticingly ruined. The kind of guy a girl like her could get completely wrapped up in and then utterly destroyed by. She swallowed. "I'm sure Isabel has a designated driver."

He nodded. "OK. Have fun tonight."

She smiled. "Thanks." She popped her door open and paused to look at him one last time. "Take care, Luke. Thanks for bringing me here."

He nodded.

"See you at the wedding if I don't see you before that."

"See you at the wedding."

She closed the door. Luke watched her until she disappeared behind the doors of the restaurant.

***

He didn't think he would hear from her that night, but around 2:30, Luke was cruelly jolted from sleep by the unrelenting ringing of his cell phone. He picked it up and saw Mila's number on his screen. "Hello?"

"Luke, it's Mila," she said in a hushed tone. "If your offer still stands, I'm going to need that ride home after all."

He fell against his mattress in silent protest, closing his eyes. "Where are you?"

"I'm at Sugar's."

He sat up. "How did you get from Baldwin's to Sugar's? That's all the way on the other side of town."

Mila bit her lip. "Long story. But somehow we met up with these guys and ended up here. Isabel's ready to pass out. One of her friends is taking her home. But these other girls, they're hanging around these guys and…I don't know. I'm just a little uncomfortable with the whole situation."

Luke pulled on a pair of jeans. "OK. Stay where you are. I'll be there in a few minutes."

"I can't stay at Sugar's. They're closing the place down."

"Go to Clem's across the street," Luke said. "They're open all night. I'll be right there."

He disconnected the call and got ready as quickly as he could. He was at Clem's in fifteen minutes. Mila was standing in the entryway talking to some burly guy with lots of hair.

Luke got out of the truck and caught Mila's eye. She waved at him just as he was opening the door. The burley guy looked over his shoulder. His gray beard was stained like he had eaten something weeks ago and hadn't gotten around to cleaning it out. He smelled like a mixture of cigarettes and alcohol.

"That your boyfriend?" he asked Mila.

"Yes," Luke answered before she could say anything. He held his hand out to her and she slipped hers inside his.

"You shouldn't be letting your girl run around on the loose all dolled up like that," the guy said.

66

Luke nodded. "You're telling me." He lowered his eyes and smiled at Mila. She smiled back, and he pulled her forward out the door.

"Thank you," Mila said as soon as they got outside.

They crossed the street, and he let go of her hand and pulled the truck door open for her. She climbed into the truck and Luke closed the door, then got in on the driver's side and started it back up. The warmth she felt from him just a minute ago appeared to be gone now. She wanted it back. She knew that she shouldn't, that she was somehow poking a sleeping dragon, but still, she did.

"Do you think you're OK to drive?" He pulled the truck out and started down the road. "I could take you back to Cobra's if you think you can drive." She looked fine to him. He didn't think it would be a problem anymore.

She nodded. "Yeah."

He looked at her. "Why do you sound disappointed about that?"

"Sorry. That's not what I meant. I just had visions of Colt sitting on the front porch with a shotgun."

He laughed. "You're giving him way too much credit. He's not going to be on the porch with a shotgun. I'm sure he's asleep in his bedroom, and he doesn't care what time you get home."

"Right." She cocked her head, unconvinced. "But do you know how he has that way about him that makes you feel like you're getting scolded by the principal even if he doesn't say a word and has no right to say anything anyway?"

Luke knew exactly what she was talking about; he had seen him do it many times. "I'm sure you have nothing to worry about, but if it will make you feel better, you can stay at my place tonight. He'll just think you stayed at Isabel's."

She paused to study him for a moment. There was nothing underhanded about the suggestion. Not by the way he looked anyway. The way he operated, well, that was a different story. She didn't know that side of him. She closed her eyes for a minute to survey her options. Either way she was headed into the den of a lion. One was far more dangerous than the other, though. She opened her eyes and looked at Luke. She had always been drawn to danger.

"If you don't mind going back to your place…" She said the words so quietly she wasn't sure if he heard them.

He shook his head. "I don't mind."

He drove the rest of the way to the farmhouse, parked the truck and got out to help her out. It was hard not to notice the way she looked sliding out of the truck in that little red dress. As soon as she was steady on the ground, he let go of her and turned toward the house. She could catch the truck door herself. His attention was focused on trying not to think about the way she looked in that dress.

He unlocked the door to the house and stepped inside, throwing his keys on the counter and turning to look at her. "I'll find you something to sleep in." He couldn't stop his eyes from scanning her up and down, just for a second, before they met hers again. "Assuming you don't want to sleep in the dress."

She smiled, all of a sudden nervous. "Thank you." She waited by the door as he went down the hallway, slipping off her shoes and trying to figure out what she was supposed to do next. The answer should have been simple. It should have been nothing. As a matter of fact, she should not have even been standing there with the opportunity to consider it.

He came back down the hallway and handed her a folded pair of sweats, a long-sleeved tee and a toothbrush. "You can have my bedroom. Second door on the left. The bathroom is right across the hallway."

She took the toothbrush and clothes and smiled shyly. "Thank you."

He nodded. "Good night, Mila."

She watched with disappointment as he kicked off his shoes, pulled off his button-down shirt so that only a tee shirt and jeans remained, and settled down on the couch. What she was disappointed in, she had no idea. It wasn't like there was going to be a liaison between her and Luke for the short time she would be in States. And anyway, she had Gabe waiting for her in London. Shaking her head at her wayward heart, she turned away from him and headed down the hallway.

Luke laid on the couch and tried to get comfortable. Some people didn't mind sleeping on couches. He was not one of them. He doubted he would get much more sleep tonight, but he was no

68

stranger to sleepless nights. He closed his eyes and pulled the blanket his grandmother had knitted up to his chest, exhaling and trying to relax. Actually, this wasn't so bad. He must have been more tired than he thought. He settled in further, enjoying that peaceful feeling that only the verge of sleep can give you.

"Luke." He opened his eyes and saw no one. Mila must have been calling him from down the hallway.

"Yeah," he said.

"Could you come back here please?"

He sat up. "Are you OK?"

"Yes, I just need you to come back here."

He stood and walked down the hallway, stopping at the doorway and running a hand through his hair when he saw her. There was nothing special about what she was wearing or how she looked, except for the fact that it was Mila. Any other girl with her hair falling down around her shoulders and no make-up on, wearing an old shirt of his and a pair of his sweats, would not have looked like that. Old shirts and sweats were not supposed to make a girl look irresistible.

"What's the matter?" He felt like he needed to be cautious, even though he knew she wasn't trying to get him to come to bed with her.

"I can't sleep in this big cozy bed while you're out there on the couch."

He shook his head and took a step back, offering her an easy smile. "I'm fine on the couch."

She tucked a piece of hair behind her ear and nodded. "Yeah. I knew that's what you were going to say. But I feel bad about calling you, and I feel bad about taking you up on your offer to stay when you're out there sleeping on the couch. I know you're trying to be a gentleman…but it's just me."

Just her. He almost laughed out loud.

"Please stay? For me? I would feel so much better."

He knew her well enough to know that she wouldn't be stupid enough to get tangled up with a guy like him. The way he saw it, he could argue with her for the next half-hour or he could just relent while he still had a chance to get some sleep.

"OK," he said quietly, ignoring her smile as he crossed the floor and got into bed beside her. She crawled under the covers and turned out the light. There was enough moonlight filtering in that he could still see her lying there in all her natural beauty.

She looked up at him in a way that made him want to go to her, to pull that beautiful body to his and kiss those tantalizing lips. He closed his eyes and rolled onto his back. Colt's sister. He shouldn't even be thinking about it.

"Luke?"

He opened his eyes and stared up at the ceiling. "Yeah."

"I was just thinking. I know you're going to get mad at me for saying this, but I really think you should talk to your dad."

"I can't," he said patiently.

She propped her head up on her elbow. "I know you have good reasons not to go see him. I understand that. But I think you will regret it if you don't. And that would be a big regret. It's not like picking the wrong flavor of ice cream at Chubby's. I mean, this is huge."

He turned to his side to look at her. "I can't do it because he's gone." He saw the surprise register on her face. "Alicia called me today. He's dead."

She closed her eyes, and he could see the genuine regret she felt for him. Then she opened them again. "I think you should go to the funeral then."

"No."

She bit her lip. "Luke, if you don't go, then it will just be over and you'll never have any closure and that's just going to be so bad." Her words were so soft, and he knew they were coming from a good place.

"Maybe that could happen, but I don't think it will." He smiled at her, barely able to stop himself from touching that beautiful face and her soft luscious hair. "Let's just go to sleep, OK?"

She nodded. "OK."

"Good night, Mila." He closed his eyes.

"Good night."

She tried to fall asleep. Gave it an honest effort for a good fifteen minutes. But her mind was racing, and she knew there was only one way to stop it. She propped herself up on her elbow again. "Are you still awake?" she whispered.

"Yes," he whispered back, and then thought he might immediately regret that.

"I can't stop thinking about it. I know I'm probably crazy, and I know you want to go to sleep and I'm really sorry…."

"OK," he said wearily. "I'll go."

Her eyebrows shot up. "You will?"

He nodded. "I will go if we can stop talking about it now."

"You promise?"

"I promise."

"And you're not just saying that?"

"Mila." He smiled. "I'm agreeing to go *if* we can stop talking about it."

"Right. OK." She blinked several times. She was so relieved that he agreed to go and so proud of him. It wasn't going to be easy, she knew, but eventually he would be glad he went. She was sure of it.

His eyes were closed, but he couldn't have been asleep yet. "I'll go with you," she whispered, and he opened them again, looking at her from across the bed. "So you don't have to go alone."

"OK."

She smiled. "OK."

Again he closed his eyes, and he felt her move closer to him, felt her hair on his shoulder and her body just inches from his. Against his better judgment, he let her stay there.

Chapter 10

Peyton kept her phone off all weekend. When she finally turned it on Monday morning before school, she saw 54 missed calls from Trevor and 35 from Zoe. She selected to delete all the voicemails without listening to any of them. She had nothing to say to either of them.

By lunchtime, she had to shut her phone off again because Trevor had not stopped calling. She was sitting at a table by herself in the cafeteria when something unusual happened – a group of popular kids, most of whom she didn't know, motioned her over to their table. She glanced around herself as if she didn't believe they were motioning for her, but she was the only one at the table.

Then she remembered. Her car ride with Dylan last week. He said it would be her ticket into the popular crowd. Not that she wanted anything to do with them, not really. She got up and carried her tray to their table. Everyone was friendly toward her except for Autumn and Bianca. It was clear that they didn't want her around, but they never did.

She ignored it. As a matter of fact, she basically ignored all of them. She was still brooding over the events of the weekend when Dylan got up to take his tray to the tray return and sat down at the table next to her, his back to the table itself.

"You don't seem to like my friends," he said quietly.

She shrugged.

"I know. You don't have any plans on staying so you may as well not make friends, right?"

Lunch was over, and students were beginning to file out. Dylan stood and waited for Peyton. They started toward the cafeteria exit together. "I just don't see the point in having friends."

"Well, for starters, they make life a lot more fun."

Again she shrugged.

"Why do you have such an attitude about life?"

"Why do you care?" She would have liked to walk away from him, but they were both headed to the same chemistry class.

"I don't know. I guess because I like you, Peyton."

"Well, I'll let you in on something, then. I'm not worth the effort." Without waiting for a response, she walked into class ahead of him and took the last seat at one of the chemistry stations so that Dylan wouldn't be able to join her.

Luckily, he didn't pursue her, or the conversation, any further.

***

Dylan waited in the hallway after chemistry was over. "Come with me," he said quietly when Peyton walked out the door. She eyed him with a little bit of surprise and a lot of suspicion. He nodded his head indicating the direction opposite where their next classes were. When he took a few steps in that direction, she followed him.

He took her to the auditorium, backstage behind the curtains.

"What are we doing here?" she whispered.

"Skipping class," Dylan said. "Drama club doesn't use the stage until after school. No one will find us here."

"Uh-huh. Right. So why are we skipping class?"

"Because I wanted to talk to you."

She rolled her eyes.

"What's wrong with you today? You're brooding more than you normally do, which I didn't think was possible until today..."

"Again, Dylan, why do you care?" She sat down on a step ladder in front of him.

"We already went over that part. Now spill it."

She sighed heavily, looking up at the ceiling. "I broke up with Trevor this weekend."

For a moment, he looked like he was happy to hear it. She looked at him like she was appalled, and he turned stoic. Supportive if she didn't know better. "What happened?"

"He wasn't who I thought he was. I just…" She looked away. "I never want to see him again."

"That bad?" Dylan sat down on an amp near Peyton. "What did he do?"

She wiped a tear that had escaped down her cheek. "I went to a dance at my old school on Friday. Got all dressed up to see him again. I missed him so much." She willed herself to stop crying, but more than that, to stop feeling like there was something wrong with her, that she would never be worthy of anybody's love. "He was with another girl."

Dylan shook his head, looking to the ground. He knew how she felt about Trevor, and he was torn between feeling genuinely disappointed for her and wanting to kick his ass. He realized quickly that only one of those things was going to help her and looked back up at her with empathy in his eyes. "Then he's a fool," he said quietly.

Peyton looked to the ground. "Well, he was with my best friend, so…"

Honestly. It was beyond him how anyone who had the love of this amazing girl would ever throw it away like that. He sat facing the result of the mess Trevor made, and all he wanted was to make everything better for her. But there wasn't much he could do. He knew that. "I'm so sorry, Peyton." He shook his head again. "He doesn't deserve you."

She needed to suck it up before she turned into a puddle of helpless tears right before his eyes. "Anyway, he has my signed copies of the *Star Wars* comic books, and I want them back. But I never want to talk to him again."

"So how are you going to get them back?"

He watched as Peyton covered up the pain so quickly, giving him a grin that told him she was up to something. "I'm going to have to break into his house." She said it so matter-of-factly, like they were talking about the weather or penny loafers or vanilla ice cream. "Which I can do without any help. I just need someone to get me there."

"That would make me an accessory to a crime." He shouldn't have liked the sound of that, but he did. Calculated risk and a hint of danger, just like the girl herself.

"Yeah," she said. "So, what do you think? You in?"

Dylan stood and reached his hand down to hers, pulling her up. "I'm in."

He took her hand and together they snuck out of the school.

***

Dylan pulled up across the street from Trevor's house and cut the engine. He checked the time. It was a little before 2:00. No one should be home or getting home anytime soon. They waited a few moments, watching the house to make sure it was empty.

It was a gloomy afternoon, which only served to make the neighborhood look drearier than it already was. The street was lined with a mix of houses that the owners were trying to fix up and houses that the owners had given up on. Trevor's house was somewhere in between. The front steps and the porch looked a bit unstable, and the house itself would have probably looked better if it weren't painted a dark shade of gray.

"How are you going to do this?" Dylan asked, never taking his eyes off the house.

"I've done it a thousand times. It's no big deal."

"You're going to pick the lock?" Finally he looked at her.

Peyton nodded, pulling off her seatbelt. Dylan felt a surge of anticipation as she glanced at him, opened the door and slipped out of the car. She didn't wait for him to catch up with her on the street, and she was already working the lock when he joined her on the porch. He squatted down next to her and watched. It took less than a minute for her to clear the lock. She put her hand on the doorknob and turned it, the click of the latch the only sound to be heard before the door yielded to her. She looked at him and smiled, and for a split second, he could see the thrill in her eyes.

"Pretty impressive, Wilson."

She shrugged, a slight blush creeping across her face, then stood and pushed the door open, and he followed her inside.

The house was cleaner than Dylan expected. He always imagined that people like Trevor cohabitated with perpetual piles of dirty laundry and dishes stacked up for weeks in the kitchen. It was nothing like what he thought. The house was neat and tidy, although there was a faint hint of a musty smell that seemed to fade almost immediately after he stepped inside.

He closed the door behind him and silently followed Peyton up the steps to Trevor's room, which was also surprisingly neat and clean. A small folded pile of laundry and a key on a key ring were the only things on top of his dresser. The bed wasn't made, but other than that, the room was in order.

Peyton kneeled beside Trevor's bed and bent down to look underneath. The stash wasn't there. She tried in between the mattresses as Dylan started opening up drawers. Then she slid the closet door open.

"I think I know where they are," she said, and Dylan walked over to the closet. "Way up top on that shelf. I just can't reach them."

"In that box up there?"

"Yeah."

Dylan reached for the box and brought it down carefully. He put it on the bed for her to open. When she did, the first thing she saw was a picture of them. They were sitting by a fire at a party, Peyton on Trevor's lap and Trevor's arms wrapped around her. His eyes were lowered so they looked like they were closed, his lips pressed against the side of her neck. Her blood drained as she looked at the picture, remembering what life was like before her dad ruined everything. *You and me are forever.* That is what he told her that night after two of their best friends broke up.

She stared down at the picture, her hands shaking, and in one swift movement ripped it in half. The sound of the paper tearing would haunt her for a long time, she knew. She threw the picture on his bed, then picked up the box and looked at Dylan. "You ready?"

Dylan lowered his head, keeping his eyes on her. "You want me to carry that?"

She shook her head. "No. It's my stuff. I'll take it."

Together they walked out of the house, Peyton locking the door behind her, and drove off to wherever Dylan would take her. Today she didn't care.

They drove past the city limits before he spoke. "You OK?"

76

"Yeah," she said softly. "I got my *Star Wars* collection back. How could I not be OK?"

He glanced at her and she smiled, a beautiful smile that was covering up a shattered heart. "Look, Peyton. The guy's a douchebag. I know you think you loved him…"

"Back off, Dylan." She looked out the window.

He nodded once and kept driving. "Do you want to go back to my place? My parents won't be home until later."

She gave him a look, and he realized how that must have sounded. Damn. He couldn't seem to get anything right with this girl.

"I didn't mean it like that," he clarified.

"Right," she said. "I don't care where we go."

Dylan drove the rest of the way to his house without attempting to speak to her. He would just say the wrong thing anyway. He pulled into his driveway and clicked the garage door opener.

"*This* is your house?"

"Yeah," Dylan said, as if it were no big deal.

"Mansion is more like it," she mumbled.

He shrugged. After 17 years, he was used to all the money his family had. He always thought it was a good thing. There was a certain sense of security that went along with it, not to mention the opportunity that a lot of other kids didn't get, like meeting his favorite professional hockey player when he was 11. But now, with Peyton, it made him feel awkward. He pulled into the garage and dropped the door, then turned to her. "My parents are both physicians," he said by way of apology, and she nodded.

He got out of the car and thought briefly about going over to her side to open the door for her. But again that seemed like it would be awkward, so he just waited for her to get out. They walked across the garage, and he noticed Peyton taking it all in – the three-bay garage, the extensive work area and the elaborate indoor golf game his dad had set up on the far wall, complete with his favorite beer on tap.

He opened the door to the laundry room and waited for Peyton to go inside. "Nice place," she said when they got into the house itself. He threw his keys on the kitchen counter, and Peyton looked around. The décor of the dining room and kitchen looked like something you would see in a fancy Italian restaurant. The living room featured a huge stone fireplace and French doors leading into another living room. Dylan gestured to the French doors. "That's the family room. We can hang out there. Do you want something to drink?"

"No, thank you," Peyton said quietly. She felt like she didn't belong there. But she followed him into the family room anyway and sat on the couch next to him while he clicked on the TV.

"What kind of shows do you like?" He realized that despite his efforts, he knew almost nothing about her.

"Documentaries."

Dylan took pause, but he didn't see any indication that she was kidding. "What kind of documentaries?"

She shrugged. "Any kind."

He found one on the evolution of dolphins. "Is this good?"

"I've seen this one." He held out the remote control, but she didn't take it. "I can watch it again. Have you seen it?"

"Can't say I have."

She nodded earnestly. "Then you should watch it. Didn't you ever wonder why mammals evolved to live in the sea?"

"I never thought about it," he admitted. He sat back on the couch, putting his arm around her. For a moment she felt tense but he ignored it, and eventually she settled against him. He almost let out a sigh of relief. Within several moments, she was asleep, and he was engrossed in the documentary on the evolution of dolphins.

Chapter 11

Luke stepped outside of the funeral home and looked across the canopy area at Alicia. She was slim and pretty, a blonde beauty. Her eyes were a soft green, and her hair fell down her back in waves. But for all the beauty she possessed on the outside, she seemed rather tortured on the inside. He couldn't imagine why. She and her sister, Brianna, were the chosen ones. What did Alicia have to fret about?

He watched as she puffed on a cigarette.

She inclined her chin in his direction. "Thanks for coming," she said, blowing out smoke and tapping her cigarette to shake off the ashes. "I'm glad you did. I'm sure everyone is."

He nodded, just looking at her.

"What?" she asked. "Are you surprised what a wreck I am? Do you know why I'm a wreck?"

He looked away, wishing he could be anywhere but here, but then stepped closer to her, as he wasn't interested in making any more of a spectacle of either of them. He'd had enough of that throughout the duration of the viewing. He didn't answer her question, but she continued anyway.

When she lifted her hands, he saw that they were shaking. "You think you lost because he abandoned you. But the truth is, life without him was probably better than life with him."

He had to stop himself from rolling his eyes. So Alicia was the victim here. Luke wasn't interested in any of this. If it weren't for the deal he made with Mila, he wouldn't even be here. He bowed his head and closed his eyes, thinking that it might have been better to just let her keep talking that night. Right now, anything seemed better than this.

"You don't know what it's like to have a father who never approved of you no matter what you did. Straight As, basketball, volleyball, swim team." She rattled them off with a certain amount of disdain in her voice for each one. "None of it was good enough for him. And forget about having boyfriends or any kind of social life. I spent my whole life trying to be what he wanted and it still wasn't good enough. You don't know what it was like."

Luke looked to the ground and then looked back up at her. "And you don't know what it was like to grow up without a father," he said quietly.

Her eyes turned soft and, in spite of herself, she felt a surge of sympathy for him.

The doors to the funeral home opened and Kim walked out and stood beside Luke. "I don't think I can take any more of the whispering and indiscreet looks," she said to Luke. "I've never felt like such a spectacle in my entire life."

"I felt like that all day, too, sis." Luke put an arm around her shoulders and gave her a squeeze. Alicia looked at them with envy and the desperate desire to have the kind of relationship they had. The kind of siblings who stuck together instead of competing with one another for the approval of their father.

"Can I have one of those?" Kim asked Alicia, pointing to her pack of cigarettes.

"You don't smoke, Kim," Luke said, releasing her and leaning against one of the pillars of the building. "You don't need that."

"I don't either," Alicia said. She locked eyes with Luke. "Smoke, that is."

He held her gaze. He knew what she wanted, some kind of amicable conversation, but he wasn't going to give it to her. For the life of him, he would never understand why she kept trying to pursue a relationship with him that he clearly didn't want. She wasn't so relentless with Kim. All of her attention, and all of her emotions, seemed to be focused on Luke.

"You don't even know me, Luke," Alicia said, her eyes filling with tears. "You're my brother and sister, and we don't even know each other. I just want to know you. Is that so horrible of me?" Tears rolled down her cheeks and she looked up to the sky, wiping them away.

Luke ran a hand through his hair and glanced at Kim.

"Sweetie." Kim reached a hand out to her. "It's not horrible at all."

Luke stood back and watched. The drama was playing out in an even grander manner than he had imagined, and as far as he could see, there was no escape from it.

But then, like an angel to the rescue, Mila walked up beside him and grabbed his hand. "I don't mean to steal him away," she said to his sisters. "But if you could just excuse us for a minute." He squeezed her hand in a gesture of a thank you, and she led him down the sidewalk toward his truck.

"Thanks for the save," he mumbled, when they reached the truck.

"Well, it's my fault you're here to begin with," she said, and they stood side by side with their backs against the truck. Luke looked up to the gray sky, wishing with all he had that this could just be over.

***

Mila slid into the truck next to Luke. Finally, it was over. The funeral, the viewing, the grave site. All of it – over. And every aspect of it was terrible. He'd met relatives he never knew existed, and he felt obligated to smile and shake hands with everyone who approached him. He even had to smile politely as people shared stories with him about his father.

All of that was bad enough. But being there at the graveyard with all these people, most of them strangers, all he could think about was the last funeral he'd been to. The one where they buried the love of his life.

Without a word, he started the truck, turning down a lane in the cemetery that would get them out a little more quickly.

"Are you OK?" she asked him after they got onto the road.

"Yes," he said.

"You're thinking about Scarlett, aren't you?"

"I don't want to talk about Scarlett," he said harshly, and she relented, staring out the window at the ugly, gray day.

***

"What's the matter with Luke?" Lizzy whispered to Colt in the kitchen as they mixed together some mud to patch the drywall. He had put in an obligatory effort to be friendly when he first got there, but then he seemed to fall deep inside himself, remaining in his own quiet world as he worked on sawing support beams in the garage. Colt didn't like to see him like that. It reminded him too much of how he was those first few months after Scarlett died.

"His dad's funeral was today," Colt said. "And my sister made him go." He looked down at the ground. "And I'm sure that didn't go well."

"Oh," Lizzy said quietly. She poured spackle into her little bucket and climbed up onto the sink counter, stretching to reach the top of the wall with her putty knife. He watched her for a second, admiring the way she took to fixing up the house like she'd been doing this her whole life.

From the moment he saw her in her little white tee shirt and work overalls earlier that day, he had been losing the battle to stop himself from thinking about how cute she looked. And when she wrapped a blue hanky over her forehead, making her blue eyes shine even brighter, he was downright smitten.

He loved Alaina, there was no doubt about that. But still, there was something about a country girl. And there was something about Lizzy.

He grinned as he watched her spackle where the wall met the ceiling, a hunk of mud splattering on her face.

"Darn it," she said, like she meant serious business.

Colt laughed and reached for a rag. "Here you go." He handed it to her.

She smiled in an embarrassed kind of way, only making herself look all the more adorable. He wanted to climb up on that countertop and wipe the spackle off for her, but instead he turned back to the larger bucket of mud and went on about his business on the other side of the kitchen.

He would be seeing Alaina tomorrow, and the timing of the trip couldn't have been better. He was going to get himself into

82

trouble if he didn't get a hold of himself. He had no intention of throwing away a two-year relationship for a girl who just happened to be there, even if she was the cutest thing he'd ever seen. He grabbed some more mud on his putty knife and smeared it on the wall. The house would be done soon, and life would be back to normal. He should have been relieved by that thought, but instead he felt a twinge of disappointment. He refused to acknowledge it as he continued smoothing out the mud on the wall.

Chapter 12

Colt sat behind the wheel of his truck, smiling when he caught sight of Alaina for the first time in what had been far too long. Her visits to Tennessee were getting to be fewer and further between ever since she made the cover of *Vogue* a few months ago, catapulting her career into unprecedented territory. He stared at her, trying to freeze the moment, knowing that all too quickly they would be saying goodbye again.

Her eyes scanned the pick-up lane and landed on Colt as he stepped out of the truck to meet her on the sidewalk.

"Laney." She let out a giggle of excitement as he pulled her close and hugged her so tight he lifted her off the ground. Setting her back on her feet, he looked into her gorgeous happy emerald eyes. "How is it that you're still mine?" he asked. "I keep waiting for you to tell me that some famous actor is stealing you away and taking you off to places far more exotic than Honeybee."

"I *love* Honeybee." She smiled. "And I especially love you."

He touched his forehead to hers. "I especially love you, too," he said softly, then kissed her on the cheek. "What do you think about getting out of here and going someplace where there aren't a hundred other guys gaping at you?"

She smacked him on the arm. "Stop it."

She protested those comments every time, but the fact of the matter was that it was true. There was never a time that Alaina went unnoticed. It used to be only because of how perfectly beautiful she was. Nowadays, he wasn't convinced that people didn't recognize her from some of her modeling gigs.

He grabbed her suitcase and her hand and walked her to the truck. Once inside, she slid across the seat and laid her head on his shoulder, looking out the windshield as they drove down the country road that took them away from the airport.

"I've had enough of my job," she murmured, wrapping her arms around him. "Enough with the airports and the hotels and the cameras." She closed her eyes. "These next few days, I just want to be your girlfriend."

He gave her a squeeze, just as happy to be her refuge as he was that she was his.

***

The drive back felt shorter than the drive to the airport, but that was probably because he had a beautiful woman on his arm telling him stories about photo shoots and career opportunities, along with the gossip about some of the girls she was modeling with. The life that she lived apart from him felt like some kind of otherworldly bubble, a fantasyland that didn't really exist. He could imagine it, but he'd never actually seen it. He had only ever been to New York once to visit her and meet her mother, and that was only for a weekend, long before she started to become well known on the modeling scene.

"Enough about me," she said, pulling away from him so she could look at him. "What have you been doing since the last time I was here?"

He looked at her out of the corner of his eyes and smiled. "Waiting to see you again?"

She smacked him lightly on the arm. "Besides that."

"I told you about that house I'm working on with that girl from the shelter," he said. "So outside of work, and outside of trying to keep an eye on Peyton and make sure Luke's OK, that house has been taking up most of my time."

"Do I get to see it?"

He pulled her to him again. "You get to see anything you want."

"Mmm…" She looked at him suggestively, and he smiled, holding out his arm so she could snuggle into him again. Keeping his eyes on the road, he kissed her on the top of the head. She smelled like heaven.

It was another hour before he finally pulled the truck into the driveway, shut it off and gave her a squeeze. "Welcome back." He buried his nose in her hair, taking in the sweet scent of her.

"Thank you," she said, remaining in his arms for just one moment longer before she pulled away to slide across the seat and wait for him to get out and open the door for her.

Outside of the truck, she stood before him, her hands against his chest once again. "How about that kiss I didn't get at the airport?" Alaina had this way about her where she could be equally classy and proper at the same time she was undeniably hot and sexy. She could make a man go completely out of his head if he wasn't careful. "Don't get me wrong, I love your old-fashioned southern ways, but I don't see anyone around here but you and me."

He exhaled a breath, then bent his head and kissed her as politely as he could, trying his best not to devour her right there.

She smiled, a warmth in her eyes that he missed about her all the time. He took a step back to let her pass, then grabbed her suitcase and followed her up the steps of the porch. Once they were inside, he closed the door behind them and pulled her back into his arms.

"Laney," he whispered in her ear. "There are a million things I want to do with you this weekend…" He kissed her earlobe.

"Mmm," she murmured, smiling at him in that sexy way, wrapping her arms around his neck.

"But right now I can't seem to keep my hands off you." He looked into her eyes.

She smiled. "Then don't," she said, closing the small gap between them with a kiss.

***

It was late in the afternoon when Colt called Lizzy to ask if they could come by so Alaina could see all the work they'd been doing these past few weeks.

"I'm at the house right now," said Lizzy. "Come on over."

"OK. Mind if we stop after we grab a bite to eat?"

"Not at all." Lizzy took a quick peek at herself in the mirror. *What's the use*, she thought. She was never going to measure up to some supermodel. She didn't even know why the thought crossed her mind.

"Great. See you then." Colt ended the call and looked at Alaina. "All set to go see the house after we eat." He turned down the road to the café that Alaina loved. They featured mostly vegetarian health foods and apparently they had the best cup of green tea she had ever been served.

They sat down near a window after they placed their orders, and Alaina's phone rang. "I'm sorry, but I have to get this," she said. "It's my agent."

Colt nodded, and she smiled, turning slightly away from him to take the call. He watched her as she spoke, and somehow he knew. He knew this was going to be the call that would change their lives forever.

He waited as she talked to her agent about her trip and what the weather was like in Tennessee. He tried to think of what he would say if it didn't work out the way she wanted it to this time, but he knew those words would be unnecessary.

"OK, yes," she said, and he could see a change in her demeanor, like they were getting down to business. "Oh, my stars. Are you kidding me, Shell?" She shifted in her seat, barely able to contain herself. "Yes. OK. New York City Headquarters, 10AM on Monday. OK. See you there."

She ended the call. When she looked across the table at Colt, there were tears in her eyes.

"What did she say?"

"I, um. Wow." She looked at him. "I'm going to Paris. And Brazil. And Germany."

"What?"

She closed her eyes for a second, and a tear rolled down her cheek. Even tears were perfectly beautiful on Alaina. Sometimes it was like she wasn't a real human being.

"Colt, I just got a major contract. A major, major contract. Like a million dollars a year with bonuses. That kind of contract."

He leaned forward. "What?" He knew what she said. He just didn't exactly believe it.

"I don't know. They want to sign me on an international tour for some big names in the fashion industry. And Rae Lynn Banks is starting her own clothing line. She wants me, too." She placed her fingertips on her temples and lowered her head, still trying to comprehend it all herself. Colt touched her arm and her eyes met his. "I – I can't believe it." She smiled. "A million dollars? One *million* dollars? Do you know what I could do with a million dollars?"

He knew exactly what she would do with a million dollars. Put her mother up in whatever kind of house she wanted and buy a new place in New York City, something more upscale than the hole she lived in now.

"So, you're the most beautiful girl on the planet and now you're a millionaire? Maybe we should go ring shopping this weekend." He smiled. There was a twinkle in his eye that Alaina loved.

She got up and sat down on his lap, looking him in the eyes. "I would have gone ring shopping with you a long time ago," she murmured. He looked her up and down, not knowing what to say. If anything, this threw a whole new set of issues into their relationship. There was no way he could seriously consider getting her a ring. It was too much to think about right now.

But she seemed like she was serious. He was relieved when she broke into a smile and her eyes lit up with excitement. "I have to call my mom." She kissed him on the cheek and jumped up. "I'll be right back." She ran out the front door of the café and stood on the sidewalk dialing her mother.

He was happy for her in a dreadful kind of way, if that was possible. He loved the girl, and he wanted all her dreams to come true, and then some. He just wasn't sure where they were going to fit into each other's lives with all the changes that were inevitably coming their way. There was nothing he could do except sit tight and see where this new path would lead them.

***

Lizzy heard the truck outside, opened the door and stood on the porch to wait. Her heart sank just a little seeing them together, Colt holding the door open and helping Alaina out of the truck. Lizzy could only imagine. She would feel like the luckiest girl in the world. She hoped Alaina felt that way.

Colt shut the truck door and took her hand, and Lizzy found herself giving an exaggerated smile, mostly to cover up her intense feelings of inadequacy. Alaina was gorgeous like she'd never seen gorgeous before. So pretty she didn't even look real. It was like she was airbrushed right onto her grandmother's sidewalk.

Her eyes shifted from Alaina to Colt. Together they looked like they just walked off the set of a happily-ever-after movie.

"Lizzy," he said when they got to the steps. He stood aside and turned to Alaina. "This is Alaina."

Alaina smiled, and she looked even prettier if that were possible. "I've heard so much about you," she said. "It's nice to finally meet you." She held out her hand and Lizzy shook it, feeling awkward. She was Colt's girlfriend, for crying out loud. She should have stepped forward and given her a hug.

"Would you like to see inside?" she asked.

"I would love to." Alaina was so pleasant it was impossible not to like her.

Colt eyed Lizzy. He wasn't sure why she seemed so fascinated with Alaina. He'd seen reactions to her before, but something about Lizzy made him feel uncomfortable. It was like she shrunk back, like she felt like less of a person herself because Alaina was around.

That was irritating. The last thing he wanted to do was make Lizzy feel bad about herself. But maybe he was reading her wrong. She turned to lead them into the house before he could think anything more about it. He grabbed Alaina's hand and walked up the steps and into the house. Lizzy watched while he showed her all the different things they were working on. She hadn't anticipated that she would feel embarrassed in this situation, but at the moment she felt like a charity case.

It didn't matter. She would do anything to get her grandmother back into her house. She pushed her feelings aside and concentrated on Colt and Alaina again. It was cute the way he called her Laney when he talked to her. Any time he had ever mentioned anything about her to Lizzy, he always used her proper name. And it was nice the way Alaina was so interested in the details of Colt's life. Their body language told her they were close despite the fact that they were apart from each other for weeks at a time. It was clear that they were so taken with one another that

Lizzy's heart sunk even further. A part of her, a bigger part than she knew until now, had been hoping their relationship was much more superficial than it appeared to be.

They only stayed for a short while, and Lizzy was relieved when they were gone. Trying her best to put thoughts of Colt out of her mind, she went back to deciding which curtains she would keep for the kitchen. She couldn't wait to see her grandmother's face when they got her back into her house where she belonged.

***

Mila and Luke were in the kitchen at his house elbow deep in peaches.

He wasn't quite sure how she had managed to talk him into this, but he was wearing an apron around his waist and making a peach custard pie. Mila had been at Colt's when he stopped to drop off a key for him to one of the houses they were going to be working on, and they had gotten to talking about his grandmother's peach custard pies.

Now here they were. And it was so much better than being at a funeral surrounded by memories that seemed like they would haunt him for the rest of his days.

He stole a glance and caught her licking the spatula. Her eyes locked with his as she licked more batter from her fingers. "It's not very good," she said in an effort to downplay her actions as she carried the spatula to the sink and rinsed it off. "Custard pie batter is never good. It's nothing like raw cookie batter."

He nodded once, not even trying to hide the fact that he was completely taken by how adorable she was standing in his kitchen in her apron, her hair pulled back in a messy bun, her deep, soulful eyes staring innocently at him.

"Ready to try this?" she asked.

He smiled. "I'm ready."

They each poured their fillings into their pie crust, topping them off with cinnamon and nutmeg, and Mila carefully placed them in the oven, then set the timer and turned to Luke. "They're supposed to bake for 45 minutes, but we should check on them in a half-hour."

Luke nodded, untying his apron and tossing it aside. "Do you want a beer? Or is that the wrong thing to offer someone like you?" He gave her a lopsided grin, fully aware that he was dealing with a hundred-dollar-bottle-of-wine kind of girl. It wasn't necessarily bad, and it wasn't her fault. Not really. She was just swept up in the life she had discovered in London. It was probably what all the big-time advertising executives drank.

"I can drink beer," she protested.

He leaned against the counter, looking at her with interest. "Really?"

"Of course I can drink beer. Are you kidding me right now? Do you know how much beer I drank in college?"

"All right, then," Luke turned and walked toward the refrigerator. "Two beers coming right up."

She watched as he popped the bottles open and walked to the cupboard to pour hers into a proper beer glass. It was a light amber color, bubbling with freshness when he set it down on the counter in front of her.

"Aren't you going to pour yours into a glass, too?"

"I like mine out of a bottle." He took a sip, his mischievous eyes never leaving hers.

She picked up her glass and drank a small amount. The truth of the matter was he had her number. She didn't like beer. Much preferred a nice glass of wine. But she wasn't going to say that now.

He watched her with amusement. "Give me the beer," he said.

"Why? I love this beer."

He smiled. "I'll get you a glass of wine. We both know that's what you really want." He took his beer and put it in the fridge, then grabbed a bottle of wine out of the cupboard and looked at the label. "How do you feel about Bordeaux?" he asked, and her eyes lit up.

"I *love* Bordeaux."

He grinned, then worked the cork and poured her a glass, bringing both the glass and the bottle over to the countertop.

"Thank you," she murmured.

He lifted his glass. "Cheers."

***

Peyton walked up the dark alley near Trevor's house. She had thought of a few more things that she wanted back. She knew it was far riskier to be here on a Friday evening than it was to be there during the day when he would be at school and his dad would be at work. That was why she hadn't asked Dylan to bring her this time. Instead, she got her grandmother to drop her off at the mall, telling her she was going shopping and then meeting some friends for a movie. As soon as she got there, she walked in one door and out another to catch the bus that would take her to Trevor's side of town.

She had to walk approximately one mile to get to his house and when she got there, she saw that it looked dark. The porch light was on, which was a good indication that no one was home. Before she attempted to get into the house, she would need to see if there were any cars in the garage. She crept slowly toward it and climbed a pile of logs to get high enough off the ground to see through the window.

And that was when someone grabbed her from behind. Someone who was a lot bigger and stronger than she was. A gloved hand covered her mouth so she couldn't scream, but she writhed about, kicking her assailant in the shin with her heel and then sending her elbow crashing into his ribs.

"Peyton," the person rasped. "It's Dylan."

She stopped struggling and let him carry her by the waist through Trevor's yard and a little ways down the alley before he removed his hand from her mouth and set her back on her feet.

"What the hell are you doing here?" she demanded.

"What are *you* doing here?" he countered. "In a neighborhood like this on a Friday night in the dark?"

She shoved her hands into her jacket pockets, licked her lips and looked down at the ground. "I have some unfinished business here."

"Like what?"

She looked up at the sky. "Like nothing. Nothing you need to know about. What are you doing here? How did you know I was here? And why did you just try to kidnap me?"

"I stopped by your house to see if you wanted to go to a party at Ethan's tonight," Dylan said. "Your grandmother told me she dropped you off at the mall so you could go to a movie with some of your friends, which I know is a lie because you're not interested in making friends. The rest of it wasn't too hard to figure out. And that was hardly a kidnapping attempt."

"You shouldn't have come here."

"I had to make sure you were OK."

She threw her hands up. "No, you don't! You don't have to do anything for me! I never asked you to look out for me."

"Obviously somebody has to."

She glared at him. "I was managing fine on my own."

"What were you doing here?"

She rolled her eyes. "I needed to get something."

"So you were going to break into his house again, now, when you could easily get caught?"

"I wasn't going to get caught."

From the alley where they stood, they could see the headlights of a car shining down the street. "Thanks, see ya later, man." It was a voice that Peyton knew all too well. It was Trevor, getting out of someone's car and running up his porch steps.

Her eyes met Dylan's. She wanted to kick him in the shin again, for all the smugness on his face right now.

He put out his hand. "Come on. Let's get out of here."

She looked at his hand, kicked her foot against the black pavement and then put her hand in his. He closed his hand around hers in his usual self-assured way and walked her down the alley to where he had his car parked.

Once inside, he started driving her back toward her grandmother's house.

"I would have been fine," she mumbled. "So what if Trevor would have found me there? I would have just talked to him then."

He nodded, trying not to look too amused. He knew that he had just totally saved her ass just as well as he knew she was never going to admit that out loud.

"I wish you would just let it be," he finally told her after they had driven a few miles in silence. "Whatever it is can't be that important. If it was, you would have picked it up the first time we were there."

She looked out her window, arms crossed in front of her chest, brooding. She was not about to respond to him.

"If you need whatever it is that badly, I'll take you back," he said, looking across the car at her. "You can't do it in the dark, and you can't do it by yourself."

She turned and glared at him, irritation seething. "You know, Dylan, you're actually a better parent than my dad was to me," she said. "I should probably be thankful to you."

"You should definitely be thankful to me," he agreed.

They drove a few more miles before he spoke again. "Look, I know it's tough. I know that the guy was everything that you ever thought was good in life and he turned around and stabbed you in the back in one of the worst ways possible. He broke your trust and took your best friend from you all in the same day. I know that couldn't have been easy."

He paused and waited for her to give him some smart-alec retort or tell him to mind his own business, but she just stared out the window, so he continued. "Peyton, you're a tough girl. Tougher than any girl I've ever known. Not to mention beautiful and smart and funny and so determined," he said. "With one *seriously* wicked elbow." He half coughed and half laughed, bringing his hand up to his chest.

She turned to him and smiled, the prettiest smile in the world. It was such a shame she didn't smile more often.

Dylan pulled up to the road by her grandmother's house and parked the car.

"Thanks for coming to get me tonight," she said softly, and there was something about her tone of voice and the way she looked at him that made his heart start to pound. She slid across the seat toward him. "I'm sorry that I beat you up." She lowered her head and smiled, then her eyes met his again. "Do you think I left a bruise?"

He swallowed, then gave her a half grin, trying to look a lot cooler than he felt. It wasn't what she was saying, it was the way she was saying it that had him unnerved.

She slid onto his lap and straddled his legs, her back to the steering wheel, and pushed his jacket open. He kept his hands to his sides while she looked into his eyes, licked her lips and pulled up his sweater and tee-shirt, bending to inspect his chest.

Under the shirt, he was quite stunning. Sculpted from countless football workouts and perfected with the kind of beauty that only youth can grace a person with. His abs were also spectacular, she thought, as her eyes trailed down his belly and then back up to his chest.

"Nope," she said. "No bruise." She let his shirt fall back down. "You're going to be just fine." She smiled.

"Peyton." He reached up to stroke her hair. She didn't flinch. Didn't move to get away. He put his hands on her hips and slid her down his lap until their bodies met, and she threw her arms around his neck. He was going to try to do this slowly, but she kissed him before he could even figure out what his next move was going to be.

There was so much fire in this girl. He felt it in her kiss just as much as he felt it in the rest of her body. Damn, he wanted her like he had never wanted anything in his life. He threaded his fingers through her gorgeous hair and shifted his body against hers, longing for so much more than just a kiss. Too quickly, she pulled back, staring down at him, her hair tousled, but the rest of her far more collected than he was.

"This doesn't mean I'm changing my mind about us," she said as he stared up into her eyes trying to catch his breath. "I just wanted to make sure you were OK." She slid off of him and opened her car door, then turned to look at him one more time. "Thanks for the ride," she said. "Good night."

She got out of the car and headed toward the house. Dylan watched her walk away and sat there for a few moments staring at the closed door that she'd just run through before he drove off into the night.

***

It was getting late, and they were drinking too much alcohol. Well, Mila was anyway. The buzzer hadn't even gone off yet, and she was near the bottom of her second big glass. She was going to need to pace herself a little better after this.

She walked to the kitchen to check the timer, assuming the pies were just about done. She and Luke had been sitting on the couch for the last half-hour talking, and she found herself falling further and further under his spell. Or maybe it was the wine. She glanced his way as she stood before the oven waiting for the final seconds to tick down. Somehow she doubted it was the wine.

She had no excuse to be having these kinds of feelings. It wasn't like she didn't have intentions with Gabe as soon as she returned to London. She felt smitten when she talked to him on the phone just a few nights ago. And just this morning, he had sent her the sweetest picture of himself holding his sister's yellow Labrador retriever puppy. She'd wanted to leap into that picture when she saw it. In that moment, she had wanted nothing more than to be with Gabe again. But now…

Luke joined her in the kitchen when the buzzer went off, chasing any thoughts about Gabe directly out of her mind. He stood by the sink and watched her pull the pies from the oven and place them carefully on top of the stove. There was something so thoughtful about the way she took so much care with them, or maybe just about the way she was there, trying to recapture a part of his childhood that he had lost along the way.

He poured her another glass of wine without asking and handed it to her. "Thanks for doing this," he said, holding onto her glass just a second longer than he needed to. She took pause and looked at him. "I mean it. Thank you." She smiled, and he let go of the glass.

She gestured to the pies. "Those are going to need to cool for a little while. We may as well get comfortable."

He led her back to the living room, and she noticed when they sat down that he hadn't gotten himself another drink, only her.

"Are you trying to get me drunk?" she asked, a smile on her lips as she sat against the arm of the couch, turning toward him.

She looked incredible tonight, and he was pretty sure she didn't even know it. Mila was nothing like so many girls he knew, the kind of girls who would show up at his house in slinky dresses with a six-pack of beer. It wasn't that he didn't appreciate those girls, but right now, they only served to show him how different Mila was. How special she was. She was wearing jeans and a red sweater, her hair pulled up with a few stray pieces framing her face beautifully. It was like she wasn't even trying, but still she looked like an angel.

"Why would I be trying to get you drunk?" He smiled slowly. It had been a long time since he flirted with a woman. Neither that, nor actually enjoying a woman's company were necessary when he was actively avoiding developing any kind of real connection with anyone.

She looked down at her glass, a blush creeping across her face, then took another sip and looked at him. He motioned her over with his finger. "Come here, cutie," he said, and she moved closer to him, settling against him as he put his arm around her.

Cutie. As in Colt's kid sister kind of cute or something more than that?

"Tell me about London," he said, taking her wine glass from her and putting it on the coffee table so she could snuggle in closer.

"It's amazing." He imagined the dreamy look in her eyes as she spoke. "The museums, the boutiques, the royal family. In the wintertime, they have skating rinks set up all over the city." She pulled away to look at him. "You should come to London sometime. I could show you around. I think you would like it."

He smiled and then slowly lowered his gaze to the floor. "We were going to," he said, and then looked at her. "Scarlett and me. We talked about travelling like that on some kind of romantic getaway all the time."

"What stopped you from doing it?"

"She said she couldn't decide where she wanted to go between England and France and Italy. I told her we could go to all three, but she didn't want that, either." He shrugged. "I think the truth was that she didn't want to be away from her daughter for two weeks."

Mila's eyes grew wide. "She had a daughter? I didn't know that."

He nodded, a certain fondness in his eyes. "Ava."

Mila pointed to the mantle across the room. "Is that who's in that picture over there?"

"Yeah." Mila got up from the couch to get a closer look. Ava was a little blonde girl with baby-fine hair and huge brown eyes. The picture was such a close-up that the only background you could see was what appeared to be blurred out leaves on a tree behind her.

"She's beautiful!" Mila exclaimed, staring down at the picture in her hands. Then horror gripped her heart. "Luke, did she….was she in the car with Scarlett…?"

"No," he said, and she noticed that the harshness he normally carried in his voice when he talked about Scarlett wasn't there. "Scarlett was alone. She just dropped Ava off at daycare."

"Where is Ava now?"

"With her dad."

Mila placed the picture back on the mantle and crossed the room to sit on the couch with him again. She picked up her glass of wine and sat against the arm of the couch so she could look at him while they were talking.

"Do you ever get to see her?"

Luke shook his head. "No. No, Jay doesn't want me to see her. We're not on good terms." He fidgeted, repositioning himself and looking across the room at the picture of Ava on the mantle.

Mila cocked her head. Obviously they wouldn't be friends, but she asked the question anyway. "Why not?"

"He thinks I stole Scarlett from him." He turned back to her again. "I didn't. She was done. She was already moved out of his place when I met her. She was a single mom with the most beautiful little girl." He smiled affectionately. "He wasn't done trying to make it work, but she was. I don't know if he ever accepted that. So when I lost her, Jay sent for Ava's things, and that was that."

"When was the last time you saw her?"

He swallowed. "At the funeral. She was so sad. Those big brown eyes filled up with so much hurt. And there was nothing anyone could do to make it better. I tried to comfort her, but Jay didn't want me to. I only got to talk to her for a couple minutes. When it was over, I picked her up and gave her the biggest hug and I knew…I knew it would be the last time I would see her."

"Oh, Luke," Mila whispered, tears dancing in her eyes.

"Well, she needs to have her life with her dad, you know." He said it in the most casual way, but he wasn't fooling her for a second. It mattered, maybe even more than anything else in his life right now.

Mila leaned forward and touched his arm. "She needs you, too. You were a big part of her life. You're probably the biggest connection she has with her mom."

He leaned his head back against the couch and looked up at the ceiling. "Thing is, I have no legal rights to the girl. I'm at Jay's mercy. There's nothing I can do."

"You could talk to him."

He shook his head. "He won't listen to me."

"That was then," Mila insisted. "Then, when emotions were still raw. Now that some time has passed, you should try again. It might be a different story this time. Isn't it worth a shot?"

"I don't know," he said softly, more than a hint of defeat in his voice. "It's not that I don't think about it. It was one thing to lose Scarlett, but another thing entirely to see that little girl lose her mother. Sometimes I think it's best to just leave it alone and let Jay handle it."

"I understand." She wanted to press the issue further, but something told her not to. "Do you think those pies are ready?" she asked, standing and putting down her glass of wine. "Because I don't know about you, but they smell darn good to me."

He looked up at her, and she saw the darkness in his eyes almost disappear as he smiled at her. "I can't wait to try those pies." He stood and followed her into the kitchen, hoping this night wasn't going to end anytime soon.

Chapter 13

Colt stood silently watching Alaina as she tossed things into her suitcase. His eyes fixated on the sexy pink bra she had been wearing the first time he saw her in what had been far too long. He wanted to turn back time and start the whole weekend over again. He felt like this every time, but it was even stronger this time.

He remembered every detail of how that bra looked on her, the lacey edges underneath his fingertips and then against his cheek. He took a breath and settled his gaze on her. She was fussing with a pocket zipper on her red leather jacket, not even noticing any indication of how much he was going to miss her.

"I want to come see you in New York," he said quietly.

She stopped what she was doing and looked up at him. "You want to spend some time in New York?" She asked it in such a way as to not make him feel like she was trying to paint him into a corner, but there was still a tinge of hopefulness in her voice.

He stepped closer. "When things settle down a little. When you know better what's going on with your schedule."

She smiled. "Nothing would make me happier." That was what she said. What she didn't say was the part about him moving to New York City. She didn't have to say it. He understood that's what she wanted. It was what she'd wanted ever since they had the conversation a year-and-a-half ago about being exclusive.

He tucked a lock of her hair behind her ear and smiled. "Just don't get swept off your feet by some romantic Italian guy who doesn't speak English when you're over there in Italy."

She batted her eyes. "I would never. I only have eyes for you. You know that."

He nodded, then looked to the ground. He had to admit it was pretty amazing that Alaina had been faithful to him all this time. It was hard to do that when they spent so much time apart, and he imagined it was even harder for her with the amount of men she must have had vying for her attention.

"I'm going to miss you," he said softly, looking into her gorgeous jade-colored eyes.

She smiled and kissed him on the cheek. "I going to miss you, too."

He sighed and looked at the clock. There was nothing more to do other than let her go again. He picked up her suitcase and followed her out the door. It should have gotten easier over time, saying goodbye to her like this after a short visit together. But it never did. He followed her down the hallway, stopping for a moment to say goodbye to Mila.

She should have spent some time with her, Mila thought as she crossed the room to give Alaina a hug. This was the woman her brother was in love with, and she barely even knew her.

"Congratulations on your contract," Mila said as she took a step back from her. "Next time we're both in town, we really need to go shopping together or something."

Alaina nodded. "That would be great." Colt knew she was just being polite. Alaina hardly ever went shopping. She didn't need to when most of the designers she modeled for gave her clothing from their line so she could be a walking advertisement for their product.

They said their goodbyes, and Colt followed Alaina out the door. He tried to stay upbeat, but the whole thing felt like a death march this time.

When they got to the airport, he parked the truck and turned to look at her. She smiled demurely, eyes moving from him to the floor of the truck and back up to him again. He reached across the seat and touched his finger on her chin, lifting her face just slightly so he could look into her eyes. And then he kissed her. It was a soft, sweet kiss, but it surprised her nonetheless. He was just so private about his love life that kissing her in the truck at a crowded airport took her completely off guard.

"What was that for?" she asked.

"I love you, Laney."

She radiated the glow of a woman who had the world at her feet. "I love you, too."

He looked at her just a few seconds longer and then moved to get out of the truck. She waited for him to grab her suitcase and help her out. He put his arm around her as he walked her to baggage check-in. When they reached the check-in line, she checked her bags, and he pulled her to him, kissing her on the forehead. He held her there for a moment.

She didn't know what she had done to get all this extra affection, but Alaina loved it. It never occurred to her that it might mean anything other than the fact that he would miss her so much when she was gone. It never crossed her mind that he might be desperately trying to hold on even as he felt her slipping away.

"I have to go," she said regretfully, looking into his eyes.

He nodded, backing away and holding her hands until only his fingertips were touching hers. "Have a safe trip back," he said. "Call me when you get to New York."

"I will."

"Let me know how things go tomorrow."

She nodded. "I'll do that, too."

"I love you."

"I love you, too." She smiled. "Talk to you soon."

Again he nodded, and she turned and walked through the doors of the airport. Colt watched her until he could no longer see her, then walked to his truck without looking back.

Chapter 14

Mila stared at Isabel as she recited her wedding vows to Michael. When they were growing up, there were dozens of celebrities they dreamed of marrying someday. They would go to concerts and make up fantasies about backstage passes that would lead into meaningful relationships with their favorite rock stars. Yes, they dreamed about weddings together. But she never imagined it would be like this. Seeing her so happy as she promised her life to Michael was overwhelming in a lot of ways.

She looked across the room and found Colt, imagining that his would be the next wedding she'd be home for. The thought of having Alaina as a sister-in-law was intriguing and altogether unfamiliar. Aside from the appreciation both women shared for fashion, she didn't know what they had in common. She couldn't even think of one memory of the two of them doing something together. She was pretty sure that was because there weren't any. And there seemed to be something very wrong about that.

As the pastor prayed over the bride and groom, Mila's eyes almost involuntarily moved from Colt to Luke. It wasn't the first glance she'd stolen at him today, and it wouldn't be the last. He basically looked magnificent in his light blue shirt and dark blue tie. Most people looked better one way or another –either in casual clothes or all dressed up. Luke could pull off either ensemble with ease. She honestly didn't know which look she preferred on him.

He caught her staring at him and smiled, then quickly turned his head, but she could still see the smile on his face. She had to stop herself from beaming back at him, so as to not raise any suspicions among any of the guests, namely her brother.

Finally the ceremony came to a close. Isabel and Michael were introduced as husband and wife to an applauding audience, and they walked down the aisle together. Mila stood at the altar and linked arms with her partner, took a deep breath and started down the aisle. When she got close to Luke and Colt, she glanced over for just a second, long enough to see Luke wink at her. Her heart started pounding furiously, and she quickly refocused on the remainder of her walk down the aisle.

She tried to act casual when he approached the receiving line, but her stomach was jittery and her palms were sweating. She pulled him into a hug, just like she had done with every other guest, but as soon as he put his arms around her, she knew it felt different. She tried to pretend it wasn't, but it was.

"You look beautiful," he whispered in her ear, and her heart did an erratic thing inside her.

She pulled away from him and looked up into his eyes. "Thank you. So do you."

He smiled, shaking his head and looking down at the ground. It was the truth, but clearly not the kind of compliment he was comfortable with. The next person in the receiving line came through before she had a chance to talk to him any further.

***

The pictures of the wedding party were unsurprisingly thorough and grueling. It felt like days before they were released to the limo and driven to the reception hall. The first part of the reception was a whirlwind. It wasn't until the meals were served that things started to become less of a blur. And that was about when she noticed the brunette sitting at a table with Luke and Colt, her attention focused acutely on Luke. She wasn't at the table when they first came in. She had moved from whatever table she was assigned to in order to sit with them.

Her heart felt like it was falling to her stomach as they cleared the dance floor and the DJ announced the first song for the bride and groom. She wasn't sure what she had expected from him, especially given the fact that she was going back to London in a few short weeks. Still, she wanted something more from him than what he was giving her.

When the song was over and the dance floor opened up to the rest of the guests, Mila noticed Colt slip outside. She glanced over at Luke's table and saw him fully engaged in conversation with the girl and turned on her heel, walking through the doors to get some fresh air and talk to Colt.

It was a chilly day, but not too cold to take a breather outside for a few minutes. She walked past two men who were standing there smoking and approached her brother. "What are you doing out here?"

He didn't answer her right away. She could see that something was on his mind, but there was no telling what it was. "Just getting some fresh air."

She didn't believe him, but she knew he wouldn't tell her even if there was something the matter. "Have you heard from Alaina? Is she back in New York yet?"

"Yeah, she's back."

Mila cocked her head. "You OK, Colt?"

He looked at her. "Yeah. Why would I not be OK?"

"Just checking." She put her hands up in a show of surrender. "Who's the girl drooling all over Luke in there?"

"That's Debbie Truitt," Colt said. "We did some work on her house after she split from her husband." He looked out over the parking lot. "I'm not a fan of hers," he said quietly. She must have been a special kind of obnoxious for Colt to say anything like that about an acquaintance. "He isn't, either," he added, focusing his attention back on Mila. "He just can't seem to get away from that one."

Mila shrugged, trying not to look too disappointed in the way that her silly romantic notion of Luke didn't seem to match up to any kind of reality. The truth of the matter was he could get away from her if he wanted to. He could walk right out here and hold out his hand to Mila and pull her onto the dance floor. But he wasn't going to do that. He wouldn't because there was nothing romantic going on between them. It was all in her head.

"Or he doesn't want to," she said out loud before she could stop herself. "I guess it would be kind of fun, you know, living that kind of life, where you're an attractive guy and girls fall all over themselves just to be around you. Why not have a little fun with that?"

Colt stared at her, silently assessing his sister's sudden interest in his best friend. He could tell she was trying to hide how she felt, and he thought better of lecturing her about falling for someone like him. She should know better. She didn't need him to say it out loud. But still, he felt like he needed to set the record straight. She was wrong about him that first night she saw him at Cobra's, and she was still wrong about him today.

"I don't think he's the guy you think he is," Colt said. That much was becoming obvious, Mila thought miserably. And now it was clear to Colt that she was carrying a torch for him. As if she weren't already embarrassed enough about the way she was falling for his meaningless flirtations. It probably wasn't even flirting to him. It was probably just the way he acted toward all the girls, which was why they all fell so hard for him.

She silently chastised herself. She knew better than that. But still somehow, she didn't.

"You knew the guy he was before you left," Colt continued. "The guy who would hook up with just about any girl who was interested. But Scarlett changed him. Did you ever think Luke would fall for a woman with a little toddler running around? Can you even imagine?"

Something inside Mila's heart spilled over, a warm pile of mush radiating from her chest. Colt was saying the opposite of what she thought he was going to say, and she found herself struggling to hide the glimmer of hope he had just brought to life inside her.

"He's not taking every girl in town home like you think he is. As a matter of fact, I've seen him say no a lot more than I've seen him say yes. He's not out there having the time of his life and not caring who he hurts. He's just trying to get through this." He shook his head. "You can't even imagine what it was like. I'm telling you, Mila. However bad you think it would be, take that and multiply it by a hundred."

She looked down to the ground. She didn't need more reasons to want to run to Luke. But Colt had just provided them to her, and now all she wanted to do was go back inside and pull him away from Debbie Truitt.

"Scarlett must have been something else," she said softly. She wasn't ready to discuss all these feelings she was having for him, certainly wasn't ready to have them beaten down by Colt. It was one thing to stick up for his friend. It would be another thing entirely to know that Mila was developing real feelings for him.

Colt shrugged. "She was OK, I guess." He looked away, not volunteering any further information on the matter.

"You didn't like her?" She was prodding, but she knew her brother. And she knew that there was something he wasn't saying.

He looked at her again. "It's not that I didn't like her. I just thought Luke gave up a lot for her, and I never thought she appreciated him like she should have."

"What's that supposed to mean?"

He grinned slowly. "One has to wonder why you care so much, Mila."

Quickly, she looked down, her cheeks ablaze. "No reason," she murmured.

"Well, just in case there is a reason, which I know there wouldn't be, or at least I know there *shouldn't* be, all I have to say is that I thought Scarlett used her mom status to control their relationship. Scarlett and Ava were always number one. There was no mistaking that."

"If it was so bad, why did he stay with her? He can have any girl he wants."

Colt shrugged. "He fell in love with her. And I wouldn't say it was bad. I'm just saying that relationship changed him. He's not the person you knew when you left."

She tried to imagine him like that, but it seemed unfathomable. "I better get back inside," she said eventually. "Make sure nobody needs me for anything."

"Sure," Colt said. "I'll be there in a minute."

Mila walked back in to see that neither Luke nor Debbie were sitting at the table anymore. It didn't take her long to figure out where they had disappeared to. There was a second open bar upstairs for anyone who wanted to step away from the crowd and watch the dance floor from above.

She wasn't going to let Debbie Truitt spend the evening with him. Not when she knew that he didn't even want that. She crossed the floor and walked up the grand staircase, the one that the wedding party had made their entrance on just hours before. When she got to the top of the steps, she saw him, drink in hand, tie loosened up as he leaned over the half-wall and watched the dance floor below.

She glanced in the area of the bar and saw Debbie standing near one of the plush red chairs talking to an older gentlemen. She was keeping one eye on Luke and making sure there wasn't much distance between them, Mila could see that much. Not that she could blame her. He looked downright edible tonight.

She paid no further attention to Debbie and took a few steps closer to Luke. "Hey," she said, leaning against the half-wall.

"Hi." He swirled his drink and she looked down at it.

"What are you drinking?"

"Whiskey on the rocks." There was something sad in the way he spoke, and she wondered if he was thinking about Scarlett. Wondered if he had thought about marrying her and this wedding was just another cruel reminder of the life he couldn't have.

"Rough day?"

He gave her an easy smile and shook his head. "Open bar."

"Luke, would you like to dance?" She wanted to dance with him. But she also wanted to get him out of there, away from Debbie and into their own little world. It was quickly becoming her favorite place to be, and she was pretty sure he was happy there, too.

"I'm not a very good dancer," he said. That was a lie. Surely he would know she knew that. She briefly wondered why he was turning her down, but quickly decided to give him just a little push. This was supposed to be a fun night, not one to be ruined by the ghost of his former lover. She would never say that out loud, but she wanted to take him away from his demons, even if it was just for a little while.

She held out her hand. "It's a slow song. It doesn't require a whole lot of moves."

He looked down at her hand and smiled, then put his hand in hers and let her lead him down the steps. Mila didn't dare turn back to look at Debbie, as she was sure the visual exchange would not have been pleasant. They walked to the dance floor and Luke slipped his arms around her waist.

"So," she said as they started moving to the music. "Did you agree to dance with me because you wanted to get away from Debbie or because you really kind of wanted to dance with me?"

He cocked his head. "How do you know Debbie?"

"I have my ways."

"You have your brother," he corrected her, and she smiled. "And I think it was a little bit of both."

"But mostly," she said softly, her eyes shining and her smile captivating. "Mostly it was the second thing."

He smiled back at her but didn't answer. Instead, he pulled her to him so that she could no longer look at him like that. Mila laid her head against his shoulder and closed her eyes. She felt settled, like she was exactly where she was meant to be.

***

At the end of the night, long after Colt had gone home, assuming she would be spending the night at the hotel with the rest of the bridesmaids, Mila slipped out to the patio to find Luke.

"Thinking about going home?" she asked, as the party was winding down inside. "Are you OK to drive?" His eyes locked with hers and he gave a slight nod. It was unnerving, the kind of look that made her feel like she was under scrutiny. She pointed over her shoulder. "You can always stay here at the hotel with me and drive home in the morning. All the bridesmaids have their own rooms so it wouldn't be a problem."

He stared at her just a beat longer. The woman was so inviting, so much more spectacular than what he remembered. He remembered her, all right. It would have been impossible not to notice her back in high school. But today, with that fancy dress and those soft hazel eyes and wine colored lips... How could *any* man be held accountable for his actions around a woman like her looking the way she did right now?

Slowly, he smiled, bending his head down and running his hand over the back of his neck, then looking at her. "I think we both know that's not a good idea," he said, and something inside of her jolted. He was feeling the same way she was. It was the first time he'd confirmed it with words. But what did it mean exactly?

She stood before him, desire naked in her eyes. She looked so damn beautiful in that dress. Luke averted his eyes, looking to the ground. She touched his arm and his eyes snapped to her again. "I'm just saying…" she said softly. "If you need a place to crash…"

Oh, *hell*. Before she could finish her sentence, he planted a hand on either side of her face and kissed her. She couldn't lie to herself. There was a part of her that always wondered what it would be like to kiss Luke Hunter. To know why so many girls seemed to go mad over him after just one day together. And as she opened her mouth to his, she knew. Knew what every girl who had ever kissed him must have known. There was something insanely sexy about him. It was like a spell that was impossible to resist.

She was just about to be swept away, right there on that patio in the shadows of the night, when he pulled away from her. She couldn't explain what was happening, but she felt stunned by his kiss. She opened her eyes, looking up at him, an expression of surprise on her face.

He closed his eyes, and she thought he looked shameful, maybe even regretful. His eyes met hers again. "I shouldn't have done that," he said. "I'm sorry."

Her heart was pounding as she reached her hand out and took his, leading him through the grand French doors back into the hotel. It wasn't until they slipped into the elevator and she let go of his hand that she realized, with some embarrassment, that her hands were shaking.

The elevator doors opened and she grabbed his hand again, leading him to her hotel room door. Quickly, she fumbled for her key, not wanting to give him time to protest. And then she actually sighed with relief when he followed her inside. *What was she doing?* She closed her eyes and inhaled a deep breath. The door latched shut behind them.

She looked up at him, standing on her tip toes to kiss him again.

His hands found her waist again, and he squeezed her close, forcing himself all the while to not pick her up and carry her to the bed. For the life of him, he didn't know why he followed her up here. He should have told her goodnight and insisted on going home.

But he didn't. And now here he was, still a complete mess over Scarlett and unsure if he was ever going to allow himself to fall in love again, standing in a hotel room with what appeared to be Colt's very willing sister.

Colt's sister, he said to himself over and over again. But it didn't stop him from kissing those lips, wrapping his arms around her and leaning over her to kiss her on the neck. She moaned as he kissed her there, and he felt her loosening his tie, pulling it off and unbuttoning the first few buttons of his shirt.

He looked down at her, and she closed her eyes, her lips luscious and her chest heaving. She opened her eyes and looked up at him, every bit the sexy woman. He stared back at her almost gravely at first, and then his lips tipped up to an easy smile. She didn't smile back. He took a step back and stood upright, pulling her up with him. She looked at him with questioning eyes.

"Luke," she whispered, reaching up to touch his face. He let her touch him for a moment, then took her hand and kissed it before he moved her away from him again.

"I shouldn't have kissed you," he said. "And I shouldn't have come up here with you."

"Why not?" she asked, her eyes shining with the sting of rejection. "I thought you liked me."

"Oh, it's not that," he said, giving her a half-smile. "Come on, Mila. You know we can't do this."

She looked down to the ground and licked her lips, then looked up at him again. "I'm not a child, Luke," she said. "I'm no different than any of the other girls you go home with on a whim."

For a moment, he was silent, just staring at her. "You're not a child," he agreed. "But you are different from other girls."

"Why?" she asked, fully aware that she was beginning to sound like a spoiled brat who was about to take her ball and go home. "Because I'm Colt's sister?"

He nodded. "Yeah," he said in a way that indicated that this much should have been obvious. "That's part of it." He backed up and leaned against the desk. "But that's not all of it." He saw the confusion in her eyes and knew he would have to explain himself further if he didn't want her to walk away feeling rejected. He really didn't want to get into this, but he followed her up here, and now he was going to have to give her an explanation. "I'm a mess, Mila. I know it probably doesn't look like it to someone who just blew back into town a few weeks ago. It probably doesn't look like it to a lot of people, but I am. And when people are a mess, they make stupid, reckless decisions."

He watched as her eyes softened and she began to understand that he was turning her down out of respect. "I lost my whole world when I lost her," he said, crossing his arms over his chest and looking down at the ground before looking at her again. "You don't just bounce back from something like that."

Her eyes filled with tears as a rush of emotion bubbled to the surface. Embarrassment and rejection started to fall away as her heart swelled for him.

"Don't look at me like that, either," he said, uncrossing his arms. "Like you're going to save me. The same way every other girl looks at me."

She dropped her head and looked down to the ground.

"I'm sorry if that sounded harsh," he said quietly, and when she looked back up, he saw that the tears were falling down her cheeks. He crossed the short distance between them to wipe the tears from her face. "It's just...irrational thoughts make people do irrational things. You're not here to save me. Got that?" She looked up at him, her eyes huge, and gave a subtle nod. He smiled. "I just wish you weren't so damn tempting," he said, trying to lighten the mood.

She bit her lip and looked down at the ground again. Truth was, he had never seen her like this before, so open and so vulnerable. In that moment, maybe it was he who wanted to save her. He took a step back and took a breath, trying to put a little distance between them, gain some perspective, stop feeling so crazy around her.

"Do you remember Dennis Hawk?" she asked quietly, and he nodded. Dennis Hawk was Mila's boyfriend when she was in tenth grade. Just before school let out that year, he was killed in a four-wheeling accident, and later that year, his father was sent to jail for involuntarily manslaughter. "Losing Dennis was nothing compared to what you're going through, but I want you to know that I understand a little bit anyway. And I'm so, so sorry I didn't think about that before I put you in this position. Of course you're not over it. Of course you feel like you're a mess and your life will never get back on track again."

He stared down at her, a certain comfort coming with her words, a comfort in knowing that there was someone in his world who had been through a loss like his. He truly believed that she did understand.

She reached up and touched his face, and he closed his eyes. "Stay with me tonight," she whispered, and he opened his eyes. She could so easily pull him back under her spell, and he wasn't sure he would be able to stop himself a second time.

"I can't," he said, regret thick in his voice.

She smiled. "I don't mean it like that. I just mean it as two people who could use a friend and a break from the rest of the world. Stay with me tonight, as my friend."

He backed away, shaking his head. "Mila, I am like, *super* attracted to you," he admitted. "Look at you." His eyes moved down the length of her dress.

"I can change," she said quickly. "I'll be right back."

Before he could respond, she brushed past him, grabbing her bag and heading into the bathroom, closing the door behind her. He glanced at the closed door and waited for her to come back out. He wasn't staying, but he would at least tell her goodnight.

When she came back out, she was wearing little black shorts and a white shirt with long black sleeves. He swallowed. That outfit, and the way her hair was now falling loosely over her shoulders, was even worse.

"Like I said, I have to go." He made a move toward the door, pausing only to give her a quick smile. "Goodnight, Mila."

She reached out and touched his arm. "I'll make sure that nothing happens between us tonight," she said, looking at him with soft eyes. "Please stay? For me?"

He didn't want to. But even as he looked at her, he felt himself losing the battle.

She was impossible to say no to. Which was exactly why he shouldn't stay. "All right," he finally said. "But I'm serious. Nothing can happen between us."

He waited for her to nod in agreement before he walked past her, sitting on the far end of the couch. She crossed the room and sat down on the opposite side, looking at him as if he were the most important person in her world. Inwardly, he sighed. He hated that look, and he hated it even more on her.

***

It was almost three in the morning. They should have been asleep a long time ago, especially after the long day Mila had, but her head was buzzing, and sleep was the last thing on her mind. She had thus far failed to convince Luke to join her in bed. He was lying on the couch in the moonlight, his feet propped lazily on the arm closest to the bed.

She had just finished telling him about how she lost her first job over in London. Mila had fallen victim to a catty wench in the office who didn't like her and before she knew what was happening, she was out the door.

"I didn't know you lost your job in London," Luke said. "I thought life was just a big bouquet of roses over there."

She bit her lip. "I didn't tell anyone I was fired," she said softly. "It was the worst day of my life. I was so scared about the future, and I had no one to turn to. But I didn't want anyone back here to worry about me. I guess I wanted everyone to *think* it was a bouquet of roses. It never is, though, is it? No matter where you go, no matter what you do…"

He watched her as she talked. Ever since he had known her, he always thought she was one of those women who was bound to be successful in any career she would choose because she was just that ambitious. She always dressed the part, and she was willing to put in whatever kind of extra commitment it took to perform to the highest level. He couldn't imagine her losing her job and not telling anyone about it. Her family would have worried sick about her, of course. She was right about that much.

"Anyway," she said. "Your turn. Tell me about the worst day of your life." As soon as the words were out, she wished she could magically retract them. "I'm sorry. I wasn't thinking."

"That's because it's three in the morning," Luke said, and she heard him sit up. He rubbed his eyes and stood. "You still OK with me sleeping in that bed?" he asked. "I don't like couches."

She moved closer to the edge of the bed. "There's plenty of room for you," she said. It was a king-sized bed. There was more than enough room for both of them.

114

He pulled back the covers and laid on his back, his hands behind his head under the pillow. "Long version or short version?" he asked. It took her a minute to realize that he was continuing their conversation and answering the question she had asked before he came over to the bed with her.

"The long, uncensored version," she said. "The rip-my-guts-out-and-make-me-cry-like-a-toddler-who-just-dropped-her-ice-cream-on-the-sidewalk version."

His eyes slid to the side, and he looked at her with an adoring smile, then laughed softly. She was giving him an out, he knew. An opportunity to claim that something like losing an ice cream cone was the worst thing that ever happened to him, but he wasn't going to take it.

"The day they called to tell me that Scarlett was in a bad accident, that was for sure the worst day of my life up to that point. But what happened after that day, that was worse."

She turned on her side to look at him, and his gaze remained fixed on the ceiling. The whole thing felt too close, too intense. He never talked about this. And he probably wouldn't be right now if it weren't three in the morning and she weren't going back to London in a few weeks.

"The worst day actually came three days after the accident, when her parents signed the consent to let her die."

Mila swallowed. Her heart drooped. She had never even thought about everything he must have been through.

"Did you not want them to sign it?"

"They had to sign it," he said. "She wasn't going to get better. And between the time they made the decision to sign it and the day they pulled the plug, there were small moments of clarity. Like we all knew it was the right thing to do. It almost felt like we were giving her a gift, but that wasn't what I felt like the day it happened. I was holding her hand, searching for any sign of life, anything that would prove the doctors were wrong. And I was praying for a miracle. Literally kneeling by her bedside begging God to give her back to me. And then I felt a hand on my shoulder. It was a preacher, coming to pray for her and for all of us." Mila stared at him, absolutely mesmerized, a vaguely sick feeling in her stomach. "And then the doctor came in, and I knew it was time. My stomach felt like it was twisting inside out. I was so unsettled and panicked inside, trying to figure out a way to save her before it was too late. Because if anyone was going to save her, I felt like it should have been me."

"Oh, Luke," Mila whispered. She touched his arm. He didn't seem to notice.

"The doctor explained that he was going to disconnect her from the respirator and that it would happen quickly after that. Her mom started sobbing. The doctor pulled out the tubes, and I just closed my eyes. We were supposed to be comforting her, telling her it was OK to go and that we loved her. Her mother and father did that. Me? I just stood there with my eyes closed and listened to her trying to breathe on her own. I knew it didn't mean anything. They told us she would do that. When I opened my eyes again, I saw her heart monitor, and she wasn't gone yet. I kneeled down beside her again and took her hand. And then..."

He turned on his side and looked at her. "Well, I guess you know how the story ends."

She nodded, wiping tears from her eyes.

He gave her a gentle smile. "I'm sorry. I wasn't trying to make you cry."

"No, it's OK." She nodded, wiping away the last trace of her tears. "I wanted to hear it."

He looked her up and down and then continued, trying to make the story a little less grim. "Colt was there when we came out. I was in such a daze. But I remember he hugged me and said, 'I love you, man. We'll get through this.' And then I saw that your mom and dad were there too. They all lined up to hug me, but it turned into one big messy group hug." He laughed softly, even as more tears welled up in her eyes. "And I was so thankful, so thankful that they were there. I don't think I will ever be able to make them understand how much that meant to me."

Mila exhaled shakily, wishing she could have been there with the rest of her family, and not 4000 miles away in her own little bubble hearing bits and pieces of news from home instead of living it with the people that she loved.

"I'm sorry I wasn't there," she said quietly.

Unexpectedly, he pulled her into his arms and kissed the top of her head. "Don't be. It wasn't a good place to be."

"But I wish I would have been there for you."

He moved far enough away to look at her again. "It wouldn't have made a difference," he said. "Not then. So don't feel bad about it."

She nodded. But obviously it did make a difference who was there for him that day or he wouldn't have mentioned it. She wasn't surprised that it was her family and not his own.

She reached over and touched his face. "I am so sorry," she whispered. "So, so sorry."

For a moment, he didn't say anything, just looked into her boundless, beautiful, sincere eyes. "It's probably good for me to talk about it," he said. He knew for a fact that it was. He could already feel a shift, a lightening of the load he had been carrying since the day he lost her. "I've never talked about that before."

She nodded, her eyes intense, as she took in every word, every touch, every movement.

"But please, don't do what everyone else in this town did," he said. "Don't look at me with pity. I know people mean well, but it just makes it worse."

"OK," she said. "I won't pity you. But can I hug you? Please?"

He smiled and pulled her back into his arms. She sighed, feeling like she could stay there forever.

Chapter 15

Luke inhaled a deep breath. He hadn't said anything to Mila about it this morning, but he decided that he was going to go to Jay's to give Ava her birthday present. He was parked on the side of the road outside Jay's house, under the pine trees that lined the sidewalk. The sun was shining brightly and there wasn't a cloud in the sky. It felt like the perfect day to see Ava.

He picked up her birthday present, a wooden train he had made her in his garage. The whole time he was making it, he wondered why he even bothered, knowing he was probably never going to give it to her. In the end, he decided it was like therapy. Spending time doing something for Ava was the closest thing he had to spending time with her. But now, here he was, gift bag in hand, stepping onto the sidewalk. He couldn't get his head around how nervous he was as he knocked on the door.

If no one answered, he would just leave the present at the door. Tomorrow was her birthday. Surely Jay would see to it that she got all her presents. But it turned out he didn't need to worry about that because as he was formulating Plan B, the door swung open and Jay stood before him.

It was impossible to miss the disdain on his face as Jay looked at him, then the gift bag, and quickly determined what he was doing there. He stepped outside and pulled the door closed behind him.

"Hunter," he said roughly. "What are you doing here?"

"It's Ava's birthday tomorrow," Luke began as he held up the gift. "I was hoping you would let me give her a present."

Jay crossed his arms over his chest, not at all warmed by the gesture.

"Look," Luke began. "I know you would rather me just walk out of her life and never turn back. I tried to do that, but it didn't stop me from wanting to see her. I look at her picture every day, and I know it won't be long before I don't even recognize the face in that picture anymore." He paused, hoping that he would see Jay start to soften, and then continued. "I love that little girl. And the thing is, she loves me, too. I just want to know her." Luke looked away. He didn't think Jay was going to change his mind. "I just…" He looked at Jay again. "I never meant any harm to you, or to her, or to anyone. I know you lost someone you cared about that day, too. But I lost everything that mattered to me. And you're the only one who can give me back a piece of what I had." He looked down to the ground. He didn't know how to make Jay understand.

He inhaled slowly and then exhaled, trying to figure out a way to accept Jay's response. He wouldn't have a choice in the matter. He would need to walk away – for good this time. Even if he didn't feel like his dignity was intact, at least he would know that he tried.

He held up the present. "I get it, Jay. I do. Would you be willing to give this to her? You don't have to tell her it's from me. It's just…I made it for her, and it has her initial on it and if you don't mind, I would like for her to have it."

Jay looked at the package, and then back to him again. "I don't see why I should give her the present." Luke nodded, pulling it back to his side. "You're here now, you may as well give it to her yourself."

He looked at Jay with confusion. It hadn't even sunk in that he was going to let him see her, even as he watched Jay turn to open the door.

"Don't make me regret this, Luke," he said, pushing the door open. "Ava! Honey, there's someone here to see you! Come see who it is."

"A visitor? For *me*?" From inside the house, Luke heard her little voice, and his heart that had felt dead for so long, melted.

He waited for the moment he would see that pretty little face again, that bright smile and those big round eyes just like her mother's. And then Jay stepped aside and there she was, like a little angel in a blue princess gown, the smile on her face a vision he would never in his life forget.

He dropped down to meet her at eye level, opening his arms for a hug.

"Luke!!!" She squealed and ran to him, jumping into his arms and wrapping her little hands around his neck, then sitting against his leg and looking up at him with all the goodness and innocence he had remembered about her.

Again she squealed and launched herself into his arms. Tears filled Luke's eyes as she hugged him with everything she had in that little body. He quickly wiped them away, not wanting her to think there was anything bad about this visit. His eyes found Jay's. "Thank you," he whispered.

To Ava, he said, "Do you know what tomorrow is?"

She sat back down on his leg, her smile taking over all of her features. "My birthday! I'm going to be four!" She held up four fingers.

"That's right," he said. "I wanted to wish you a happy birthday. And..." He turned to pick up the gift. "I brought you something."

Ava jumped off his leg and clasped her hands together. "You did? For *me*?" She looked at Jay. "Can I open it today, Daddy?"

Jay smiled. "Of course you can, sweetheart."

Luke handed her the bag. Eagerly she pulled the present out and ripped off the wrapping paper. He had done a shoddy job of wrapping it, but she didn't even notice. As soon as she saw the train, she started jumping up and down. "A train! A train! A train! It's just like when we played with the trains together!"

Luke smiled. "Yeah," he said. "And do you know what that 'A' is for on the side?" He quickly wiped away another tear while she was looking down at the train.

She looked up at him. "Ava?"

He laughed and pulled her to him. "That's right," he said. He hugged her, wishing the moment could last longer, an emptiness bubbling into his heart when she pulled away.

"Do you want to come play trains with me?" she asked.

"I would love to do that," Luke said. "But I can't today. Listen." He looked into her eyes and paused, as if he had something important to say. "I hope you have a very, very happy birthday."

She nodded. "Thank you, I *will*." He laughed, taking another moment to enjoy her presence before he stood, and she immediately hugged his leg. "Thank you for my present." She looked up at him. "I love it *so* much!"

"I'm so glad you like it. Happy birthday."

"Go on back in the house, princess," Jay said. "I'll be there in a minute."

"OK, Daddy," Ava said, then paused to look at Luke again. "Bye, Luke!"

He smiled and waved. "Bye, sweetheart." She disappeared into the house, and Jay closed the door behind her.

Luke exhaled, thankful for a million things in that moment. "Thank you, Jay," he said again.

Jay pulled out his cell phone. "What's your number, Luke?" He looked at him expectantly. Luke rattled off the digits, trying to hide his surprise, as Jay punched them into the phone. Then he looked at him. "I'll give you a call sometime," he said. "You can come get Ava and take her out shopping or something. Little girl loves to shop." He grinned. "She wears me out with all the shopping."

Luke laughed, unable to process all the raw emotions that were coursing through him. "Shopping buddy, yeah, OK. I'll take anything I can get."

Jay nodded. "You're right about one thing, Luke," he said. "Ava loves you."

"I love her, too, man," Luke said. "Always will."

***

Lizzy hung the last picture in the living room with the utmost concentration. When Colt walked back in after taking the last of the tools back out to his truck, he couldn't help but stop and watch.

121

"Looks good," he said as she tipped up the right side a smidge so that the picture hung perfectly straight.

"Thanks." She stepped back and scrutinized the picture, a fishing boat tied to a pier in the foreground with the backdrop of a small village. "It looks like the town my great-grandparents lived in," she said. "I think my grandma will love it."

"I think she will, too," Colt said. "She's lucky to have a granddaughter like you."

She turned to look at him. "Know what I'm lucky to have?" she asked. "You." He lowered his head and she continued talking. "I know I've said this, like, a million times, but I can never thank you enough for everything you did."

When he looked up again to let her know it was OK, that she was more than welcome for anything that he had done here, there was a look in her eyes that almost screamed danger to him. It wasn't that she was looking at him with the shining eyes of someone with a schoolgirl crush. It was the depths of kindness, softness, warmth, and it damn near pulled him under.

"You know you don't have to thank me, Lizzy," he said softly. "Anyway, you took Luna off my hands. I was desperate that day."

She cocked her head. "It's not the same thing. So just know that I will always be grateful to you. And we'll leave it at that."

He smiled, backing away a little. Now he saw the look. One that told him he better get out of there. "I guess we're done here, then. I'll return everything we didn't use tomorrow." He kept his tone matter-of-fact, almost business-like.

She nodded. "I'm just going to take a quick look to make sure I didn't forget anything, and I'll be right out."

"Yeah. OK." He turned and walked to the door, waiting for her to come back and trying not to think about how cute she looked with her hair braided in two pigtails and a blue bandana around her head. There weren't a lot of girls who could pull that look off. But it was so natural on her, so perfectly cute.

She walked back out into the foyer area and untied the bandana, pulling it off her head. "All set," she said with a smile that suggested a sincere admiration for him. He turned and opened the door, holding it for her to go through first.

122

When they got to her house, he parked the truck and looked across the seat at her. "Let me know what she thinks of the place, OK?"

"Yeah," Lizzy said, looking him up and down and wishing there were a way to prolong the night and, ultimately, her time with Colt. "You bet."

He smiled. "Good night, Lizzy."

"Good night," she said. "See you at the shelter sometime?"

He nodded. "See you at the shelter sometime."

She got out of the truck, and he watched her walk to her apartment before he drove away. Good thing this was over, he thought, as he drove the streets that would take him home.

***

Mila had spent the day with her mother and two aunts. She had been forced to rush out of the hotel room a lot sooner than she would have liked, but she had plans to meet them all for brunch. The four of them spent the day at her aunt's lovely home, complete with a huge white stone fireplace and plenty of hot cocoa and finger foods. It was such a cozy day, and it was great to catch up with her aunts. From the time she was a little girl, Mila had always felt like her aunt Sheri understood her even better than her own parents did sometimes. She was especially supportive of her move to London once Mila decided that's what she wanted to do. She always felt that her aunt Sheri shared some of the same spirit of adventure that Mila had.

She didn't get to see these people that she loved so much nearly enough. When their time together was over and she hugged them goodbye, Mila was already formulating a plan to get together with them again next time she was in town. She would not let two years pass again before she saw them. It was a promise she made to herself, even if she didn't say it out loud.

On her way back to Colt's, she took advantage of her time alone to give Gabe a call. It would be just about bedtime over in London, and she hoped she wasn't calling too late. It wasn't often that she called instead of emailing due to the cost of calling, but she needed to hear his voice, especially after everything that just happened between her and Luke.

She glanced in her rearview mirror as the phone rang in her ear. *What are you doing kissing another guy and inviting him to your*

123

hotel room when you have Gabe waiting for you to come home? She averted her gaze from the mirror as soon as he picked up the phone. All the tension she felt just a moment ago seemed to disappear as soon as she heard his voice.

"Hello, Love."

"Gabe." She closed her eyes and exhaled. "I hope it's not too late for me to be calling you."

"Of course not." She loved that English accent. Missed it so much, and hadn't even realized it until she had him on the line.

"I'm just calling to see how your day was." She took the long way home, not wanting to end the call even when she knew she had to. It was equally as delightful to hear his voice as it was to hear about his day. By the time they hung up, she knew that she needed that call, and she would probably need to call him several more times before she got back to London.

She slid her phone into her purse, gathered her things and walked through the front door of Colt's house. He was sitting in the kitchen looking over an accounting spreadsheet for the business.

Mila grabbed an orange and sat down at the bar stool.

"How was your visit today?" he asked, not even looking interested in her response as he started writing something down on the paper in front of him.

"Good." She started to peel her orange. She wasn't even remotely hungry, but she needed something to focus on that wasn't Luke or Gabe or her brother, who just might be able to see through the exterior and catch a glimpse of the turmoil she was creating in her life. "It's always good to see them. You know that." She didn't look up from her orange as she spoke, and he didn't seem to notice. "How are things with you and Alaina?"

That got his attention. Almost immediately, she could tell there was something going on, but she couldn't quite put her finger on what it was.

"Good," he said. "I'm going to New York to see her sometime."

That was different. Colt never talked about going to New York. He didn't like it there. And Alaina had no qualms about leaving her busy life behind every couple weeks to spend time in Tennessee with Colt. "Heading out to the city, huh? Are you trying to warm up to the idea of living in New York?"

It was meant to be a joke, but judging by the look on his face, there was nothing funny about it. "Actually, I am."

Her heart sank. She wasn't sure why, but it did. "Are you serious?"

"Yeah."

"New York City," Mila said. "That's…so far away."

"Says the girl who moved to London." He shook his head.

"But that was me," Mila said. "This is *you*."

"And your point is…?"

She shrugged. "I don't think you'll like the city. And I always thought you'd take over the family business and, just, stay here. You love it here, Colt."

"Well, there's a problem with that. I'm here. She's there. And she just got signed to a big contract, her career's taking off, and she needs to be in New York City."

"That's the worst time for you to think about moving up there. You don't know how things are going to go once she starts travelling more. You should wait and see how things shake out."

"Or I could move to New York and she wouldn't have to travel to see me. I would just be there when she's home."

"What's the difference if she travels to see you or not? She's already going to be travelling all the time now anyway. You'd be in New York all by yourself with no friends, no family, no job, no place like Cobra's."

"What do you care where I live anyway? You live in a different country, remember?"

She bit her lip. "I know," she said quietly. "I just always thought you would be here."

He started writing down numbers in the book, clearly not asking for her opinion or willing to discuss it any further. An unsettled feeling that she couldn't shake came over her. She would never want to stop him from doing whatever he wanted, but she couldn't see him being happy in New York. And she always thought of him as the strongest link in the family. As long as he was around, she never had to worry about anything.

She grabbed a bottle of water and walked back to the bedroom she was occupying. She would just have to wait and see how things played out with them. Waiting had never been her strong suit, but in this case, she didn't have much of a choice.

***

From the time he got into his truck after he left Jay's house, Luke was fighting the urge to call Mila. He had waited all day to talk to her. Now, as he drove toward Colt's, he was all but bursting with hope that she would be back from her visit with her aunts. The distance from where he was to Mila never seemed so far. When he finally pulled up to the house, he sighed with relief upon seeing her car. She was there. Right where he needed her to be. He jumped out of the truck and walked to the porch to knock on the door.

When Colt answered, Luke tried to contain the enthusiasm he felt about seeing his sister. He wasn't exactly sure how Colt would feel if he knew about the time they'd been spending together or how close he was starting to feel to Mila. He definitely didn't approve of any kind of close relationship between them when they were in high school, but that was a long time ago. He didn't think he would care, but that didn't mean he didn't.

"Hey, man, what's up?"

"I was looking for your sister, actually."

Colt eyed him for a beat and then opened the door wider. "Come on in."

"I was going to ask her to come out here."

"Really." Luke held his gaze. He would have been willing to have whatever conversation Colt wanted to have with him about Mila any other time. But right now...right now, he just needed to see her. He'd waited long enough.

"I just need to talk to her about something," he said quietly, and before Colt could respond, she was standing in the doorway beside him.

Luke smiled at her, his eyes absolutely shining. "Hey." He said it softly, but she didn't miss the excitement he was trying to subdue. She couldn't imagine what was going on. He backed up against the railing and tried to look casual as Mila stepped outside and closed the door behind her, leaving Colt to return to the accounting book he had been working on all night.

As soon as the door clicked closed, Luke lunged forward, pulled her to him, lifted her up and spun around.

Looking down at him, she giggled. She was beautiful. That lush brown hair and those big doe eyes. And that beautiful, perfect, happy smile.

126

"What are you doing?" she asked, her voice full of excitement for whatever it was that was going on.

He put her down and released his grip. "Guess where I was today?"

"Cashing in a winning lottery ticket?" she ventured.

"Better than that," he said. "I went to talk to Jay about Ava."

Her heart rate quickened. "You did?"

"Tomorrow's her birthday so I asked him if I could give her a present. Not only did he let me see her, but he took my number and said he would call me sometime so I could spend some time with her." He smiled excitedly and opened his arms again. "Can you believe that?"

"I'm so happy for you," she breathed, and he pulled her to him again.

"I couldn't have done it without you," he said. "I was just going to let her birthday pass and keep feeling sorry for myself."

She pulled away. "You're not feeling sorry for yourself," she said quietly. "You're dealing with something no one should ever have to deal with…"

"Mila, thank you," he said. "I haven't felt this good since she was here. I almost forgot what it felt like to feel good." He leaned forward and kissed her softly on the cheek.

She felt a serious tug on her heartstrings. When he pulled away from her, he saw tears in her eyes.

"You're crying. Why are you crying?"

"Happy tears."

He wiped them away and smiled. "Yeah," he murmured. "Happy tears."

"So when do I get to meet her?"

"I don't know. I'll let you know as soon as he calls me."

Mila sniffed, holding back more tears. They both knew the chances were pretty good that she would never meet Ava because she would be gone before Luke saw her again.

"I would like that," she said, smiling through all the confusion in her heart.

Chapter 16

The first thing Colt noticed about New York City was how impossibly congested it was. The second thing was how cold it was. Way colder than Tennessee.

But he was back with Alaina, and they had a couple days to spend some time together. Her plans for the day involved taking him around the city to show him all the things they could do when they had more time. They covered what felt like an endless amount of miles before she took him to a pizza shop that she had always wanted him to try.

When they stepped inside, the overwhelming smell of fresh dough and seasonings filled his senses. After all the smells of the city, most of which were not favorable, this was a welcome change. For a fleeting moment, it almost made him feel like he might be able to call this city home someday.

They sat down at a bistro table near a window and looked at the menu. "All of these pizzas are amazing, but I think you'd like the pepperoni and sausage with extra cheese the best," Alaina told him.

He cocked his head. "I'm surprised you would even know what that tastes like." Alaina was one of the few people he knew who really did treat her body like a temple. She almost never ate or drank anything bad, at least not when he was around her.

"I've been known to indulge in a piece of pizza every now and then," she said with a subtle smile.

"We have to go with your suggestion, then." He should have made it a point to visit her in New York a long time ago. Now that he was there, he could see that it was important to her.

"OK." She closed the menus and put them aside, sliding out her chair. "Relax. Take in the atmosphere. I'll be right back."

He watched as she walked to the counter to order. It didn't take long to see that even in New York City, Alaina still got noticed. He quietly observed the way men looked at her and wondered if she ignored them every time like she was doing now.

He guessed that she probably did. In the two years they were together, he had never been tempted to the point where he do anything to throw away his relationship with Alaina. There was something special between them, he knew, or they never would have made it this far.

She returned to the table, and as they talked, he found himself getting caught up in the excitement of all there was to see and do in the city. It wasn't long before their pizza was delivered to their table, and just by looking at it, he could tell it was going to be one of the best pizzas he had ever eaten.

He was right. The cheese felt like it was melting in his mouth, and the flavors of the sauce were the perfect complement to all the cheese. "This *is* amazing," he told her, wiping his face with a napkin after he swallowed his first few bites. "Incredible pizza. Excellent choice on the toppings and the extra cheese."

Her eyes twinkled and he felt humbled and oddly smitten by her in that moment. Walking around the city had been fun, but she really nailed it with the pizza. It was such a thoughtful way for her to welcome him into a place that just might someday be his home.

When they finished eating, she paid the bill and grabbed his hand, leading him out into the cold winter air. He linked his arm in hers and tried to focus on her warmth as opposed to how frigid it felt outside.

"Where are we going next?"

She looked at him out of the corner of her eye and smiled. "I'm taking you to a whiskey bar in Soho." She turned her head to steal a glance. "I haven't been there yet but a friend of mine swears it's the best whiskey bar in the city. You should be a good judge of that, don't you think?"

Sweet heaven, he loved this woman. He couldn't remember a time in his life when anyone had planned an entire evening based on what he would want to do. Not that he needed anyone to do that for him, but when someone did, it was completely unexpected and appreciated. It occurred to him that she would have done this all along had he given her the opportunity, but he never made plans to come to New York. Once again, he felt a pang of guilt for being a terrible boyfriend.

"I think we should definitely check this out," he said, keeping up with her confident stride. He took a few more steps before he stopped dead in his tracks. "Laney."

She stopped, a look of uncertainty on her face. "Is everything OK?"

"I love you, Laney." He bent his head and kissed her in a respectable manner at first, but then he took her by the waist and pushed her against the building and opened his mouth to hers, pulling away after one magnificent moment. He kissed her on the lips and then the forehead, his eyes smiling the entire time.

"Did you just kiss me like that right here on the crowded sidewalks of New York City?"

He nodded, looking her in the eyes despite the embarrassment he felt for allowing his feelings to overpower him like that.

"Did you like it?" Her tone and her smile and her eyes were all so playful and inviting. "Do you need to do it again to see if you liked it?"

"I definitely liked it."

She placed her hand on the back of his head and pulled his face to hers. "I think you should do it again anyway," she whispered in the sexiest of ways.

She pulled him closer and once again he pressed his lips to hers. It was so out of character for him, but there was something exciting about kissing the most beautiful woman in the city and not caring who saw them. He allowed himself to get swept away for just a moment before he pulled away from her, this time for good. He patted her on the butt. "Come on." He turned to start down the sidewalk again, holding his hand out for her to take it.

She was still in a daze when she grabbed his hand and continued on their way to the bar. She didn't want to make too big of a deal out of it, but the fact of the matter was, he never kissed her like that in public. She wasn't sure what was going on with him, but this was one change she could get used to. It wasn't that she felt the need to become an exhibitionist, but she loved the way he couldn't seem to stop himself from kissing her.

Eventually, they made it to the whiskey bar, where Colt ordered a single malt scotch for himself and an Irish whiskey for Alaina. When they were served, he raised his glass, and she did the same.

"To us." He smiled as she clinked her glass with his, a happiness in her eyes that he wanted to see go on forever.

"To us," she said, and he took a sip, watching her intently as she put the glass up to her lips. He laughed as she made a face the instant that the liquid touched her tongue. He rubbed his hand on her back as she put the glass down.

"You didn't like it? Have you ever had good Irish whiskey before?"

"You call that good, huh?"

Again he laughed, such a happy and sincere laugh that she laughed along with him. "So you didn't like it, then?"

She pursed her lips and thought about it for a second. "Actually, I think I kind of did."

He gestured to the glass. "Try it again, then."

She picked up her glass and put it to her lips again, swallowed another sip and nodded her head yes.

"Yes, you like it?"

"Yeah," she said. "I could drink more of this. I could become a whiskey drinker with you."

He held up his glass again. "Bottoms up," he said, taking a long pull of his Scotch.

***

Mila felt like she had walked right into the past. She had driven to Luke's house for a second round of attempts at making peach pies like his grandmother used to. But before they made it to

131

the kitchen, they got to talking about all the good times they had at this place when they were growing up and it belonged to his grandmother. Their discussion prompted a short stroll to the barn, where she stepped inside and looked around in wonder.

Everything – the smell of hay, the bales that were stacked in the corner, the ladder built into the wall that led to the loft – was exactly the way she remembered it. She inhaled a deep breath and took in the smell of the place, feeling herself relax as her mind was transported to a simpler time.

It was here that Luke and his friends gathered on any given weekend during the school year and any day of the week during the summer. There had been more make-ups, break-ups and hook-ups around the campfire and in this old red barn than Mila cared to remember. Her sharpest memory was the day she caught Marcus Maloney making out on a bale of hay with Clarissa Samuelson the summer between her junior and senior year.

Marcus Maloney. The biggest crush she had ever had in her life. The boy who had led her to believe, with his flirtatious winks and mischievous grins, that he had a thing for her, too. She remembered the way her heart had slammed into her chest when she realized what was happening. She had opened the barn door to get more oil for the tiki lights, and there they were. Clarissa with her legs draped over his. She thought he had given her a remorseful shrug, but she had murmured an awkward apology and turned away so quickly that she couldn't be sure.

"You thinking about Marcus Maloney?" Luke asked, looking at her out of the corner of his eye and giving her a knowing smile.

She smacked his arm. "Shut up, Hunter. How did you even know about that?" She felt a flush of embarrassment. She hadn't thought her feelings for him or about what happened that night were that obvious. But if Luke noticed it, did that mean everyone else had as well?

He shrugged. "I don't know. I guess I kind of kept an eye on you. You're Colt's little sister. Of course I noticed you." He looked around the barn. "All the memories at this place…" His voice trailed off. "And all you can think about is Marcus Maloney." He laughed then took a step back in anticipation of another blow.

Mila put her hands on her hips and looked at him defiantly. "It was a defining moment of my teen years. Do you know how much I liked that guy? At least he meant something to me, which is more than I can say for the dozens of girls you made out with on the hay bales."

"It wasn't dozens," Luke protested, then did some quick calculations in his head. "OK, maybe it was."

She laughed. "I know it was."

"But it wasn't on the hay bales," he defended. "I always took them to the pent house." He pointed to the loft.

"*Much* classier." Mila rolled her eyes.

Luke walked over to the ladder and took a step up, then leaned away from the wall and looked at her. "Come up to the pent house."

Her brows knit together. "I'm not going up there with you."

He grinned and climbed a few more steps. Lord, that boy was dangerous looking. Her boots clicked against the wooden floor as she walked across the barn to the ladder. Luke had just disappeared through the square cut-out that led to the loft.

When she reached the top, he already had the doors swung open, and the fresh air brought new life to the staleness of the winter months that hung inside. He sat at the edge of the loft with his legs hanging off the side. He twisted to look at her and patted the floor next to him.

She cocked her head. "Aren't you afraid you're going to fall sitting that close to the edge?" she asked as she moved closer.

"I've fallen out of here at least a dozen times." He looked down to the ground. "It's not that bad of a fall."

She approached him and looked down, assessing the distance between the loft and the ground. "*That* makes me feel a lot better." She sat down next to him anyway. It was a chilly evening. She pulled her coat tighter and then Luke put his arm around her. She looked out into the night. On a farmland that was nothing but nature for 200 acres, the stars seemed to go on forever.

"It's beautiful," she said, her voice full of enchantment.

"You know why Marcus Maloney hooked up with Clarissa instead of you?" Luke asked, pulling her closer as she laid her head on his shoulder and took in the masculine scent of him.

"Because she was prettier than me?"

She felt him shake his head. "Nope. No way. You were the prettiest girl in high school."

She turned to look at him. "I was?"

He smiled down at her. "Yeah. You were. But everyone knew you weren't the kind of girl who would be making out with Marcus Maloney on a bale of hay."

"I might have been that kind of girl," she said.

"You weren't. And even if you would have been, Colt would have kicked your ass, only after he kicked the ass of the person who was caught making out with you. Everyone knew that. He was even ready to fight me once over you."

"Over me? Why? What did you do?"

"Well, I didn't actually *do* anything. Remember that night the cops came because Jimmy Tanner's mom reported us for underage drinking?"

"Oh, yeah. Everyone scattered in different directions. It was like a bomb went off. Every man for himself."

Except it wasn't every man for himself. She distinctly remembered that she was talking to Luke near the side of the barn, and her heart was doing this funny pitter-patter thing that made her think she liked him in more ways than she cared to admit. When he saw the cops in the distance, he grabbed her arm and pulled her into the barn, where they climbed the ladder and hid in the corner behind the mother lode of hay bales. At the time, there were easily a hundred bales in the loft.

And they waited. Luke hadn't thought the cops really cared that they were drinking. As a general rule, they tolerated a certain amount of lawlessness in their town, and as long as nobody got hurt, they tended to turn a blind eye to kids having their fun. He was ready to go face them if the situation called for it, but it didn't play out that way. He heard Colt talking to one of the police officers, listened carefully as the conversation turned to one of Colt's cousins who was also on the police force. In the end, the cop told him to just keep it down and stay out of trouble, and then he was gone.

"After the cop left and we came out of the barn together, he gave me a look. You know that look, right? The one that tells you you're in trouble?"

Mila laughed. She knew the look all too well. "What was the issue?"

"He didn't like me running off with you like I did."

"But you were trying to protect me."

"That wasn't the point."

She shook her head. "I'm so embarrassed."

He squeezed her a little closer. "Don't be. All it takes is a moment sometimes. Just a moment, and something shifts. And who knows what happens after that? I'm glad he looked after you the way he did. You were a special girl. And the guy I was in high school didn't deserve the girl you were. Trust me, I didn't."

Briefly she wondered if he had felt anything like she had that night, but opted to back off after his conversation with Colt.

"What about the guy you are now? Does that guy deserve a woman like me?" It was a bold question. She might not have asked it if it weren't for the fact that she was snuggled into his arms and not sitting face-to-face with him.

"Probably not." Given another second, she would have protested, but he twisted her around to face him, and there was an intensity between them that just about made her heart stop. "But that doesn't stop me from wishing that I did."

Sweet heavens. She had promised herself that there would be no more escapades with Luke. But every time she was around him, no matter what her intentions were, she couldn't seem to stop herself.

His hand was on her chin, lifting her face to his, so close she could just about taste the kiss that was coming. But he didn't kiss her. He just looked into her eyes and waited. For what, he didn't exactly know.

He looked to the ground, and when their eyes met again, there was more intimacy in that moment than anything she had ever experienced in her life. There was something so naked and honest about him. She could see everything in his eyes: the heartbreaker from high school, the kind and caring partner he was with Scarlett, the broken pieces that she so desperately wanted him to patch back together. The storm in his eyes was dangerous and beautiful at the same time.

"I disagree," she asserted finally. "I think that you do deserve a woman like me."

He grinned. "Is that so?" There was something so irresistibly southern about that grin and the way he said those words. Something about him that felt right, despite her feelings for Gabe.

135

She was about to be swept away, and she felt completely powerless to stop it.

He didn't hesitate another second to lower his head and kiss her then, a kiss that held so much confidence and so much restraint. At a basic level, his confidence made her feel safe. Beyond that, it made her want more of him. So much more.

Her hands found his chest and lingered there. The feel of his hard body along with the quickening cadence of his heartbeat only served to make her feelings stronger. The effect he had on her in that moment was dizzying.

"I think a woman like me…is exactly what you need," she said when he pulled back from her just an inch and looked into her eyes.

He didn't respond, just lowered his lips to hers again and moved his hands from her hair to her waist. He could give himself a minute. That was all he would do.

She moved to get closer to him, kneeled before him and then leaned into him, kissing him with more passion than he was prepared for. His heart pounded wildly as he discovered this stunning part of her, and all he wanted to do was let her keep going. But he knew he couldn't. He dropped his head back to force her to stop kissing him like that only to have her rain sweet kisses down on his neck.

"You have to stop that," he whispered hoarsely, and it sounded just about as helpless as he felt.

He forced himself to hold still as her lips moved from his neck to his ear and she moved to put one leg on either side of his thigh. "Are you sure that's what you want?" she whispered, tickling his ear with her breath and then with another kiss.

His breath involuntarily hitched. His hands gripped her at the waist, ready to push her away if he needed to. She opened her eyes and assessed him, then smiled seductively. "I could be misreading you, but it doesn't seem like that's really what you want."

She lowered her head, and her soft lips met his, and once again he didn't stop her. His hands at her waist also betrayed him as she moved closer so their bodies could melt together as she kissed him. Those hands that were supposed to stop her were on her back, longing to touch her soft skin as they held her to him.

He wasn't going to stay in control for much longer. In fact he may have already lost the battle, and the girl was doing nothing to stop that from happening. She was dangerous. Far more dangerous than he would have ever known to give her credit for. And if she were any other woman…

"We have to stop." By the grace of something stronger than he was, the words were out before he could think about it. He didn't say it in a very convincing tone, but it was a start. She pulled back and looked into his eyes. "I can't do this with you," he breathed, still not making a move to push her away from him. He didn't know what he was going to have to do to make her understand how badly she was tempting him right now. He had already explained to her all the reasons he needed to be careful with her. He hoped that was enough because right now, he didn't think he had the brain power to explain it again.

"OK," she said quietly and fell down against his chest. He waited for his heart to stop pounding so furiously, holding her in his arms and focusing on nothing more than breathing in and breathing out. How in the world had she been able to do that to him so quickly with just a kiss? One minute he was telling himself everything was under control, and the next…

"Mila?" He stroked her hair as he held her.

"Um hmm?" she murmured, her eyes closed and her face pressed against his chest.

"Are you always that commanding when you decide you want something?" He had never seen anything like it before, at least not from a woman as classy as she was.

She opened her eyes and pulled back to look at him, her cheeks flushing. "I wasn't being commanding."

He pulled her against him again and kissed her on the top of the head. "Yes, you were," he whispered. "It was so sexy. So incredibly hot and sexy." He felt her settle against him again, and he knew he couldn't trust himself to hold her like that much longer, not with those images of her relentlessly flashing through his head.

He gave her a tiny push. "We should go inside and see about making those pies." Yes, the pies. The whole reason she was here tonight to begin with. Why they sidetracked to the barn was beyond him. Not that it mattered. The only thing that mattered now was getting her into the kitchen and putting some space between them.

"Mmm…" she murmured, cozying against his nice, warm body. "You're right. We should." She didn't make a move to go anywhere, though. She wasn't quite finished enjoying the sweet feel of his warm body against hers.

He smiled to himself at her innocence. At least that's what he thought it was. She was either completely unaware of how much she was affecting him or she was just an evil temptress, and he couldn't see her being a girl like that. "So we should do that, like right now," he added, urging her forward again.

She opened her eyes. "Yes, OK. Right now."

She pushed away from him and stood, holding her hand out to help him up. The cruelty of her body leaving his took a moment to absorb, but he hoped she didn't notice that as he reached up and touched her hand, fighting the temptation to pull her back down on the floor of the loft with him. He wasn't finished with her yet. But he had to be. He stood and turned away from her, pulling the doors to the loft closed.

"Can't wait to make those…pies," he heard her say.

He locked the doors to the loft and turned to get a read, but he was already almost certain that it was sarcasm. Somehow there was nothing even remotely offensive about her, even if she was ridiculing him for doing nothing shy of protecting her from the trouble that he was.

He half grinned and took her hand, leading her across the loft to the ladder. "You're going to thank me for keeping my hands off of you someday."

He stepped down the ladder and waited at the bottom to help her down. Once back on solid ground, she turned to him and looked up into his eyes. "That didn't actually feel like you keeping your hands off of me. If I remember correctly, your hands were in my hair…" She touched her hair. "On my hips…" He watched as her hands traveled down her body and landed on her hips.

So she *was* an evil temptress.

"Yeah." He nodded and squeezed his eyes shut, placing a fist on his forehead and trying to remove the images of her that had been burned into his brain. He dropped his hand and looked her in the eyes. "I know. I'm sorry."

She licked her lips. "No apology necessary," she said softly, then turned to walk toward the house so they could start working on baking peach pies.

***

Mila pulled two recipe cards out of her purse, each adorned with a drawing of a cornucopia at the top and each featuring a different recipe in Mila's very unique and very pretty handwriting. Lord. Even her handwriting was pretty. Had he ever thought that about *any* girl? She placed one card in front of him on the counter and the other in front of herself. She looked at her card. He looked at her.

"I talked to my mom about it, and I think these two recipes have some serious potential." Her eyes met his from across the counter.

He was having a hard time concentrating on anything other than those lips. With some effort, his gaze dropped to the recipe card. He knew he needed to focus, to stop thinking about that kiss in the loft.

"But I have to ask you," she said, a warm smile crossing her lips. "What happens if we get this right?"

"If we get this right, I would be forever grateful." He said it without hesitation, like he meant it.

"Mmm."

He looked up. "What?"

She stopped gathering ingredients and stole a glance. "I was just wondering what that means. When someone is forever grateful to you, does that mean they would buy you a plane ticket to the US if you're stranded in London? Or pick you up at the airport in New York if you missed your connector and needed a ride all the way back to Honeybee? Would that forever grateful person go so far as to give you the shirt off their back if it was freezing cold out and you needed another layer?"

He cocked his head. "A plane ticket to the US. What does that run? About a thousand dollars?"

"Almost exactly."

He twisted up his mouth as if he were giving the idea some serious thought. "You missed your connector. Because of something you did or something you couldn't control?"

"Does it matter?"

139

"Of course it matters."

"It shouldn't matter. You're forever grateful. Remember?"

He thought about it for a few more seconds. "OK, fine. I would do all those things." He turned away from her, moving toward his pie crust and then looked over at her from across the counter.

"Really?" she asked.

"Maybe not that last one. Do you know how much I hate the cold? Is that why you threw that one in there?"

Mila laughed. Actually, she didn't know. And even now that he mentioned it, she couldn't remember one time he complained about the cold. "You're hung up on that last one. Hmm."

He took pause, trying to figure out what she was implying, then looked at her innocently. "What?"

Mila started measuring out her ingredients. "That last one? That's the one that *really* counts."

He ran a hand over his face. "All right, fine! I would do it. But I wouldn't like it." He looked down at his recipe card to start getting his ingredients together and went about making his pie. As he sprinkled the cinnamon onto his peaches, he looked at her again. "Mila? You know I would do any of those things for you anyway, right? And that last one, I would be happy to do it for you."

She smiled, and he knew that a piece of his heart would be hers forever.

***

Alaina led Colt up the narrow staircase that led to her apartment. It was the same as just about every other apartment in New York City – 300 square feet of space to live in. Not enough room to breathe, let alone live.

She unlocked the door and pushed it open, stepping inside and turning to take his hand and yank him across the threshold.

"I love having you here," she said, her voice and her eyes brimming with passion.

They had a great night, but still there was a nagging feeling in his heart that said that even with all the great nights in the world, this place would never feel like home to him. He pushed that aside and focused on Alaina.

"I had a really nice time tonight," he said softly, reaching out to touch her cheek and then her hair. "Thank you for making it so special."

She shook her head. "The only thing special about tonight was that you were here. It was all you."

He disagreed, but he wasn't about to argue with her, not with the way she was looking at him right now.

She leaned closer to whisper in his ear. "Do you know what my favorite part was? That kiss…" Her lips grazed his ear as she spoke, and it was all he could do to hold still and let her finish. "On the sidewalk. That was so hot."

He swallowed, and already his throat had gone dry. His hands threaded through her gorgeous long blonde hair as her lips met his in the most tantalizing way.

It took everything in him to resist the urge to carry her off to the bedroom, but the one thing that stopped him was the idea that after these few days together, it would be a while before he would see her again. Women needed romance, he understood that. They needed to feel sexy and wanted. He wanted her to be able to take her time so he could make her feel that way, because she was all those things and so much more.

She pulled his sweater over his head and discarded it on the floor beside them. As her kisses grew more urgent, his hands slid down her body and found her waist, and he wrapped his arms around her and pulled her close for just a moment before she inched away and started to unbutton his shirt. His breath was hot and heavy against her neck, his cheeks aflame with desire as she worked one button at a time, slowly releasing him from the prison that his clothing had suddenly become.

"Alaina," he breathed, before she was even halfway finished with his shirt. The weight of her gaze burned into his eyes, and finally he pulled her to him, dragging her down the short hallway and into the bedroom, closing the door behind them.

**

The pies were on the coffee table next to them, and Luke and Mila had already decided that the recipe he made was better than any of the other pies they had attempted thus far. Her piece of pie had been abandoned on the table, and they were sharing a piece of his pie. It was good, but it still wasn't the same as his

141

grandmother's. He wondered if they would even come close before she headed back to London. He knew he could probably find someone else who would be willing to bake pies with him, but it wouldn't be the same without *her*.

He watched as she took her fork and grabbed a healthy piece of cinnamon-and-peach heaven, noting that there was very little pie left on the plate for them to finish. Instead of taking another piece, he put the plate down on the table and leaned forward, just inches away from her.

"That's a pretty big bite," he said, his face serious but his eyes playful. "Are you going to share that?"

She gestured to the table. "You have seven more slices on the table. Have at it."

"I'm saving that for later. You took the best last bite. All I have left on my plate is the tiniest chunk of peach and some crust."

"You poor thing." She didn't pity him at all. If it wasn't obvious by the way she said it, it was unmistakable when she took the remainder of the piece that was on her fork and closed her mouth around it, sparing not even a crumb for him.

"So that's how you're going to play it?"

"You have *seven more slices* on the table." Her mouth was full of pie when she spoke, but somehow she still managed to look ridiculously cute.

He backed away, trying to overrule the desire he had for her. But that quickly became useless when she took her fork and pulled off a juicy sliver from the pie, then leaned into him and held it up to his lips. Suddenly, he had very little interest in the pie.

Without eating the bite, he took the fork from her and placed it on his plate, his hand gripping her at the waist and holding her strongly against him. He didn't speak a word, and he didn't hesitate to kiss her in spite of all the intentions he had to leave her alone.

His heart pounded furiously as he lowered his head to the arm of the couch, allowing her to settle on top of him and kiss him on the neck exactly as she had done in the loft. He reached up and touched her hair, closing his eyes and inhaling the sweet coconut scent along with the seductive scent of her perfume.

There were so many reasons he couldn't let this happen. London. Scarlett. The mess his life had been before Mila came home.

The mess it would be once again when she left. His heart, all bruised and broken, and hers, so beautiful and vibrant and lovely.

He felt her hand on his cheek, urging his mouth to hers again, felt the softness of her lips along with the wicked promise of her tongue. She tasted like vanilla and nutmeg and cinnamon and peaches.

He tried to pull away, lowered his face and his eyes and smiled, but she tipped his face toward her again, and the seductive look in her eyes gave him no option other than to kiss her again. Every time his lips touched hers, it felt like a jolt of electricity running through him. Each time, it became stronger and he became weaker.

His hands slid under her shirt at the small of her back, and her skin felt like fire beneath them. She moved one of her hands to his stomach and felt the hardness of his abs beneath his shirt. Her teeth nipped at his lip before she bit down lightly, the most erotic thing he had ever seen.

His head fell back against the arm of the couch, and he felt her soft lips on his chest. He inhaled a shaky breath, trying to figure out why he let himself get in to this position yet again. It wasn't his fault – not entirely. The girl was impossible to resist.

"All right," he grunted, squeezing his arm around her.

She stopped to look at him, her eyebrow quirked up in question. Or maybe seduction. He couldn't quite tell. He took a breath, trying to calm the erratic beating of his heart. After a moment, he reached up and touched her hair.

"I'm sorry." He lowered his gaze to where his eyes looked like they were closed, and he looked truly ashamed.

"Why do you always apologize when you kiss me?" she whispered, touching his face softly.

His blue eyes snapped to hers. "I don't know what else to say."

"Why do you have to say you're sorry at all?"

For a moment, he didn't respond. His fingertips touched her face and ever so softly, he ran them across her cheek. "You are so beautiful." Again he lowered his gaze and sighed, then moved to sit up, forcing her to move away from him so that at the very least, she wasn't on top of him anymore.

It wasn't enough. He stood, taking a few steps away from the couch and hooking his thumbs in his back pockets, turning to face her. "I already told you why I can't get involved with you."

Mila nodded. She had reasons of her own to not get involved with him. Her future in London. Gabe. Things he didn't even know about.

He sat against the arm of the couch. "I'm trying to keep myself in check. I'm just not very good at it when I'm with you."

She smiled in the most understanding of ways. "It's OK." She touched his arm and he looked at her hand, then at her, and forced a smile. The frustration on his face was apparent. She removed her hand from his arm and looked to the ground. "It's getting late," she murmured, looking at him again. "I should go."

He nodded regretfully, then quickly reconsidered. "Or you could stay."

"You want me to stay?"

Again he nodded, the unspoken promise in his eyes that he wasn't going to touch her again. She understood what was in his eyes, and she understood why.

She bit her lip and nodded. "OK." The word floated quietly in the air between them, and she saw a flicker of happiness in his eyes despite the grave look on his face.

"OK, you'll stay?"

She nodded. She knew what he needed more than anything. Companionship. Some way to feel like the world wasn't some cold dark place filled with hopelessness and ruin. "Of course I'll stay. I would do just about anything for you, do you know that?"

He didn't know what he did to win that kind of loyalty, and he doubted she would ever understand how much her friendship meant to him. He had no way of expressing that. Not in a way that she could comprehend. No one could unless they had been through this themselves. Empathy was one thing, and he appreciated empathy. He believed people could imagine how he felt. But when they were done imagining it, they got to go on with their lives, unaffected by the devastation he was living with every hour of every day.

He pulled her closer, hugging her to his side with one arm and ignoring all the reasons he wanted to kiss her again. He just held onto her, trying not to think about the day he would need to let her go.

***

Colt laid awake beside Alaina, who had fallen asleep a long time ago cuddled against him. She looked like an angel as she slept. He had been watching her for the past hour, trying to figure out which life he wanted: a life in New York with Alaina or a life in Tennessee without her.

In spite of how incredible the entire evening had been, he still felt like he didn't belong in the city. And the thing about New York was that there was no escaping the city. In other cities he'd spent time in, like Nashville, there were places you could go where you could feel like you were in the country. People owned cars and lived in houses with yards. Life here would be pavement, brick and mortar, taxicabs and subways.

Alaina stirred next to him and opened her eyes and smiled. There was so much trust and affection in that smile. "I love you," she murmured. "Thank you for coming here." She closed her eyes and fell right back to sleep.

In that moment, he might have committed. But she was asleep again before he could say anything, so he closed his eyes and tried his best to shut off his mind.

Chapter 17

Mila sat in her mother's car in the mall parking lot staring down at her phone. She had spent the afternoon in retail therapy as she tried to compare her unexpected feelings for Luke against her feelings for Gabe. At the end of the day, she was no closer to resolving anything, but she knew as she sat in that car, in that moment, it was Luke's voice she couldn't wait to hear again.

It had been ten hours since he hugged her in the doorway of his house and sent her on her way. Ten hours since she felt the warmth and happiness that only he could give her.

It was crazy. She could not fall for Luke Hunter. It would be one of the biggest mistakes of her life. But it might have been too late for the stern warnings. It may very well be that the only thing that was left to do was scold herself for allowing it to happen after she got back to London.

She dialed his number, looking out into the sky where the sun was just about ready to start setting. She missed these Tennessee sunsets. There was nothing like them anywhere else in the world as far as she knew.

"Hello?" He answered on the second ring, cutting off her thoughts about Tennessee and sending her heart soaring.

"Hey." She smiled as a feeling of contentment settled over her. "How are you doing?"

"Good." He said it in a light-hearted way, like he hadn't just spent the entire day obsessing over her like she had over him.

She refused to reel herself in. The feelings between them were real, whether he wanted to play it cool or not. She needed for him to know how she felt without putting on pretenses. And right now, all she wanted was to see him again. "Do you want to come to my mom and dad's for dinner? I'm heading over there now."

He glanced at the clock in the garage. He would want to get cleaned up before he went over. "What time?"

"About an hour from now," she said. "Pot roast, I think."

He smiled. The menu didn't matter. God help him, he would go to the moon if she asked him to. "I would love to go to your mom and dad's for dinner tonight."

Her heart pounded. "See you there," she said in a flirty tone. She ended the call and started driving toward her mom and dad's, unable to wipe the smile from her face the entire way to their house.

***

Mila felt like a schoolgirl getting ready for her first date when she heard the knock at the door. She knew who it was, but she looked up in anticipation anyway when Hallie jumped to her feet.

"I'll get it!" she announced, running over to the door.

When she opened it, Mila saw the affection in Luke's eyes when he looked at Hallie, then bent to meet her at eye level. She imagined, not for the first time, what he must have been like with Ava. She took a sip of her sweet tea in an effort to tone down her own feelings of affection.

Peyton gave her a look. Drat. That must have been pretty obvious. She took another drink and turned away from Peyton, walking to the kitchen island, where she put her drink down and leaned over the countertop, watching them.

"Luke!" Hallie exclaimed. "Are you coming for dinner?"

"I am," he said.

"Did you know I made the mashed potatoes? We used to make them at our house out of a box but my grandma showed me how to make them out of *real* potatoes."

He laughed. "Did you know that's the very best kind of mashed potatoes?" Hallie's eyes widened in excitement and anticipation. "I can't wait to try them." He looked past her to everyone and said hello, his eyes settling on Mila for just a second before he stood and stepped into the house.

There was a time in her life when she liked exclusivity. No matter who she was with - a best friend, a boyfriend, anyone who was the center of her attention at the moment – she preferred an environment where it was just her and that person without all the unnecessary distractions of other people buzzing about. It wasn't the case with Luke. She wanted to share her family with him, and she wanted him to want to be a part of everything that was her.

These next few weeks were going to pass too quickly. She knew that now, standing there trying not to stare at him as he stood in her mom and dad's kitchen.

***

Colt was home when she got back from dinner, kicked back on the couch with his feet up, drinking a beer. "How was dinner?" he asked.

"Good." She slipped off her shoes. "How was New York?"

"Good." The way he said it, she knew he wasn't going to give anything away.

"How's Alaina?"

"She's good, too."

"When did you get back?"

"About an hour ago."

She sat down on the chair. "Did you two talk about anything life altering?"

He laughed. "No."

"Do you think you could be happy in New York?"

He leaned forward and ran a hand over his face. "I don't know," he said honestly. "But for her, I would try it."

"Does that mean you're going to?"

He shrugged. "I don't know what it means. How are Peyton and Hallie doing?"

That was it. She wasn't going to get any more out of him than that. She tried to make peace with herself over the fact that he wasn't going to be around much longer. She knew what he was going to do even if he didn't. It didn't settle well with her, but she was going to have to find a way to be OK with it.

Chapter 18

It had been one hell of a day at work. In a way, it was good to be back, but the work they did day in and day out could sometimes be grueling. Colt sat at the bar with Luke drinking his whiskey and trying to figure out the next step of his life. Moving was a big deal, no matter how you sliced it. Yes, you could always move back. But once you made the move, things changed. Things would change between him and his family. Expectations would change between him and Alaina.

No longer would he only be seeing her every couple weeks, stopping his world to spend time with her. If he moved, she would become a part of his world, and she would be a consideration every time he made a decision. Like what to pick up at the grocery store. And where he was stopping for dinner on any given night. And he was sure it would only be a matter of time before she would be looking for a ring on her finger.

This was so much more than a decision about whether or not he wanted to move.

"I don't see it," Luke said. "You're just too much of a country boy."

"I could adjust," Colt said quietly. "I love her, man. I have to make some kind of an effort."

Luke studied him for a moment. He understood Colt well enough to know that he would have to give it his best shot before he walked away – if he walked away. "I get it," he said. "As long as that's what makes you happy. Did you tell your dad about it?"

"I haven't made any decisions yet," Colt said. "There's nothing to tell."

Luke was just about to say something when the door to the bar opened and in walked a pretty little blonde girl who was clearly looking for attention. Boots all the way up to her thighs. A slinky black dress that barely covered her bottom and clung to her in all the right places. It took him several seconds to realize what Colt knew the moment she walked in. It was Lizzy.

She smiled at Colt and gave a little wave. Colt sat up in his chair and watched her walk over and sit down beside him. He wasn't looking at her with admiration. He was looking at her like he was completely caught off guard, and not in a pleasant way.

"What are you doing in this place?" he asked her. "What are you doing in *that outfit*?" It came out harsh, but he didn't care.

"Just thought I would swing by on my way from a party," she said. "I wanted to see what all the fuss was about, why you like it here so much."

"This is no place for a girl like you looking like that." His eyes were hard when they fell upon her, but she remained unfazed. She wanted him to see her like this, to know that other guys might find her desirable. She wasn't just cute, sweet little Lizzy like he thought she was.

She ordered a drink, and the bartender placed it in front of her. "Looks like I'm staying a while anyway," Lizzy said. "How you doing, Luke?"

"I'm fine." Except for the unshakable feeling that this was not going to end well. "You?"

She took a sip of her drink and offered him an inviting grin. "Good."

Just under the surface, Colt was boiling. Luke saw it even if Lizzy didn't. He thought for sure he was going to yank her out of her chair and insist she cover herself up, but he didn't.

Lizzy glanced around the bar, crossing her legs in front of her. "So, are all these people your friends?"

He turned and looked her up and down again and was just about ready to do something about her when Billy Daniels and two of his friends approached. Billy stood next to her and ordered something from the bar, then turned to leer at her while the bartender was getting his drink.

"Come here often?" he asked her, tongue-in-cheek.

Lizzy smiled demurely, a blush creeping across her cheeks. "No, it's my first time here."

"I know that," Billy said. "I would've remembered you."

Colt swallowed. It was an effort to not clench his hands into fists and take Billy down right then. But he couldn't do that. He was just talking to her. And she seemed to be enjoying it. What was he going to do about it?

He tried to focus on his conversation with Luke, but he couldn't help but keep one ear out for Lizzy and that slime ball.

"You should come with us to Knuckles," he heard Billy say.

"Knuckles, where is that?" she asked.

"It's just a few miles from here. I could drive you. It's a lot more fun than this place. Music....dancing...body shots..." He rested his hand on the small of her back and looked down at her suggestively, waiting for her response.

Nope. Not going to end well, Luke thought, and Colt slammed down his amber whiskey so hard it sloshed out of the cup. He stood, turning to Billy, and pushed him. Hard.

"Stay away from her, Billy," he warned.

Luke sat back and assessed the situation. Not only were they outnumbered, but Billy also had at least 40 pounds on Colt. It would be a tough fight and one that he didn't want to get into. He wanted his fighting days to be behind him. But he didn't know if there was going to be much of an option. He waited to see how it was going to play out.

"What's it to you, Wilson?" Billy snarled, shoving Colt back.

He ignored Billy and grabbed Lizzy by the arm. "You're coming with me," he said.

"What if she doesn't want to go with you?" Billy asked loudly, puffing up his chest. The entire bar fell silent, watching the drama unfold.

"It's OK," Lizzy said. "Please. I don't want a fight."

Colt took her by the arm and turned away from Billy, escorting her out the door. He was probably gripping her a little too strongly, but he didn't care.

Luke watched Billy stare Colt down as he walked out the door with Lizzy. Colt didn't notice, nor did he care, and Luke was pretty sure Billy was just doing it for show anyway. He muttered something under his breath after the door closed and stalked off with his friends.

Outside the bar, Colt led Lizzy to the enclosed porch that served as an entrance to the restaurant portion of the establishment that was currently closed.

"What are you doing?" he demanded. "What are you doing here dressed like that? Do you have any idea what kind of people you could run into at this place? Do you know *anything* about Billy Daniels and his friends? And you were going to take off with them to Knuckles and do body shots? Body shots? What were you thinking, Lizzy?" He was yelling at her. He knew he shouldn't be, but he couldn't stop himself.

Lizzy's eyes filled with tears. "I'm sorry. I didn't mean for that to happen. I just…"

"You just what? Wanted to get yourself raped?"

"No," she said, tears spilling down her cheeks, tears that immediately softened him. "I knew that wouldn't happen. I knew you were here. And I just wanted you to see…" She looked to the ground.

"See what?"

She sniffed and looked up at him again. "The way you look at Alaina. Like she's beautiful. I just wanted you to see that maybe I could be beautiful, too." She wiped tears from her cheeks. "I'm sorry," she whispered, willing the tears to stop.

Colt was too stunned to do anything, couldn't even move. It almost felt like a punch to the gut. He blinked. Once. Twice. She wiped away more tears.

"This is so stupid," she said dejectedly. "I'm such an idiot." She turned to walk away, and he reached out and grabbed her arm.

"Don't go," he said quietly.

"Why?" she asked. "Haven't I humiliated myself enough for one night? Let me go, Colt." She wiped away more tears.

"Lizzy…"

"Don't worry," she said. "I won't go back in the bar. And I won't go anywhere else. I'm just going to go home."

His head was still spinning. He didn't know what to say, so he just stood there looking at her, trying to find the right words. "Lizzy," he said softly. "I do think you're beautiful. You didn't need to put on an outfit like that for me to see that." He wanted to tell her more, like how he also thought she was smart and funny and so incredibly kind, and how he'd never met anyone like her before, and if it weren't for Alaina...

Finally she looked at him again, and he hated the hurt he saw in her eyes. A small smile curved her lips. "You do?" she asked, her voice so small and innocent.

He took a breath. He was so close to kissing her, but he forced himself to stand still. "I do," he said, not sure if it was an admission he should have made given the current circumstances. "But I hate the outfit. Absolutely hate it." She looked down to the ground. "I wish you would burn the thing."

After a minute, she looked up at him again, and the sadness in her eyes was still there. "I'm sorry," she said softly. "I made a complete fool out of myself. I'm going home now."

She turned and walked out the door. He let her go, still dumbfounded by everything that just happened.

***

Hours later, Colt was still trying to clear his head when Mila slipped in the door and closed it quietly behind her. She was expecting Colt to be asleep at this hour, but he was on the couch watching a game on TV.

"Where were you?" he asked as she pulled off her coat.

"Well, I had dinner at Mom and Dad's and then..." she hesitated.

"Then you went over to Luke's house," he finished for her.

She smiled, looking down for a second before she met his gaze again. "How'd you know?"

"Well," Colt said. "I have eyes. It's pretty easy to see."

She sat down on the chair. "So are you going to lecture me? Or threaten him like you did in high school?"

He shook his head. "You're an adult now. You make your own decisions."

154

She gave him a questioning look. "Why did you threaten everyone to stay away from me in high school?"

"It wasn't *everyone*. He was bad news in high school. You wouldn't have wanted to get mixed up with him." He looked back to the TV again and then at her. "He's not that guy anymore," he said, getting up from the couch. "But if you weren't leaving to go back to London in a few weeks, I would still tell you to be careful. He's not in a good place. Usually when relationships start with at least one person not being in a good place, they don't end well."

She nodded. He still had a way of making her feel like a child who just got scolded. He looked at her and gave a quick smile, so quick that it was totally insincere. "Good night, sis," he said, and walked down the hallway.

Chapter 19

Trevor parked his car on the street next to Peyton's grandmother's house. He hadn't wanted it to come to this, but she wouldn't take his calls. And short of kidnapping her, he could think of no other way to see her. He stepped out of the car, ready to face her for the first time since that ugly incident at the dance.

He was stupid. Stupid. Stupid. *Stupid.* There was no excuse for his behavior, but he knew he could still get her back. All he had to do was apologize and remind her of all the reasons they belonged together.

He walked down the sidewalk and onto the porch, rang the doorbell and stuffed his hands into his pockets. Momentarily, Peyton's grandmother was at the door.

"Mrs. Wilson?" Trevor said. "Ma'am?" He lowered his head in a gesture of respect. "My name's Trevor. I was wondering if Peyton was around. I really need to talk to her."

Colt abruptly stopped the conversation he was having with his dad about updating the kitchen. He looked over his shoulder at Peyton, who was in the living room helping Hallie with her homework. The way the color had drained from her face was enough of an indication for him. "I'll handle it," he said quietly, and she nodded, closing her eyes and exhaling in dramatic fashion. Her chest was tightening. She was starting to break into a cold sweat.

Colt crossed the floor. "Let's take this outside," he said, putting a hand on Trevor's shoulder and all but pushing him back onto the porch. He pulled the door closed behind him not noticing when it clicked back open, and Trevor stood by the steps, turning to face Colt.

He wanted to crack him across the face like Peyton had, wipe that arrogant look out of his eyes and teach the kid a lesson about respect. Not that it would do any good. There were just some people in the world who refused to see the error of their ways. Those people never changed.

"Listen, I know what you must think of me," Trevor began.

"If you knew what we thought of you, you wouldn't be here," Colt said.

"I have to see her, man," Trevor said, like they were friends, guys who understood each other. Colt turned his head and looked down, trying to temper himself. "I have to explain that I made a mistake, and I'm sorry."

Colt took a step closer. "Listen, Trevor." He said his name like it was some kind of a disease. "I know what you're doing. I know you want to try all those lines about how much you love her and missed her and how you were so desperate you didn't know what to do. But you and I both know that's bullshit."

Trevor looked down to the ground in an acknowledgement of shame and embarrassment, which was better than what Colt had given him credit for. When he spoke again, his tone wasn't quite as harsh.

"You're just going to go confusing her heart and making her think you could work this out. She deserves better than that. She deserves better than you."

Trevor looked at him with defiance in his eyes.

"And I know you're used to dealing with her dad who didn't care about anything and wasn't really much of a dad. Right, Trevor? But she's with us now. And we care, you got me?"

"Look, it's not what you think," Trevor said.

"It's *exactly* what I think. You're not welcome here. And just this one time I will ask you politely to leave and never come back. After this one time, I won't be so nice."

Trevor looked at him, trying to think of another protest. But this guy looked serious, like he was going to deck him if he didn't get off of his mother's porch right now. He shook his head as if Colt didn't get him at all, then without another word, turned and walked away.

Colt watched him leave before he turned and opened the door to go back in the house. He stepped inside and almost ran right into Peyton, who was apparently standing at the door listening to the whole confrontation.

"I'm sorry," he mumbled. Which part he was sorry for, he didn't exactly know. The fact that Trevor was such a jerk? The fact that he had shown up here tonight? The fact that she just heard that conversation?

She looked up at him, her eyes filled with tears. "Thank you," she said softly.

He looked into her sad, confused face. "Listen, Peyton, don't ever settle for a guy like that. You're so much better than that. You should be with someone who makes you feel loved and respected. You deserve that."

She closed her eyes, and tears streamed down her cheeks. He knew these were things that Richie never taught her, and it was obvious she felt undeserving of a good life. And that was just what her father did to her. The fact that her mother abandoned them was a whole other set of therapy sessions.

"You're a fighter, Peyton," Colt said. "Always have been. So damn defiant from the day you were born." She looked up at him and he smiled. "You can rise above this. Don't go back to that guy. He doesn't really care about you."

She wiped her eyes, and he saw the resolve start to steel within her. She hated feeling vulnerable, hated even more when she let those feelings show.

"Thank you," she said again.

He nodded. "Anytime."

He wished there was something more he could do. He knew Trevor wasn't going to give up that easily. He just hoped Peyton would be strong enough to let him go.

Chapter 20

Colt opened the door to the chalet. It was an unexpected rendezvous, but he and Alaina had figured out a way to swing it so they could spend a few days together in Gatlinburg before she went off to Paris. They had spent the day visiting local shops and planned to spend the evening by the fireplace.

Alaina looked heavenly in her cream-colored sweater and dark blue jeans and boots. He must have thought that a million times today, must have restrained himself from pulling her to him and kissing those gorgeously plump pink lips at least that many times. When they walked into the chalet, she pulled off her boots and poured them each a glass of wine while he turned on the fire.

She handed him a glass and held hers up. "To us," she said. "To new beginnings. To Paris and New York."

"To all of that." He clinked his glass to hers and took a sip, his eyes locked with hers the entire time. She wasn't reading him. Not at all. Wasn't seeing the doubt that had been nagging at him all day. Thought nothing of leaving Tennessee out of the equation in her toast. She wasn't doing it to be dismissive. It was the reality of the situation. If they were going to make it, Tennessee would, in fact, be out of the equation. He would be giving up everything else he loved to be with the woman he loved. It wasn't sitting well with him. It was bothering him a lot more than she realized.

Alaina walked across the room, opened the door to the deck and stepped outside. He followed her out, wrapping his arms around her from behind and looking out over the Smoky Mountains. It was the two things he loved, his two separate worlds that were about to clash. As he stood there, he tried to make that nagging feeling go away. The one that told him this wasn't going to work no matter how hard he tried.

"I love nights like this with you," Alaina murmured, her voice dreamy. "Soon we'll be able to do this all over the world. You can come see me in Venice or Paris and we can drink wine and take in the sights. Doesn't it sound so romantic?"

He had to admit that part of it sounded good. It was the part about him moving to New York and her career exploding that he wasn't sure about. He knew enough about her lifestyle to understand how vastly different it was from his. Different didn't have to be bad, he knew. Different could be better sometimes. But this wasn't the kind of different that got him excited.

Did he love her enough to make it work? Did it matter where he was as long as he was with her? He didn't know. And if he didn't know…was the answer no?

She put her glass of wine down on the deck rail and turned to him, taking his and doing the same. He looked into her eyes, trying to forget about everything but her. Alaina wrapped her arms around his neck and stared back at him. His eyes were dark, but if you looked closely, there were many different colors in them, and she always thought his eyes perfectly reflected the man he was – the solid surface and all the parts underneath. She loved every piece of him, even his strong opinions and his sometimes dominating behavior. Especially that. The thing was, he was never dominating with her. It was one of the things that made her feel like his relationship with her was so special.

She offered a small smile as her thumb stroked the back of his neck, then bent her head to kiss him. She loved the way he tasted, delighted in the way he smelled. She felt his hands on her back and then at her waist as she touched his face, kissing him slowly.

He tried to turn on autopilot as she continued her sweet assault on his lips. He thought it should have been obvious to her, that she should have felt the tension in the way he held her, the way he kissed her, but she didn't.

The last thing he wanted to do was ruin the romantic weekend they had planned right before she left for Paris. But going through the motions and making her think everything was OK when it wasn't felt dishonest. He thought they were in trouble, and he didn't think the feeling was going to pass.

He took a breath as she traced a finger down his chest, then took a step closer, pulling her to him, his eyes lowered to where they looked like they were closed. He was so sexy. So enticing. Every single time. She bent her head back as his hand caressed her neck and he kissed her again.

"Alaina." He looked into her eyes, and she was sure all the love and desire she felt for him was right there for him to see. He took a step back, his hands slipping away from her. "Alaina, I need to talk to you."

She smiled. "Now?"

Without hesitation, he nodded. "Yeah." He took a breath and held it for a second, then exhaled and looked at her. She looked puzzled, maybe even a little hurt and rejected.

"What's going on?" she asked, trying to temper her concern. It had to be something big, she knew that much. "Colt?"

"I'm sorry. I don't know how to say this."

Her heart began to pound. "Just say it."

"OK." He nodded, then looked her in the eyes. "I don't see our future being together."

She felt her heart slam against her chest. "What?"

"I loved being in New York with you. It was one of the best weekends of my life. But every time I think about living there, I go cold. I don't want to leave Tennessee. And you're going to need to be in New York. I either have to make a move or we're never going to see each other."

"That's not true."

He nodded and took a breath. "Yes, it is." The words were decisive, but she could see that he wasn't confident.

"Colt, I can come and see you between photo shoots. And you can come to New York once in a while. I'm going to have a lot of cash. I can take you with me whenever you want to go. It's not impossible. Don't make this sound like it's impossible." Tears were filling her eyes.

"How long are we going to keep up a pace like that? You being all over the place and your schedule being packed. You're not going to have time to come here. And where are we going to be two or three years from now? Still in the same place?" He shook his head. "That's not the kind of life I want."

She stared at him, her face filled with dread. "You don't want a life with me?"

"I don't know," he said softly. "I know that I don't want to move to New York. And if I don't want to move to New York so I can be with you, then what does that say about us? Shouldn't I want to be with you wherever you are?"

The tears slid down her cheeks. He knew it was harsh, but he had to get her to stop trying to work out the logistics and trivializing the conversation. It wasn't about geography. It was about the way he felt – or didn't feel – about her.

"How could you do this to me now?" As she spoke, he watched her eyes change from sad to defensive. "Now, when my life is going better than I ever imagined, now you pull the rug out from under me? Did you bring me here to break up with me?"

"Of course I didn't bring you here to break up with you," he said. "I was hoping that if we spent the weekend together I would feel differently about it." He shook his head. "But I don't."

"How could you do this to me?"

He looked at her sadly. "I don't want to feel this way, but I do. And I can't… I can't act like I don't. I'm sorry."

There was something so raw and sincere in the way he said it that she knew she had to get away from him. He said it like he loved her. Like it was breaking his heart to break hers. The last thing she wanted was to feel his love.

He would never forget the look in her eyes right before she turned and walked away.

"Alaina." He followed her back into the chalet. "Where are you going?"

"I have to get out of here."

"Laney, wait."

She crossed the room. "No, I need to get out of here. I'm sorry. I just…" She walked into the bedroom, and he knew she was going to pack her things. He took a deep breath and followed her in.

It felt surreal, seeing her throw things into her suitcase so violently. Alaina was never violent. It occurred to him that he was her rock, and that every time she was with him, she felt safe and protected. Now she was unraveling.

"Laney…"

She looked at him, her flawless face now streaked with tears. "Please," she whispered. "Just stop talking. You're just going to make it worse."

He lowered his head and the room filled with the sound of her leaving – suitcase zipping and hitting the floor, Alaina's footsteps coming closer. He looked up again. He was between her and the door, but not in a way that she couldn't get past him if she wanted to.

"When you asked me to come away with you this weekend, I thought…" Her voice broke and she lowered her eyes. Then she shook her head and looked up at the ceiling, wiping away the tears that spilled from the corners of her eyes. "I thought maybe you were going to ask me to marry you. And you know what? I would have said yes. I would have married you. And I would have figured out a way to make it work. But maybe I love you more than you love me. Maybe I *do* want to be with you, wherever you are."

She walked past him.

"Can you just wait a second? Please. Where are you going?"

"I don't know. But I can't be here right now."

He looked down at her suitcase and back up at her. She was in no shape to go anywhere, and she didn't even have a plan.

"You can't just leave," he said quietly as she stood before the doorway. "We're way back here in the woods. There's nowhere for you to go."

She lowered her head. "You're right." She turned to look at him, and he saw the heartbreak all over her face again. "Can you take me into town? I'll stay at a hotel for the night. I can make arrangements to leave in the morning."

Was he really going to let her go? Isn't that what he wanted? Looking at her right now and hearing the reality of it, the answer was no. This was not what he wanted at all.

"If you would just stay…" He gestured to the living room. "I can sleep on the couch."

"Colt, I can't." Her eyes filled with tears again. "I can't be around you right now. Please, take me to a hotel."

He couldn't think of a reason not to, not one that she would listen to anyway. "OK," he finally said quietly, grabbing the keys and following her out the door.

Every thoughtful gesture he made – holding the door for her, taking her suitcase and loading it in the back of the truck, opening the door to the truck – each thing rained down another drop of devastation on her. How could this have happened? A few days ago, she was sitting on top of the world. And now this. He meant more to her than her career, and she would have told him that if he would have given her the chance. But his mind was made up before he even said anything to her about it. He had rendered her helpless before she even knew what was going on.

"I think we should talk about this," he said as he started down the road toward town. "We're on completely different pages and I didn't know…"

"I don't want to talk about it." Her tone was tough as she stared out the window. "I just want you to take me to the hotel."

"You know I'm not just going to let this go."

She shook her head.

He gave her a minute to say something, but she didn't. "Maybe I was wrong," he said.

Alaina laughed cynically. "Stop talking, Colt. I can't have this conversation with you right now. You just turned my whole world upside down. I'm asking you for some time. Can you at least give me that?"

Eventually, he nodded. "Fine," he said, his tone resigned.

They reached the hotel, and he moved to get out of the truck. She looked at him coldly. "I don't want your help." He paused for just a second and disregarded her, sliding out of the truck and getting her suitcase out of the back. He pulled it around to the passenger side where she stood and surrendered it to her.

"Thank you," she murmured more out of habit than anything. She took the handle of her luggage from him.

"Can I go with you to get you checked in?" It was a stupid question. Of course she didn't need help getting checked into a hotel. She'd managed that on her own a thousand times.

"I'll take it from here."

He looked to the ground. "Would you please call me when you're ready to talk?"

She nodded.

"I don't want to leave you here," he said quietly.

"I know you don't."

"Is there any way I can change your mind about this?" She shook her head, and he saw that she needed him to back off. "Goodnight, then." He didn't know what else to say.

"Goodnight." She turned and walked into the hotel, leaving him to wonder if he just destroyed the best thing that was ever going to happen to him. She was a good woman, and she loved him. He was probably looking at their situation all wrong.

He turned and climbed back into the truck. It felt so empty without her being there. He always felt that way right after he dropped her off at the airport. This feeling was far worse. He started the truck and headed back up the mountain to the chalet.

***

Peyton sipped on a cup of hot chocolate as she walked through the stream of vendors outside the skating rink. It was the one weekend out of the year that the town set up a skating rink, and the place was crawling with people. Inside was an ice sculpture display that Dylan was planning to take her through, even though she'd already said it was too expensive.

As she strolled past one of the food vendors and eyed up their funnel cakes, Dylan couldn't help but notice, for the hundredth time tonight, how cute she looked. Peyton was a beautiful girl, there was no doubt about it. But tonight, with her hair falling around her shoulders and a slouch beanie on her head, her cheeks rosy from the cool air, he couldn't stop stealing glances at her. A lot of girls were beautiful. Peyton was more than that. She was something special. And for the life of him, he couldn't see how it was that she didn't know that.

She downed the last of her hot chocolate and threw the paper cup in a nearby trash can. "Thanks for the drink," she said. "I feel much better now."

165

"You know what else can keep you warm?" He gave her a mischievous grin. "Body heat."

"Is that so?" The look on her face told him that she was open to it.

"Yeah," he said. "You should give it a try." He reached out and pulled her to him, securing one arm around her as they continued down the walkway. "See? Doesn't that feel good?"

She laughed softly. "It does," she agreed. Honestly it felt good just being around him. He made her feel like a boy should make her feel, at least according to what Colt told her. And, who knows, maybe he was right about all the things he said to her that day. Maybe she could rise above everything and make a better future for herself, and maybe Dylan could be a part of that future.

"So this is why you don't want to talk to me."

Fear struck Peyton's heart as she recognized the voice immediately. "Trevor. What are you doing here?"

"Looking for you," he said. "The skating rink, one of your favorite weekends of the whole winter. I figured you'd be here." He looked disdainfully at Dylan. "But I didn't think you'd be with some other guy." He looked back to Peyton. "I thought you told me that you weren't interested in making friends at your new school. I thought that no one paid attention to you there. No one except for Dylan Showalter? That's a pretty big deal, don't you think, Peyton? Maybe worth mentioning?"

Peyton looked down at the sidewalk. Dylan hated the effect Trevor had on her, the way he seemed to be able to make her feel like she was less of a person for not doing exactly what he wanted her to do.

He removed his arm from around Peyton. "Leave her alone." He said it calmly, but he was ready to fight if he needed to.

Trevor's eyes snapped to his. "I want to talk to *her,* not *you*," he said in a condescending tone.

"She doesn't want to talk to you."

"So now she can't speak for herself?"

"She doesn't need to speak for herself." Dylan stood taller and lifted his chin, sizing him up. He remembered Trevor's name from the many times their teams clashed during football season. They weren't so tough, and neither was he. He didn't think he would fight. He just wanted to run his mouth.

166

He turned to move closer to Peyton, to take her hand and continue down the sidewalk with her, but he didn't make it to her. As soon as he took his eyes off Trevor, he struck, cuffing him right across the eye. It was a low blow, waiting until he turned to the side like that. He should have expected it, but he didn't.

Trevor shoved Dylan away from Peyton, and she watched in horror as he staggered back a few steps, regained his footing and then lunged at Trevor, landing a sickeningly loud blow to his jaw before they fell to the ground, both of them struggling briefly before Dylan emerged on top.

"Dylan!" Peyton cried. "Don't hurt him! Please!"

He was going to have to. He didn't think Trevor would stop until he made him stop. But before he could take another swing, he felt hands grabbing him roughly by the shoulders and pulling him up.

"All right, you two, break it up." The police officer pulled Dylan off of Trevor and then reached his hand down to help Trevor get up. Trevor refused the help and pushed himself off the ground. The officer stood between them and eyed them both. "Either of you want to explain what's going on here?" One had the beginnings of an impressive shiner and the other was bleeding from the lip. Off to the side stood one pretty girl, her eyes wide with horror. He already knew the story. Happened all the time.

"He threw the first punch," Dylan said quietly, his eyes on Trevor and his voice laced with disgust. "I was just defending myself." He was surprised at his own composure. With all the adrenaline rushing through his system, he should have been half out of his mind. But years of practice at staying cool in intense circumstances on the football field had apparently taught him differently.

"Come on, man, you *stole my girlfriend*," Trevor countered.

"I didn't steal your girlfriend," Dylan said, stopping short of providing any sort of explanation about how Trevor cheated on her with her best friend. Peyton had already suffered that humiliation in front of a crowd of people once. He wouldn't be the reason she would have to go through it again.

The officer remained between them until they finished muttering comments at each other. He didn't think the situation was serious enough to pose a threat to anyone as long as they could agree to go their separate ways from here. "You two boys think you can stay out of trouble?"

"Yes, sir," Dylan answered immediately.

"Whatever you say, officer," Trevor said.

The cop turned to face him head-on. He pointed at him. "I want you out of here," he said.

Trevor shrugged. "Fine by me."

Dylan held out his hand, and Peyton stepped up beside him and took it. "I'm sorry," he said to the officer. "We're leaving too." Together they started walking down the sidewalk, away from Trevor, on their way back to where his car was parked.

"She's a piece of trash anyway," Trevor yelled, and Dylan turned to face him again. "Used trash. Every time you touch her, Dylan, just remember that I was there first."

It took everything in him not to go after him again, but with the officer standing there, there wasn't much he could do. He turned once again, pulling Peyton close, and started walking down the sidewalk. The first few steps felt surreal, like they were in some kind of movie and everyone was watching them.

The police officer remained with Trevor as they walked away. When they got past the crowd of spectators, Dylan pulled his arm from her shoulders and held her hand as they continued the walk to his car.

"Are you OK?" he asked her quietly, still looking straight ahead. "I'm sorry I got into a fight with him. I didn't want that. I wanted today to be a good day."

"He didn't give you much of a choice, did he?"

"No," Dylan said, opening the door for her. He closed her door and got into the driver's side, starting the car. "My mom and dad are at some charity banquet tonight. Do you want to come to my place for a little while?"

"Yes," she said, without hesitation. She needed something good in her life, and sometimes it felt like Dylan was the only thing that was good. And she would be damned if Trevor would make her cry again. She kept a stiff upper lip the entire way back to Dylan's house.

***

Peyton stood next to Dylan in the kitchen. Since she'd missed out on the funnel cake she was going to buy before the whole incident with Trevor, he was making them ice cream sundaes. He melted the hot fudge topping and poured some on his and then hers.

"Keep going," she said softly, and he looked up.

"More chocolate?"

Peyton nodded. "Yes. Always more chocolate."

He smiled and tipped more hot fudge over top of her ice cream, then looked at her again. "Good?"

She nodded and then smiled. "Perfect." The glance they shared was far more weighted than chocolate and ice cream. She was letting him in –finally– and the girl underneath all those defenses was unlike anyone he had ever known.

While he was perfecting the whipped cream and cherry on top, Peyton found an ice pack in the freezer and wrapped it in a tea towel. She crossed the floor and eyed their desserts. They looked as good as anything she'd seen at an ice cream store.

He slid the sundae with more hot fudge in her direction. "Here you go."

"Thanks." She looked at his creation and then at him. "It's too perfect to eat."

He shook his head as if he didn't believe her. She took a bite, closing her eyes to thoroughly enjoy the way it tasted and how it melted in her mouth. "Mmmm," she said, opening her eyes to see that Dylan looked absolutely mesmerized by her. She put her ice cream bowl down on the counter. Of course Dylan's family had proper ice cream bowls, fancy scallop design and all.

He was still staring at her when she inched closer to him, every bit the tender caretaker as she pressed the tea towel gently against his eye. She backed off the pressure when he winced ever so slightly.

"You OK?" she asked as he leaned against the counter, allowing her to ice his swollen eye.

"Yeah." He was just wondering what it would be like to be loved by a girl like her. She barely even liked him, and even that was pretty amazing. "Peyton, I think you're beautiful," he said, trying to erase all the mean things Trevor said about her today.

She smiled, but he could see it in her eyes. She believed Trevor, not him.

He reached out and touched her face. "Also, you're really intriguing." She looked at him as if he must be mad. "And I want to kiss you, like, all the time. It's so distracting. English class? I want to kiss you. Lunch? I want to kiss you. Chemistry? I want to kiss you. Every day. All the time."

She looked up at him, and he could see the sweet vulnerability on her face. He knew it was something that she never wanted anyone to see. He knew it was there, of course, underneath all that attitude.

"Right now?"

"I want to kiss you."

She was right there. He could have done it, but he wanted her to admit, to herself and to him, that she wanted it, too. She looked down at the ground and back up at him, her eyes deliciously soft and hopeful.

"But the thing is, I never know if you want me to."

She dropped her head, looking at the ground. He put his fingertips under her chin and lifted her face to his. He wasn't going to get her to say it out loud, and when he saw the look in her eyes, he knew that he would have to be a fool to keep talking. He bent his neck and kissed her, careful to keep it soft and gentle. There was a lot that could be communicated in a kiss. He didn't want her to think he was just trying to get her in bed. Even though that was what she had accused him of from the first day he introduced himself to her, it wasn't the case.

He intertwined his fingers with hers, his heart pounding madly as he forced himself not to devour her right there in his mother's kitchen.

She rubbed her thumb across the back of his hands. There was something about those hands. Peyton imagined him on the football field, handling the ball and inspiring so much confidence in the coaching staff and their fans. Strong hands. Rough hands. Capable hands.

He pulled away for just a second, looking her up and down, his hand on her face and then her hair. Then he lifted her and set her down on the counter, his hands at her back as he kissed her again. She dropped her head back, an open invitation to explore her. He closed his eyes. He needed to be very careful to take this slowly.

His lips fell against her neck and she moaned. She felt it with him, things she never felt with Trevor. Dangerous things.

He dropped his head and took a breath. He wanted her so badly. But more than that, he wanted to make her feel beautiful, respected, worth the wait. Because she was.

He took a step back and she opened her eyes, touching his face, her eyes filled with desire. He looked down to the ground and took another breath. The way she touched him now was enough. There was something so soft and *loving* about it.

He looked into her eyes. She had never been more beautiful than she was in that moment.

"We should probably eat our ice cream before it melts," he said.

He didn't wait for a response. Instead he backed away from her and grabbed their ice cream bowls, handing hers to her and then walking to the other side of the island, leaning over it and taking a bite. She tasted better. A hundred times better.

He watched as she slid off the counter and took another bite of her ice cream. He wanted to tell her straight out not to believe the things Trevor said about her today, but he was hoping that if he treated her right, she would see it for herself in time.

She leaned against the other side of the island across from him and took a bite of her ice cream, then smiled. The feeling might be fleeting, but in that moment, it seemed like her life could be better than anything she ever imagined.

Chapter 21

Colt was pretty sure he hadn't slept a wink all night. After he dropped Alaina off at the hotel, he drove back to the chalet, sat down on the couch, and waited for her to call and end this silly game. As the hours ticked by and the phone remained silent, he went to the bedroom to try to get comfortable enough to sleep. He had just barely made it through the night without calling her, and now that day was breaking, he thought about calling her again. He wondered if she managed to sleep at all. If she had, it would be too early to call her.

He rolled onto his stomach and stared down at his phone, clicking on her name in his contacts and pausing when he saw her picture. It was not the most beautiful picture he had ever seen of her, but it was his favorite. She was so natural looking, so unposed. The smile on her face was so genuine that he could almost hear her laughter. He missed that laughter, and he wondered now if he would ever hear it again.

Unable to stop himself, he selected to dial her number and put the phone up to his ear. It wasn't likely she was going to answer. He knew that. But he had to try.

"Hello?"

"Alaina." He closed his eyes as a fragment of the tension in his muscles released.

"Hello, Colt." She sounded cold, as if she were talking to an acquaintance that she didn't like very much.

"Hey." It was just one word, but the way he said it felt intimate. Alaina steeled herself against his sweet voice. The truth was, all she wanted to do was fall into his arms and hear him tell her everything was going to be alright. She shouldn't have picked up the phone.

"Hey." She tried to sound breezy, as pointless as that was. He knew her too well. Disguises wouldn't work with him.

"I just wanted to see how you're doing."

Not what she wanted to hear. She wanted him to say he made a big mistake and he was sorry, that he could see now that he didn't have to move to New York or give up anything that he loved to be with her. That they would make this work.

"I'm fine." She looked at the clock in her hotel room. She would need to be out of there within the hour if she was going to catch her flight back to New York.

"I think I might have been wrong last night. Maybe I jumped the gun saying the things I said. Maybe we could figure out a way to make it work."

That was what she wanted to hear. But now that he said it, somehow it still didn't make her feel any better. "Honestly, I'm exhausted right now," she said, without a hint of affection in her voice. "I have to get moving so I can catch my flight back to New York. And then I'm going to be leaving for Paris, so I guess this will just have to wait until I get back."

He closed his eyes. He knew he couldn't force any kind of a decision out of her now, not when she had so many other things on her mind, and not after what he did last night. "Can you call me from Paris?"

"I don't know. I really don't know what to expect in Paris. I'm not sure if I'll have a lot of free time."

"OK." He agreed, once again at a loss for words. "Alaina, I'm sorry that I screwed things up last night." He wanted to say something that would erase all the hurt he caused and give her the chance to enjoy Paris the way she should. But there was nothing he could say to take it back. "I know you wanted time."

"I still do."

"OK." He took a breath. "So you'll call me…"

"I'll call you when I'm ready to talk to you. Honestly, Colt, I have to get going or I'm going to miss my flight."

"Alaina."

"Yes."

He fought the urge to tell her he loved her. "Enjoy Paris."

"Goodbye, Colt."

She ended the call, and he threw his phone down on the bed and ran his fingers through his hair. He had no right to be angry with her. She was just reacting to the situation he put them in. It was his fault. Every last part of it.

He couldn't stay there a second longer thinking about it so he hastily packed his bags and jumped into the truck to begin the long drive back to his house.

He was exhausted by the time he pulled in next to Mila's car, and he knew she was going to be asking a million questions that he didn't want to answer about what happened this weekend. He took a deep breath and grabbed his bags, stepping onto the porch and opening the front door briskly.

"What are you doing here?" Mila asked from the kitchen counter, where she was drinking a cup of tea. "You look awful."

"Thanks." He dropped his bag and ran a hand over his face, closing the door quietly behind him.

"Seriously, Colt. Why are you here? I thought you were spending the weekend with Alaina."

"I think we broke up last night." His eyes met hers from across the room. He was obviously disheveled from the moment she saw him, but now he looked helpless in a way that frightened her. She had never seen him like this before.

"*What?*"

"I told her I wasn't sure it was going to work with her career and me not wanting to move. She got upset and asked me to drive her to a hotel."

"You didn't do that, did you?"

"Yeah. Why wouldn't I?"

"Because she didn't really want you to drive her to a hotel. What she wanted was for you to insist she stay and work it out."

"Well, that's not what happened."

"You took her to a hotel?"

He shook his head. "Listen. I'm home early because we got into an argument, and she left. That answers your question. The rest of it isn't up for discussion."

"You're not really going to let her go, are you?"

He shrugged. "That's not entirely up to me. She's leaving to go to back to New York, and she'll be in Paris tomorrow. We'll talk when she gets back."

"Colt."

"Enough with the tone. It's my problem. I'll work it out with her." He kicked his shoes off and picked up his bag, taking a few steps toward the hallway.

She stared at him, trying to hide her feelings of disappointment. She didn't think it would be this way with her. Alaina was beautiful, smart, driven…and she loved Colt. Absolutely loved him. How could he push her away like this?

"Is there someone else?"

He stopped in his tracks and turned to face her. "Of course there's not someone else."

"Are you sure?"

She watched as he turned angry. "What, do you think I'm just accidentally sleeping with some other girl and forgetting about it? Why would you even ask something like that? Am I sure? Of course I'm sure."

She cocked her head ever so slightly. There was someone else.

"Now, if you'll excuse me, I've had enough judgment for one day." He continued down the hallway and shut the door loudly after he got to his bedroom.

She wasn't about to pursue the conversation any further. She was too busy trying to figure out who the someone else was.

***

Mila spent the better part of the morning baking cookies with her mother. Every year since she was little, the two of them participated in a baked goods drive to help raise money for the local homeless shelter. It started when Mila had suggested it as a heartbroken child who had seen a homeless person for the first time, and it continued until she went off to college. She never really thought much about it the last time they did it, never really missed it when she stopped.

But today she remembered everything she should have been missing: the dozens upon dozens of cookies, the wonderful women who ran the bake sale and old Mr. Humphrey, who kept track of the money and told stories about the war and his beautiful bride Louise. Every year, he would invariably pull a picture of Louise from his wallet, her face weathered with years of a life filled with the joy and heartache of raising four children. And he would say, "Look at her. My beautiful bride. Isn't she the most beautiful thing you ever saw?" And everyone would agree and think about how incredibly romantic it would be if their husbands would look at them the same way in their old age.

"Mom, does Mr. Humphrey still manage the money at the bake sale?" Mila asked, and then caught a grim look from her mother. Her heart sank.

"No. He passed away last year. Heart failure." Mary Beth released a scoop of cookie dough onto the cookie sheet and smiled. "But now he gets to be with Louise again," she added.

She supposed that was one way to look at it. But still, oddly, she missed the old man. She wished she could have seen him knowing it was the last time she was ever going to see him. She would have hugged him a little longer and told him what a special person he was.

Automatically, she finished scooping the batter onto the cookie sheet, put both of their cookie sheets in the oven and set the timer. She turned to see her mother sitting at the table, looking troubled, maybe a little nervous.

Mila sat down across from her. "Is something wrong, Mom?" she asked.

Mary Beth looked at her, unwilling or unable to say it out loud.

Mila's hand fluttered to her chest. "Oh, no. It's you and Dad, isn't it?"

Mary Beth gave her a puzzled look. "What about us?"

"You're splitting up. Colt told me about the issues you were having, but I didn't know how to bring it up, and everything seemed like it was OK, so I just hoped it was. Mom, you and Dad can't split up. Do you know what that would do to this family?"

She shook her head. "We're not splitting up. I'm surprised Colt even said anything to you about it."

"But you're OK now? You and Dad?"

"We're fine. We're good. We hit a rough patch. But after so many years of marriage, you learn to work through those."

Mila was so relieved she almost forgot there was another matter at hand. Her heart suddenly drooped. "Wait. If it's not you and Dad, what is it then?"

"Well, I talked to your brother the other day," she said, and Mila immediately became concerned. She knew there was something more going on with Colt than what he was telling her. And if it was something that made his mother this upset, it had to be something big. He was moving to New York. Damn.

Her mother continued. "You know I did my best with that kid, and I always hoped for the best for him." Mila looked at her, her eyes intense. And then she realized she was talking about Richie, not Colt. She breathed a sigh of relief as she felt the color return to her cheeks.

"I know you did, Mom," she said. "You're a great mom. I mean, look at how me and Colt turned out." She smiled, trying to lighten the mood, but her mother just looked down at the table. Whatever it was, this was serious.

"I don't think he'll be getting out of jail for a long, long time." Mary Beth's eyes may have filled with tears if she hadn't spent so many tears on Richie already. "He was arrested for drugs, but they also think he was there when someone was murdered, so he may be an accessory to murder."

Mila gasped, her mouth agape, and covered her mouth with her hand. "Are you serious?" She knew that she was, obviously. But she couldn't think to say anything else.

Mary Beth nodded.

"Do the girls know?"

"No. I'm still trying to get used to the idea myself," she said. "I don't know how I'm going to tell them, but I was hoping you and Colt could be here when I do."

"Of course we can, Mom. When are you going to tell them?"

"It has to be soon, before it hits the news."

Mila nodded. "Do you think he did it?"

"Who knows? He swears he wasn't there and didn't have anything to do with it, but what do I know? I just wish I could have done something differently. I wish I could have saved him."

"You did everything you could for him. You did more than what a lot of people would have done."

"It wasn't enough," she said sadly. "All I can do now is try to get the girls' lives back in order."

"I'll help you, Mom," Mila promised, but they both knew it was an empty promise. There was only so much she could do from 4000 miles away.

***

Driving to the animal shelter was not his intention when he got in the truck this morning, but Colt kept driving in that direction, telling himself he would divert to somewhere between here and there. There was a big part of him that knew he should just stay away from her. He might have done it, too, if things wouldn't have ended the way they did the last time he saw her. Every time he thought about it, he couldn't make sense of it. Walking into Cobra's with a dress like that was so unlike the girl he knew. Lizzy never vied for attention, never felt like she had anything to prove to anyone. He didn't know what went wrong.

He drove right past his last option to take a different path and pulled into the parking lot of the shelter, immediately noticing the sign in the window indicating that they were closed. He tried the door anyway, opening it to the familiar sound of the cowbell. Such an annoying sound, but somehow he missed it.

Lizzy sighed. She'd forgotten to lock the door again. She wouldn't turn the person away, whoever it was, but she wished for once that people would read the sign that said they were closed and come back again when they were open.

She stepped out from behind the display of leashes she was restocking and froze in her tracks. Her heart pounded, and she immediately began fighting feelings of embarrassment, self-loathing and inadequacy.

"Colt," she said, her heart racing. She wanted to tell him how much she regretted what she did, but she didn't know if it would make a difference. The point was, she did it, and she didn't think it would ever be forgotten.

178

He smiled uncomfortably, looking down at the ground, then looking into her eyes, taking in her long blonde pigtails, her camo pants and combat boots. Sweet peaches, she was cute. He missed those pigtails. He missed – all of her. "Hey," he said.

"Is everything OK?" She couldn't imagine why he would be there. But maybe he wasn't there to see her. Maybe he wanted to see Luna. "Luna's gone," she volunteered. "She was adopted. I thought about calling you, but I didn't know…" Her voice trailed off and she looked down to the ground.

"The answer is yes," he said, boldly and to the point, finding himself again. "You can always call me." When she looked back up, his heart felt like it was breaking when he saw the tears in her eyes.

"I made such a fool of myself." She looked to the ceiling, trying to stop the tears from falling, but to no avail. They dripped from her eyes, and it was an effort for Colt to not go to her and comfort her.

"I'm not here to make you feel bad," he said. "I didn't want to leave things that way between us."

She wiped the tears from her face. "I shouldn't have done that," she said quietly. "I shouldn't have even tried to get you to notice me. You have a girlfriend. A beautiful, stunning girlfriend and a beautiful relationship with her. I don't know what I was doing. That's not who I am."

He took a step closer. "I know that."

She sighed, bravely looking him in the eyes. Her heart hurt, maybe even more than her pride. "So what now?"

He shrugged, trying to look indifferent, like it was no big deal. "I thought if I didn't stop by I would never hear from you again. And I didn't want that."

More tears fell as she nodded. "I'm sorry," she whispered. "I don't mean to keep crying."

"It's OK." Finally, he opened up his arms. "Come here."

She slid into his arms, and he wrapped himself around her tiny frame. He felt her warmth as her head fell onto his chest.

"Thank you," she said quietly. "Thank you for not letting me go."

She felt so good in his arms. He fought the urge to kiss her on the top of the head, eventually loosening his grip and backing away. He looked into her eyes. He could get lost in those beautiful crystal eyes. For a moment, he couldn't trust himself to speak; he was afraid that anything he said would get him into a situation.

She felt it too, he was sure of it. Felt his attraction to her, his desire to pull her back in his arms and kiss her. He looked down to the ground and then looked away, rubbing his chin and regaining his composure.

"How's your grandmother?" he asked. "Back in the house?"

"Yes," she said, looking at him like she used to, like he was her hero. "She's back in her house, and she couldn't be happier. She said she wanted to meet you sometime."

"What did you tell her?"

"I told her you were busy, off saving the world. That you knew she was thankful for everything you did."

"I would love to meet her."

Lizzy smiled. "I could arrange that."

He felt them slipping back into something comfortable, and he knew in that moment that everything was going to be all right with them.

Chapter 22

It took less than a morning for the chatter to begin at school. If people disapproved of Peyton in the beginning, they downright scorned her now. She had to admit, it sounded awfully trashy the way she took the hero of the school and got him involved in a public fight with her scumbag of an ex-boyfriend. How embarrassing.

There were at least a half-dozen stories going around, and all people needed to see was Dylan's black eye to know that there was some truth behind the rumors. Probably the worst part of it, aside from Dylan being involved in a fight on her behalf, was that she was starting to care what people at the school thought about her. The more time that went on, the greater the distance seemed between her and her old school. And after everything that happened with Trevor and Zoe, she no longer had any desire to go back there.

She was standing in the lunch line all by herself trying to decide what vegetable she wanted with her meal when Autumn and Bianca slithered up beside her.

"Hey, Peyton. Nice job getting our star football player punched in the face," Autumn said. "Maybe this weekend you can get him shot at."

Bianca shook her head. "Seriously. What is he doing hanging out with a girl like you? Nothing but trouble."

Autumn smiled approvingly at Bianca's comment while Peyton quickly selected her vegetable and grabbed a drink, refusing to acknowledge them.

"Isn't your dad in the slammer?" Autumn pressed. "What did he do? Rob a bank? Incite a riot?"

Peyton slammed her tray down on the counter so hard it echoed throughout the cafeteria. Voices fell silent, and everyone looked in her direction.

"You don't know anything about my family," she hissed, not loud enough for anyone who wasn't standing nearby to hear.

Autumn sneered at her. "It seems like I *do* know something about your family," she said, her tone condescending and her voice significantly louder than Peyton's.

Dylan was at her side before she saw him coming. He put his arm around her waist and gave Autumn a disapproving look.

Autumn scoffed at him. "Really, Dylan? *That's* what you want?"

It was no small crowd that was watching them. Anything he said, anything at all, would provoke Autumn into saying something vengeful, something that could hurt Peyton. So instead of responding, he took Peyton's hand and led her to an empty table, sitting down across from her. She looked down at her food, unable to bring herself to eat even a bite.

"You know she likes me, right?" Dylan asked, and her eyes flickered to his.

"Doesn't everyone?" Peyton countered. "Or at least they did before you started hanging out with me."

"I don't care about that," he said. "And if they don't like me because I'm hanging out with you, then they don't know you."

She sort of smiled. He was trying his best to make her feel better. But the truth was, nothing was going to make her feel better right now.

"Me and Autumn… we had something going before you got here," he continued. "I mean, kind of, but not really. I wasn't serious about her. She's just giving you a hard time because she thinks she's the most popular girl at school, and she thinks she deserves me."

She nodded, taking a bite of her sandwich. She was relieved he didn't ask her anything about her father. Surely he must have heard Autumn's side of the conversation. Surely he must have wondered why she was at this school to begin with, but he was too good of a person to bring it up to her. She was sure he was waiting for her to tell him about it when she was ready.

And someday she would. She would tell him all about how her dad would put her in the back seat in the middle of the night and leave her in the car while he picked up drugs from his dealer. She would tell him about how her mother decided that a life halfway across the country without her family was better than a life with them.

"Thanks for the save," she said.

"Anytime." He took a bite of his own sandwich and winked at her. She smiled, involuntarily feeling just a little smitten.

***

The whole family was gathered around the living room at Mary Beth and John's house, settling in after eating tacos. It was Hallie's favorite meal, and Mary Beth thought it was the least she could do considering the circumstances.

"Girls, we need to talk to you," Mary Beth started, and then she stopped. She didn't want to tell them. It was killing her that Richie had gotten himself into so much trouble, and she knew the moment the words were out of her mouth, it was going to change the girls' lives forever.

Colt looked intensely at his mom. "Mom?" he asked, and she nodded. She would have told them herself, or maybe John could have even done it, but Colt was always there, ready to rescue them, and he was so good at cutting through the nonsense and telling it like it was.

He turned to look at the girls, both of them sitting on the couch with Mila. "Listen, girls," he said. "This is about your dad, and it's not good."

Peyton looked at him with imploring eyes. Hallie looked scared, devastated even. Mila put her hand on Hallie's and gave it a squeeze.

"He's in jail, and he's probably not going to get out for a while," Colt said.

Peyton looked at him, a mixture of rage and anguish. "What did he do?"

Colt held her gaze. "There's an investigation going on for murder."

"*What?*"

"No one thinks he murdered anyone," Colt said calmly. "But they think he was there when it happened."

"What does that mean?" Peyton asked as Mila pulled Hallie onto her lap and wrapped her arms around her.

"It means that he could be charged as an accessory to murder." His eyes held steady on Peyton's. "Which means he could be in jail for a long time."

"How long?"

"I don't know. It depends on what happened." He stopped there, not wanting to speak of the possibility of Richie assisting in murdering someone. That was too much even for Colt to grasp. He was sure he didn't do that, in the same way as every family of a person who has committed a heinous crime is sure.

"I'm so, so sorry, sweetie," Mary Beth said sadly.

Peyton looked around the room at the concern in everyone's eyes. She looked at Hallie, being cradled like a baby on Mila's lap, asking Mila if she was ever going to see her dad again. And she had to get out of there.

"I gotta go," she said, getting up from the couch and slipping on her shoes to go outside. She walked as fast as she could so no one could come after her, walked like she had a direction, a purpose, somewhere that she needed to be. But all she needed to be was away from there.

***

Peyton was a mile and a half down the road when her cell phone rang. She didn't want to answer it, didn't want to hear the words of comfort that her family was going to try to provide. There was no comfort, no consolation for something like this.

She picked up the phone anyway, if only to keep them from coming to look for her. She would rather be left alone. Perhaps if she told them she was OK, there was a chance they would do that.

"Hello?" she said, her voice raw with emotion.

"It's Mila. Where are you?"

"I'm walking."

184

"You've got to be freezing."

Truthfully, she hadn't even noticed it was cold outside. "I'm OK."

"Listen, I want to come get you," Mila began. "It's going to get dark out and you don't have a coat, and you shouldn't be alone right now." She waited for the protest, but it didn't come. "Can you tell me where you are? I'll pick you up and we can go get ice cream or just drive around or whatever you want." That was stupid. Of course she didn't want ice cream.

"I'm on Poplar Street," she said. "I'll wait for you here."

"Be there in a minute." Mila ended the call and pulled on her coat.

***

Colt was sitting in the living room drinking a beer when Mila came through the door. He looked at her with weary eyes, and she offered him a hollow smile.

"How is she?"

"Not good," Mila said. "How's Hallie?"

"The same." He leaned forward and rubbed his hand over his face. "I need to figure out what we're doing with his house. I guess the girls will just stay with Mom and Dad."

Mila walked across the kitchen and cracked open her own beer, sitting down on the living room chair.

Colt laughed, but it wasn't a good laugh. It was an ironic, sarcastic laugh. "It's gotten that bad, hasn't it? Bad enough for you to be sitting here drinking cheap beer with your brother."

She took a chug, then more than a chug. It felt so good washing down her throat, like it was going to wash all the events of the evening down with it. "I may even want to eat some fried food tonight. Do you have any fried food in the freezer?"

"Keep drinking," he said. "You'll be fine."

She didn't feel fine. She didn't think she would be fine for a long time. There was no book of instructions on how to handle things like this with your family. She just wanted Peyton and Hallie to be OK, but they were never going to be the same again. It was going to take a long time to get through this.

She couldn't imagine how she would feel if she found out her dad was being investigated for being involved in a murder. She

185

would probably feel like everything she had ever known was a lie, like she would give anything to not know once she knew.

She took another drink and felt herself relax a bit. "I could get used to beer," she said, mostly to herself.

Colt's phone rang before he could respond. "That's Laney," he said. "I'm sorry, I need to take this."

Mila nodded. "Sure." He got up and started down the hallway. "Just don't be surprised if all your beer's gone when you get back." That would be a lot of beer, she thought.

Back in his bedroom with the door closed, Colt picked up the call from Alaina.

"Laney," he said, sitting down on the bed and glancing at himself in the mirror. He looked like hell, his eyes bloodshot, his hair a mess, five o'clock shadow on his face.

"Hi, Colt."

"How are you?" He noticed how tired he sounded and hoped she didn't pick up on it.

"I'm OK, how are you?"

"OK," he said. All out lying to his girlfriend now. Or was she even his girlfriend anymore? He didn't know.

"Listen, I think we need a break."

"A break," he echoed. "What does that mean?"

"It means we're not together. Let's see how we do if we're apart for a few weeks."

It was a terrible idea, one he had no intention of agreeing to. "I want to work this out with you. I don't need a break."

"Well, maybe I do."

"Come on, Laney," he pleaded softly. "Don't put us in this position. It's not going to end well."

"It's all I can offer right now."

He didn't answer her right away. He knew she was banking on the fact that he wouldn't say no, but he also knew that he should. He should force a decision right now so that they could both move on with their lives – together or separately.

But she was right. He wasn't going to do that. "OK," he said finally. "Fine. I'll give you time. I'll wait to hear from you."

He heard her exhale a deep breath. "Thank you, Colt." Her relief was clearly audible.

"Good night, Alaina." He wasn't relieved at all. As a matter of fact, he was angry. She had to know this was a bad idea.

"Good night," Alaina said, a feeling of emptiness overtaking her. For the first time, she got the distinct feeling that things weren't going to work out between them. He didn't seem to really care. She could tell by the way he was talking to her.

He ended the call and threw his phone on the bed, falling down on his back and looking up at the ceiling, contemplating their relationship. He knew that if he didn't do something to change things quickly, he was going to lose her. He just didn't know if it was worth hanging onto anymore.

Chapter 23

Peyton stood at her locker pulling out the books that she needed for her next couple classes. As she searched for her math book, she all but cringed at the unmistakable sound of Autumn and Bianca's obnoxious giggles nearby.

"Hey, Peyton," Autumn said. "Is it true?" She held up a newspaper. "Is this your dad on the front page of the news in handcuffs? Is he in jail for *drugs* and *murder?*"

Peyton's heart pounded as she fought the urge to bash Autumn's head right into the locker beside her. She bit back the anger and embarrassment as she looked around the hallway, where people had stopped talking and everyone seemed to be waiting to hear her response.

This couldn't keep happening. If she kept allowing them to cause a scene, they would just keep doing it. She needed to figure out a way to calm down before she reacted, though. She turned back to her locker, catching sight of Dylan across the hall. She wondered if the article about her dad would finally be too much for him. She never got a chance to tell him. And now this was how he would find out. Lord, she was an idiot. What made her think she deserved someone like Dylan in the first place?

"So," Autumn continued. "Your father killed someone over drugs. You know, that's even worse than I thought." She held up the paper, clearing her throat. "Richard Wilson…" She stopped and pointed at Peyton. "Your dad, Richard Wilson." She looked down at the paper again.

Dylan should have jumped in and swooped her away. But he didn't want to stop her, not if she was going to give Autumn what she so richly deserved.

Peyton slammed her locker door shut and dropped her books to the floor, turning to Autumn. "What's your problem, Autumn?" she demanded. "You go on and on about things you don't know anything about, but everyone knows what it's really about. It's about the fact that you couldn't keep him. Isn't it? Isn't that what this is really about?" She took a step closer, and Autumn shrunk back. "It's about the fact that *I'm* the one he's holding hands with in the hallway, and *I'm* the one he's thinking about, and *I'm* the one he's kissing goodnight. *Not you.*" She ripped the paper out of her hands and threw it on the ground, taking a step closer so there was no mistaking her invasion of Autumn's space. "So if you're going to cause a scene, let's make it about what it's really about."

Autumn looked scared, completely caught off guard, like she didn't know what to do next. Before she could form a coherent thought, she lifted her hand and slapped Peyton. Peyton saw the appalled look on her face as she realized what she had just done, right before Peyton lunged at her, pushing her backwards toward the crowd.

Dylan saw the fire. Now would be a good time to step in. He took a few steps and stood in front of Peyton, stopping her before she was able to do anything that would get her into any real kind of trouble.

"Autumn. Peyton. Dylan." Dylan looked past the crowd of people and saw Mr. Murphy, the gym teacher, who was apparently showing up a little late for his hallway patrol watch. "Principal's office. Now."

Dylan kneeled down and picked up Peyton's books, along with the newspaper Autumn had been so interested in reading out loud to everyone. He paused for a second and looked at Peyton's father, handcuffs binding his hands in front of him. Then he stood and made his way through the crowd to follow Mr. Murphy to the principal's office.

That was it, Peyton thought. She saw the way he looked at the paper. And before she even started walking through the crowd, she regretted the things she said to Autumn. Their story was their own. It wasn't to be shared with everyone at school like she had just done. He would probably never forgive her for this.

"Dylan, I'm sorry," she said quietly as soon as she caught up to him.

He gave her a look, and a quick shake of his head, something that told her to stop talking. Not in front of Mr. Murphy, and not in front of Autumn. She nodded once and they walked the rest of the way to the principal's office in silence.

The three of them were escorted to the principal's office and made to sit in the small room together while the principal stepped into the hallway to talk to Mr. Murphy about what happened. Dylan couldn't hear what was being said, but he was pretty sure he could get himself and Peyton out of this if she would just keep her mouth shut.

Mr. Stockton stepped inside, looked at all three of them deliberately and sat in his chair behind his big oak desk, his gaze fixed on Dylan. He saw the bruise around his eye and wondered how he got it. It obviously hadn't just happened, so he assumed it was irrelevant in today's conversation. "Dylan. It's a surprise to see you here. You've always managed to stay out of my office in the past."

"That's because she's nothing but trouble!" Autumn pointed at Peyton. "This whole thing is her fault."

Mr. Stockton looked at her over his glasses. "Ms. Bethel, I'm trying to put the pieces together here so I can determine how each of you will be reprimanded. Right now I see that Peyton has a mark on her face apparently from being slapped and you've just had an unwarranted outburst. You're not building a very strong case for yourself."

In a huff, Autumn crossed her arms over her chest and sat back in her seat. Mr. Stockton focused his attention back on Dylan. "Do you want to give me your version first?" he asked, then looked at Autumn. "Without comment from anyone else in the room. You'll get your chance to tell your side of the story."

Dylan shrugged, looking down at the floor. "Sure," he said, looking back up at Mr. Stockton. "Autumn had this newspaper." He glanced at it again, the image of Peyton's father in an orange jumpsuit etched prominently into his mind. "She was harassing Peyton with it." He handed the newspaper over to the principal and watched as it occurred to him what the connection was by reading the name of the prisoner on the front page.

He looked to Peyton. "Is this someone you know?"

"That's my father," Peyton said.

The principal glanced at Autumn, who remained silent despite the obvious look of defiance on her face and in her posture. He looked back to Dylan. "Go on."

"Peyton was at her locker getting her books for class. Autumn was harassing her about what's in that paper, so Peyton confronted her. And when she did, Autumn slapped her. Then Peyton pushed her, but she was just defending herself."

A few chairs away, Autumn scoffed.

The principal ignored it. "So how did you get involved?"

Dylan exhaled. "I don't know. I just stepped in and broke it up before anyone got hurt."

"Broke it up," Autumn muttered. "More like you got in front of Peyton before she could attack me." She looked at Mr. Stockton. "She was going to attack me."

"She was defending herself, sir." Dylan had this humble, respectful way about himself that the faculty and staff seemed to love. He could have been an all-out arrogant son of a bitch for all the talent he possessed in sports and all the money his parents had, but it wasn't like that with him. It never had been.

"And you were just breaking up the fight?"

Dylan nodded, then looked down to the ground.

"And if I interviewed witnesses, they would tell me the same thing?"

Dylan looked him in the eye. "Yes."

Mr. Stockton looked at Peyton. "And what's your version of the events?"

"Exactly what Dylan said," Peyton said.

Again, Autumn scoffed. "Of course." She rolled her eyes.

"In your own words," the principal said.

"I was getting my books for class. She came up behind me and asked me if this was a picture of my father. She asked me if he was a murderer, and then she started reading the article out loud. Or she was going to. So I asked her what her problem was, and then I told her I already knew what her problem was."

Peyton fell silent, looking to Dylan for some kind of an indication, which he didn't give her. She looked back at the principal. "Which is…?" he prompted.

"She doesn't like the fact that me and Dylan are friends."

"Friends," Autumn muttered.

Mr. Stockton looked at Dylan. "Is that true?"

Dylan shrugged. "Seems like it."

"That's nice, Dylan," Autumn said, the anger growing in her voice. She always talked to him like they were insiders and Peyton was on the outside, a truth she couldn't change no matter what Dylan thought of her.

Mr. Stockton looked sternly at Autumn. "Go ahead and tell your side of the story. But stick to the facts of what happened, not your opinion about their friendship."

Friendship. Autumn wanted to protest, but she sensed even in the midst of her anger that she was already in enough trouble. "She's been harassing me for weeks. Practically ever since she got here. She thinks she's better than me because Dylan gave her a ride home from school or whatever."

"How has she been harassing you?"

"With her evil looks and her evil threats."

Peyton's mouth dropped. There were no threats. Ever.

"What kind of threats?"

"She told me that if I didn't stop being friends with Dylan I would be sorry. That I needed to stay away from him. She said she could make my life miserable if I didn't watch it. That she would do anything to make sure Dylan was hers."

Dylan looked at Mr. Stockton. "Come on. That's not true."

"How do you know that's not true?"

"Because I'm the one that pursued her. She didn't even want anything to do with me." He shook his head. "She didn't care about this school. She wanted to go back to her old school. She wouldn't have threatened anyone for talking to me."

The principal looked at Autumn. "Do you have any proof of these threats? Was anyone around when she made them?"

"No, of course not."

"Do you have anything in writing? A text message? Anything like that?"

Autumn shook her head. "Look, I know you're just going to take her side, so why don't you just tell me what you're going to do to me? I've had enough of this nonsense for one day." She said it in a way that indicated everyone, including Mr. Stockton, was beneath her.

"Autumn, did you approach her with the newspaper this morning while she was at her locker and start reading the article about her father?"

"Yes, but it was only because she threatened me and I was trying to stand up for myself."

"OK." She admitted it. That was all he needed. He looked at Peyton. "It's never in your best interest to engage in violence. Next time someone behaves in a threatening fashion toward you, it's best to walk away and talk to a teacher or staff about it. Do you understand?"

"Yes."

"I expect to not see you in my office again, Ms. Wilson. Is that clear?"

Beneath the surface, her blood was boiling, but she thought about the way Dylan handled things like this, and it gave her what she needed. "Yes," she said. It came off sounding respectful, even though she wanted to throw caution to the wind and not care about the consequences.

"OK. Peyton, Dylan, you're free to go."

Dylan stood and walked out of the office, waiting for her in the hallway. He didn't speak until they stepped out of the administration area and into the student hallway.

"Are you OK?"

Tears stung her eyes. "I didn't want you to find out like that."

"It's OK," he said. "Peyton, it's OK."

"And I'm sorry that I made that argument about you. I mean, it *was* about you, but I shouldn't have said those things about us in front of everyone. I'm sorry."

He slipped his hand into hers. "I'm proud of you. You did everything you had to do to get Autumn to leave you alone, and you kept yourself out of trouble. Is that a first for you?"

She smiled. "The only reason I stayed out of trouble is because you were there."

"Ironic. I keep you out of trouble, and I feel like I'm in trouble every time I look at you." She laughed. He walked her the rest of the way to her class and stood outside the door with her. "Just in case you were wondering…I want to kiss you right now."

He started to walk away, turning to smile at her as he continued down the hall. There was an odd feeling in her heart. Perhaps this was what it felt like to be happy.

***

Colt stood in the kitchen of the house that he and Lizzy had worked on so tirelessly. Her grandmother had just excused herself to go to the bathroom, and Colt leaned over the counter, his eyes fixed on Lizzy. Up until today, outside of the incident at Cobra's, he had only ever seen her in work clothes. And while she was adorable in her work clothes, today's ensemble took her right over the top.

She was wearing a blue and grey plaid shirt with the top few buttons undone. Under the shirt she wore a white tank top, and a delicate silver chain featuring a blue topaz hung around her neck, giving her that touch of femininity that drove guys like him wild.

"You want to go get something to eat?" he asked her quietly.

Her eyes lit up in a way that warmed his heart. "I would love to. Where do you want to go?"

"I don't know. Cobra's?" She looked at him with surprise, and he smiled. "Just kidding. How about Ironwood?"

"I *love* Ironwood!"

He turned when he heard her grandmother coming back into the living room. He saw an awful lot of Lizzy in her grandmother. Both little petite women with kind eyes and a pleasant smile.

"We're going out to eat, grandma," Lizzy said.

"Well, have fun." She wagged a finger at Colt. "You're welcome back here anytime, young man. I'll never be able to thank you for all that you've done."

He smiled. "You don't have to thank me."

194

He watched as Lizzy gave her grandmother a big hug, the old woman dabbing at her eyes when she released her. "I don't know what I'd do without you," she said to Lizzy.

"Well, you don't have to do without me." Lizzy smiled. "Have a good night, grandma. See you soon." Lizzy kissed her on the cheek and turned to meet Colt, who was already standing near the door. He pulled it open, and she walked through.

"Good night," he said to her grandmother, and walked out to meet Lizzy on the porch.

***

They were walking across the street to the restaurant, almost at the door, when Lizzy stopped. "Just a second, Colt." She put her index finger up. "Be right back."

He turned and leaned against the wall in front of Ironwood, watching Lizzy walk down the sidewalk as she dug into her pockets. She approached a homeless man and handed him something, then bent her head with him for a short prayer.

He watched as the man looked at her with grateful eyes and took her hands in his. Then she nodded her head at him in earnest and turned back to Colt, walking quickly toward him so as to not keep him waiting any longer than she had to. Colt looked at her, then beyond her at the grateful man, then back to Lizzy again.

"What was that?" He moved to go into Ironwood with her.

"Ever hear of the Tennessee Project?"

He shook his head.

"It's an initiative to help the homeless," she said. "I just handed him a voucher for $15. The voucher has a list of participating organizations where he can go get a cup of coffee or a pair of socks or whatever he needs."

Colt's heart melted. "Lizzy. That's so sweet."

She looked up at him with one of the purest smiles he had ever seen. "I can't save the world, but I can make a difference in a person's day sometimes."

They took their seats at a booth across from one another. "So, do you carry vouchers with you all the time?"

Lizzy nodded. "All the time."

"Where do you get them?"

"You can get them at any of the businesses that are involved in this. I usually get mine from Magnolia's."

"The tea shop?"

"Yeah."

He was just about to ask her how she got to be such an amazing person when the waitress came over to take their order. Which was probably for the best.

While he sat across from her at dinner, he couldn't help but compare Lizzy to Alaina. Alaina was a good person, there was no doubt about that. But Lizzy took good to a whole new level. He should have known that when he met her at the shelter. Anyone who devoted their life to helping discarded animals had to be someone special.

The thing about Lizzy was she didn't have much. But it didn't stop her from giving every day, in any way that she could. And it had taken him this long to see that because it wasn't something she talked about. It was just something that she did.

When dinner was over, he picked up the check and looked it over.

"Dinner should be on me," Lizzy said. "After all you've done to help with the house." His eyes locked with hers and she reached across the table to touch his hand. "It's the least I can do."

Colt shook his head and pulled his hand away. "I asked you to dinner. I'll pay."

She cocked her head, then pulled her hands back and conceded.

He paid the bill, slid across the seat and stood, her cue to do the same. He opened the door for her to walk through and followed her to his truck.

"Thanks for dinner," she said quietly as soon as he was inside.

"I should be thanking you."

She kind of laughed. "*You* should be thanking *me*? For what?"

"I don't know," he said, his eyes on the road. "When I'm around you, I just feel like I'm a better person." He turned his head to look at her and smiled slowly. "I don't know how you do that, but you do."

Her heart swelled. She didn't know what to think of him sometimes. She knew he was with Alaina and there was absolutely no chance that anything was going to go bad with that relationship.

She had seen them together; they were clearly in love. But when he looked at her a certain way, or said things like what he had just said to her, it confused her heart.

"You don't need me to make you a good person, Colt. You're a great person. One of the best people I've ever met."

He shook his head but didn't respond. He had probably already said too much.

When they pulled up to her apartment, he put the truck in park and turned to look at her. "It was nice to meet your grandmother. Thanks for going out to dinner."

She pointed over her shoulder in the direction of her apartment. "Do you want to come in?"

Yes. He did want to go in with her. He wanted to talk to her all night long, learn more about all the amazing things that were her.

"I can't." He was afraid of what could happen if he did. He needed to figure out a way to treat her like a friend, to not be so taken by her.

She touched his arm. "I'm not going to try to take advantage of you if you come in," she said, and he laughed. "Oh, and I donated that outfit you didn't like to Goodwill. It's gone. Just a memory now."

He stared at her, his mind going to that night where she was so open, so vulnerable, and then so crushed. He wanted to pull her into his arms and kiss her. For a moment he didn't think he would be able to stop himself.

"Good," he finally said. "About the outfit. I can't come in. I have to stop by my dad's place after this. We need to talk about a big project we have coming up."

Such a lie. But he had to get away from her.

She smiled. "OK," she said quietly and opened her door. "Have a good night."

He nodded. "You too, Lizzy."

He watched her run into the house and hoped he didn't disappoint her by not coming in. But hell, he didn't have a choice. She turned and waved at him before she opened the door to go inside. He waved back, not nearly as chipper as she was, and backed out of the driveway.

***

Luke put his cue stick back on the rack and turned to join Colt at one of the high tables, only to be derailed by Ashley Hilton. Ashley was the first after he lost Scarlett and the only girl he hung out with on a regular basis before Mila came to town. She understood he was in no place to give anything of himself, regardless of how much fun they had in the moment sometimes. Over the past few months, he had grown to be very appreciative of her and whatever it was they had together – until now. Now it felt awkward.

"Hey," she said in a tone that sounded confrontational until she smiled and stepped closer. "Haven't heard from you in a while. What do you say we get together this week?"

He forced an apologetic smile. He knew he owed her no explanation, but he felt like he did. No, he wasn't committed to her, nor was she to him. But she was there for him. She treated him like a friend. He wanted to do the same in return.

"I'm kind of busy this week," he offered.

She raised her brows, clearly interested. "With what? Or should I say, who?" Heat creeped up his spine. He couldn't just tell her he was hanging out with someone he might actually be falling for. He would expect to get slapped for something like that. Fortunately, before he could think of a suitable response, she smiled. "No worries, babe. You have my number. Call me when you get less busy." She winked.

He smiled uncomfortably and nodded. "Sure," he said. "Listen, I need to talk to Colt about some things, so if you don't mind…"

She stepped out of the way. "Of course I don't mind." She looked him up and down, his not-so-distant past coming back to haunt him. It was becoming clear that he needed to make some changes in his life. He wasn't the man he wanted to be, or the man he needed to be for someone like Mila. Up until now, it just hadn't mattered.

He lowered his head and walked past Ashley. Now it felt awkward to face Mila's brother. He pulled out a chair and sat down.

"Going out with Ashley tonight?" Colt asked.

Luke shook his head, looking down at the table, suddenly aware of how much of a mess his life still was and who he was dragging into his mess. "No." He raised his head to look Colt in the eye.

"Turning down a night with Ashley Hilton? That doesn't sound like you."

He closed his eyes, then looked at Colt again. He didn't know how much he knew about him and Mila or what he thought of it, but it was clear there was a purpose for his questions about Ashley. "Yeah," he agreed, wrapping his hand around his bottle of beer. "Well, maybe it's time for me to clean up my act."

Colt cocked his head. "Dude, it's none of my business, but she's not the same kind of girl as Ashley. She shouldn't be thought of in the same way."

He nodded, exhaling a breath, partially relieved that Colt took the direct route instead of continuing to dance around it. Once again, he looked him in the eyes. "I would never treat her carelessly. I promise you that." He took a sip of his drink.

Colt nodded. "I think she has her head in the clouds when it comes to you."

"Point taken." He took another drink and put his bottle down. "Hey, are you still working on that house with Lizzy? I think I left my favorite measuring tape over there."

"We're done with the house, but I'll let her know it's missing." The look of conflict on Colt's face as soon as he mentioned Lizzy did not escape Luke for a second.

"How are things going with Alaina?"

Colt's eyes looked tired. "Good," he said.

"Good, like you're moving to New York, good? Or good like you're staying in a long-distance relationship, good?"

"I don't know. Neither of those sound good to me."

Luke looked down at the table. Colt had been so edgy lately, not anything like himself at all. "You know something that I've learned the hard way?"

"What's that?"

"Life's too short," Luke said, raising his eyes to meet Colt's. "It's too short, man. Anything can happen. If you like Lizzy and you want to be with her…"

"Woah," Colt said. "Who said anything about me liking Lizzy?"

"No one has to say it," Luke said. He took a quick drink of his beer, figuring that right about now Colt was talking himself down from slugging him for even suggesting that he was anything but crazy about Alaina.

He shook his head. "I came here to *stop* thinking about all that."

Luke understood all too well about unsolicited advice from well-meaning people. "OK," he said. "But you're not yourself these days. And I know what it's like to have a mess on your hands with everyone trying to fix it for you, but I'm worried about you, man."

Colt looked across the table at him. He didn't have the energy for this conversation. Didn't have the energy for anything, as a matter of fact. "I'll be OK."

"What's going on?" he asked quietly. "Are you and her still together?"

"No, I guess." He shrugged. "I don't know. She won't make a damn decision, and she says she just needs time. So I guess I'm just supposed to wait and see what she decides."

Luke cocked his head. "What happened? I thought you were thinking about moving to New York to be with her."

"Yeah, about that," he said, shaking his head. "I wasn't sure about that. So I told her I didn't know if we were going to make it. And she got upset, and it just didn't go anywhere good after that. Then she told me she thought I took her to Gatlinburg to ask her to marry me."

"What? She thought you were going to ask her to marry you and you broke up with her instead?"

"It wasn't exactly like that." He took a drink of his beer, then nodded. "OK, maybe it was like that. Yeah, I guess I did that."

Luke shook his head. "So you broke up?"

He stared at Luke for a moment, trying to figure out how to explain something that he himself didn't understand. "That's what I would have done if it were up to me," he said. "But she just wants to not be together for a few weeks and see how it goes."

"And you agreed to that?"

"Not because I wanted to."

Luke looked down and shook his head. "Wow."

"I know."

"That's a disaster waiting to happen."

"Tell me about it."

"So what are you going to do?"

Colt shrugged. "Give her what she's asking for. What else am I going to do? This whole thing is my fault."

"Are you seeing Lizzy in the meantime?"

"No," Colt said quickly. "Well, not romantically. I mean, I took her out to dinner but that was all."

"Does she know that you're not with Alaina right now?"

Colt took a drink and shook his head. "She thinks we're still together."

"Can I tell you what I think?"

"Well, you're going to anyway."

"That's right. I am." He knew he was probably the only person in the world who could talk to him like this, which made it his responsibility to do so. "I would let her go, man."

"Let Laney go?"

Luke nodded. "If she doesn't want to make a decision that it sounds like she's already made anyway, then you make the decision. It sounds to me like she's just stringing you along, waiting for you to do something stupid, which you inevitably will."

"Thanks for the vote of confidence."

Luke smiled. "It's nothing personal. I would do something stupid, too." He took a drink. "Anyway, I think you have to let her go."

"I can't do that. I feel like I screwed this up and now I need to fix it."

"That's no reason to stay with someone."

"I love her," Colt said. "You know that."

"That's not always a reason to stay with someone either." Luke said, shaking his head. "There are a lot of valid reasons that things might not work out with you and her. Don't lose sight of that because you're so wrapped up in trying to fix your mistake."

"I can overcome all those reasons. All it takes is a little effort."

"You can overcome every reason except for one. It's a big reason, Colt. Don't stay with Alaina just because you feel like you owe it to her. I think it would be a big mistake."

Colt looked down at his bottle of beer. He wasn't going to talk about this. And now that he was, he still didn't want to talk about it.

Luke looked across the room, past Ashley Hilton, turning to get a better look when he saw someone waiting tables who looked like Lily Ann Reeva, one of his best friends for years until recently.

He leaned forward. "What's she doing here?" he asked, and Colt turned to see who he was talking about.

"Oh, I guess you didn't know about that," Colt said quietly, so thankful for a subject change. "Steve left her. So she's working here a couple nights a week to make rent while she's finishing up her degree."

Luke looked at Colt, his eyes wide. "Steve left her? What happened?"

Colt shrugged. "I didn't talk to her about it. But the rumor around here is that he met someone else."

Luke looked across the room at her. The girl had meant so much to him from the time they were teenagers. It was an unlikely friendship from the beginning, mostly because Luke wasn't all that interested in hanging out with girls as friends. But Lily Ann was different. Not only was she crazy in the most fun kind of way, but she also made him laugh out loud every time they hung out together. Lily Ann would do things most girls would never even consider, like go on mud runs with him or target practice for hours at his grandmother's farm. What started out as an endless amount of fun had through the years turned into a genuine friendship. They had been there for each other through so many things: family issues, break-ups, make-ups, everything. And then one day it was over. And it was Luke's fault, all of it.

Lord, he missed her now. He took another sip of his beer and spent the rest of the evening hoping they would have a chance to talk before he left.

They didn't. As a matter of fact, she intentionally avoided him when they walked toward the door. On his way home, Luke called the bar and asked to talk to Mary Claire, one of the nighttime managers who knew him well.

"This is Mary Claire, can I help you?" she said when she got on the line.

Luke gripped the wheel and looked out into the night. "Hey, it's Luke Hunter," he said.

"Hey, Luke." She spoke to him like she was getting a call from an old friend she hadn't seen in years. "Did you forget something?"

"No. I need to ask you a favor."

"What's that, sugar?"

"Your new employee, Lily Ann Reeva, is there any way you can look at her job application and give me her address?"

"What? Why do you need that?" She sounded completely taken off guard by his request.

"She's an old friend of mine," he said. "I need to go see her."

"Um, well…"

"Here's the thing, Mary Claire. I was a jerk to her back when I first lost Scarlett. I just want to apologize. And if I have to do it in front of everyone at Cobra's, I will. But if that happens, she'll probably dump a pitcher of beer over my head. So I would much rather do it at her place, where there won't be an audience."

He heard her laugh and hoped that was a good sign. He really needed to get that address.

"Tell you what, sugar," she said. "I'll see what I can do."

"Thanks, Mary Claire. You're the best." He ended the call, fully aware that her non-committal response meant that he wasn't going to get the address. He ran a hand through his hair. Damn, he didn't want to have to talk to her in front of everyone at Cobra's, but it looked like that's what he was going to have to do.

He pulled into his driveway and parked the truck, his phone lighting up with a message as he was getting out.

923 Long Hunter Road Apt. 7. You didn't hear it from me.

Luke smiled. *Mary Claire, thank you. You really are the best.* He walked into his house, an unfamiliar feeling of hope in his heart.

***

Colt had been staring at his phone for what felt like hours. Twice now he almost picked it up and dialed Alaina's number, but something stopped him. He made the decision earlier today that he was going all in with her. They had two years into their relationship, and he was in love with her. He could give up his job with the family and give New York City a chance. He would give it a year. If he still didn't like it in a year, he would come back.

If he moved in with Alaina, he could even keep the house in Tennessee, maybe put it up for rent for a year and then they could decide what they wanted to do. Together. They would figure out the future together.

He picked up the phone and called her. She answered immediately. "Hello?"

He smiled. "Hey, stranger."

"Colt." She said, her tone guarded and reserved.

"Listen. I know what you said about wanting time, but what if I told you that I'm ready to do whatever it takes to get us back to where we were?"

"I...I don't know."

"I'll come to New York," he said. "I'll come there as soon as you want me there...if you still want me there."

"Are you sure about this?"

"I'm sure."

"Yes, I still want you here." When she spoke the words, it was clear that she was crying.

He gripped the phone. "I can be there this weekend."

"What about tomorrow?"

"Tomorrow?"

"Tonight?"

He laughed. "Wish I could."

He would talk to his family tomorrow and straighten out his affairs over the next couple of weeks. He could be in New York and back in her arms in the next few days. As soon as he got there, he was sure the rest would feel like details. Details that should never have kept them apart to begin with.

***

Mila was in the kitchen making a grocery list when Colt walked out of the hallway. She glanced at him and then gave him a more thorough once-over. Something was different. He looked happy. Yes. That's what it was. "What are you so happy about?"

"Mila, I'm moving to New York City."

Her jaw dropped just a little. "New York City? You're getting back together with Alaina?"

"Yes, I am. I'm going to see her in a couple days."

"What are you going to do about the family business?"

"I'll talk to Dad about it. It will be fine."

She glanced around the kitchen. "What about the house?"

"I'm going to keep the house. Maybe rent it out or something. I need somewhere to keep all my stuff. There's not a lot of room in New York City."

Mila sighed, her head in her hand. "You're just not a New York City kind of guy."

"Maybe I can be," he said. "I'm going to give it a year. It's not fair to either of us if I don't at least give it a year."

"Wow. A year of your life in New York City."

"I thought you might be happy for me," Colt said. "You know, the girl who decided she was too good for her family and for Tennessee all the way back in college?"

"That's not fair at all."

"Isn't it? At least I'm leaving for a woman I love and a relationship I want to try to work out. Not because I think I'm too good for this place."

"I never thought that."

"Sure you did."

"Go to hell, Colt."

She got up and pulled her shoes on, slipping on her coat and grabbing her keys to walk out the door.

⋏⋏⋏

She had no idea where she was going or how she ended up here, but here is where she was, right outside of Luke's house, turning her lights off and cutting the engine, thinking this might not be one of the best ideas she ever had.

She stared at the house for a moment. She knew she was going to miss this house when she was gone. It was the oddest kind of memories that made a person homesick when they were away. A random trip to a department store and running into someone she was particularly fond of. A lyric to a song. The smell of spring at the lake not far from her mom and dad's house. It was all piled in thin layers in her mind. She knew it was there, but the memories wouldn't unravel into that feeling of homesickness until they were ready. She had come to expect that kind of thing. But things like this – the house she spent so much time at when she was growing up and now the new memories she would have – didn't need any kind of a trigger. She would remember it. She would miss it. She would think about it every day.

But she didn't want to miss the place before she was even gone. She got out and walked to the door and gave it a solid knock. Momentarily he answered, standing before her in jeans, a white tee shirt and an unbuttoned blue and green plaid shirt.

"Mila."

She bit her lip. "Are you busy?"

"No."

"Do you think I left here because I thought I was too good for Tennessee?"

"Yes."

"Are you serious?"

He nodded.

"You've got to be kidding me. Is that how I acted with everyone?"

He thought about it for a moment. "It was kind of like you were going to go find something classier and better than the town you grew up in and all the people you grew up with." He studied her for a moment. "No offense."

"None taken," she murmured, clearly rather offended.

He opened the door to her. "Want to come in?"

"Actually, I do." She stepped inside, and he closed the door behind her. "I got into an argument with Colt and stormed out."

"I can't imagine why," Luke said. He knew why. Colt's mind was a mess. It wasn't often that he didn't know exactly what he wanted to do and how to handle things, but this thing with Alaina had him turned upside down. He wished there was something he could do to help him, but he knew Colt needed to reach his own conclusions.

Mila sat down in the living room. "He's moving to New York City."

Luke blinked. "He's doing what?"

"I know. I think it's a big mistake. But he said he's going to give it a year. Anything other than that would apparently be unfair."

"No," he said, more to himself than to her. "No, no, no, no, no." That was it. It was too late to try to talk some sense into him. His efforts last night were in vain. Luke sat down and blew out a breath. "What about the family business?"

"He said he would talk to my dad. Apparently if it doesn't work out, he'll be back in a year."

He shook his head. "Wow."

Mila leaned forward. "So you really think I thought I was too good for this place?"

Luke smiled. "Who knows, Mila? Maybe you were."

Chapter 24

Colt sat down across from his mom and dad at their kitchen table. There was no easy way to say it, so he was just going to say it.

"Mom, Dad…I talked with Alaina last night. I'm moving to New York City."

First reaction: his mother looked worried, his dad, severely disappointed.

Colt swallowed. "I'm going to give it a year. If I end up liking it, I'll stay. If I don't, we'll figure something else out."

He watched as both his parents tried to hide their feelings.

Mary Beth spoke first. "That's wonderful, Colt. She's such a nice girl. I'm happy for you."

"Thanks, Mom." He looked at his dad.

John looked away and then forced himself to look at him. "Me, too. Happy for you, son."

"Thanks," Colt said, trying not to allow himself to be affected by the disappointment in his father's eyes. "I'm going to see her tomorrow. Then I'll be back and we'll need to plan an exit for me with the business. We can talk about all that later."

"Sure," his dad said, barely looking at him.

Colt pushed his chair out, unable to stay another minute and face the sadness that was filling up the kitchen. "Anyway, I have to run. Need to start packing for the flight tomorrow."

His mother stood to give him a hug. "Love you, Colt. Safe travels."

"Love you, Mom." He looked across the room. "Love you, Dad," he said.

"Love you, too," his dad mumbled. Colt turned and walked out the door, not allowing himself to think about how his dad was going to get a replacement for him. It wasn't Colt's business. It was his dad's. And his dad's responsibility to work it out. Anyway, Luke would be there. And it might be the perfect time for him to take a bigger role in the business. Things would work out just fine. They just needed time to get used to the idea of him not being there anymore.

***

New York City was still damn cold, Colt thought as he pulled his suitcase down the sidewalk. He caught a cab to Alaina's apartment building and when he stepped out, she was standing there, leaning against a lamp post, arms crossed and head tilted to the side, looking like the vision she always was.

"Laney." He walked over to her, put an arm around her waist and gave her chaste kisses on the lips between smiles. "I can't believe how much I missed you." He closed his eyes, thankful to be there, that it wasn't too late and he hadn't blown it with his stupidity. Thanking God for the grace of this woman giving him a second chance.

Her gloved hands were on the collar of his coat, and her eyes lit up like diamonds. "I missed you, too. I can't wait to tell you all about Paris."

"I can't wait to hear it." He followed her up the sidewalk, barely noticing the city at the moment, wanting nothing more than to spend the rest of the night together.

They walked inside and up the narrow steps to the door of her apartment. "I had a key made for you," Alaina said as she unlocked the door. "Not that we'll be here for long, but you'll need it for a little while anyway." She opened the door and turned on a few lights. "Welcome home." She kissed him on the cheek.

Those words, welcome home, resonated. Nothing about this place felt like home. As a matter of fact, he felt like he was intruding on her turf, even though she had thoughtfully stocked the kitchen with things she knew he would like and emptied out an entire dresser for him to keep his clothes.

It would be OK, though. It was just a matter of time.

They got comfortable on her couch, and Alaina handed him a yellow folder. "These are some of the places I was thinking about going to look at with you. My lease isn't up for another six months but I can get out of it sooner if we find something. I haven't contacted a real estate agent yet. I wanted to get a better idea of what you would like first."

Colt opened the folder. Every apartment she had found was more like a high-rise luxury hotel room and none of them were less than $3000 per month. With the trendy looking décor and the rooftop cafés, they didn't look like anything that could ever be called home. And all of them were deeply entrenched in the city, where there was nothing but more city surrounding them.

He looked at Alaina and wondered if that small-town girl she once was existed anywhere inside her anymore. She had left that lifestyle behind when she was in her early teens and won her first beauty pageant. Her mother, who had been recently divorced from her father, decided to take the opportunity and move Alaina from her hometown in Oregon to New York City to see if she had a career ahead of her in modeling. It seemed like once she got to New York, she never looked back.

"I'm sorry," she said with a smile. "I'm probably overwhelming you. You just got here." She pulled the folder from his hands and set it on the coffee table. "You can look at those later. Did you see anything you liked, though?"

"I see something I like right now." He opened up his arms and she slid inside, feeling the comfort of his arms around her. "I'm sorry about that weekend in Gatlinburg," he said softly. "You were right. We should figure out the future together."

"We're here now," she said. "That's all that matters."

He hoped that was true. So far he didn't feel any differently about New York than he had that night in Gatlinburg. He was just going to shift his focus to her. If he did that, he thought for sure that the nagging feeling would eventually subside.

***

Mila dipped a chip into the salsa and looked across the table at Luke. "Did you think I was a snob in high school?"

Luke smiled at her patiently. They were lunching at one of the restaurants she had wanted to hit before she went back to England.

"High school? No."

"Junior high?"

"Junior high, no way, man. Except for that one year you insisted everyone call you Amelia."

"That is my proper name," she defended.

"And then of course, there was the fact that you retrained yourself to speak without a southern accent."

"It's the proper way to speak."

He grinned. "You know, I still hear that accent coming out of you once in a while," he said. "Like when you get really excited about something. You just start talking and you can't shut it off."

She looked appalled. "You do not."

He nodded. "Yes, I do."

He was serious. "Drat."

"It's really not that bad," he said. "Being associated with people like the ones here in this town. Some of us are actually kind of nice."

"That's not how I meant it," she said quickly. "I just wanted to speak properly, that's all." She paused and made a face. "That didn't come out right, either."

She doubted she could make a person understand her appreciation for the English language. There was a beauty to language, really. A way to use words and make them into something so beautiful that it resonated timelessly through generations. You were either one of those people who understood or one of those people who didn't.

Luke straightened, getting back to the original question. "I didn't really notice it until you went to college. Maybe the summer before that. You started to get obsessive about getting out of here."

"I just wanted to see the world. It had nothing to do with not wanting to be here." His memory was exactly correct. The desire to leave originated when she was considering her options for college, but it didn't have anything to do with Honeybee. She would have felt compelled to explore no matter where she was from. She wouldn't have moved to an entirely different country if that hadn't been the case.

"I get it," he said. "I think it's great that you went to UNC and then moved to London. There aren't many people in the world who have that kind of courage."

She looked down at the table. "I don't know about courage. It was just a drive that I couldn't seem to push down."

"Why would you want to push it down?"

She shrugged. "To stay with my family, I guess. I don't see London as a permanent thing anyway. Or at least I didn't until more recently." What was she going to do about Gabe? If they did end up in a serious relationship, would he be willing to move to America with her? She could see heartbreak in her future. But heartbreak wasn't something that scared her. She had lived enough to know that the pain of bad experiences faded and the character that resulted made it all worth it. She even felt it with Luke. While she never would have wished that kind of sadness on anyone, she knew that the entire experience with Scarlett was something that would forever change him, and he would find a way to use it to make him a better person.

Someday. He wasn't ready for that yet, probably wouldn't be for a long time.

He was looking at her in a curious way, trying to determine what she meant with that last comment. Mila lowered her gaze, took her time dipping a chip and put it into her mouth.

"So what changed?" he asked.

She swallowed. "I'm sorry?"

"You said you weren't thinking about staying in London long-term until recently."

"Um." She looked down again. There was no way to make this sound good, nothing she could do to get out of it or make it sound like anything different than it was. She looked him in the eyes. "Well, there's someone over there that I think I could have a future with." Her stomach clenched as she said the words out loud. Something felt very wrong.

He kept his eyes on her and nodded once but didn't say anything.

"I mean, he's my neighbor. And I had a crush on him ever since I moved there." She laughed uncomfortably, her eyes shifting to anything but him. "And right before I left..." Finally her gaze met his again. "The night before I left, he told me that he thought he was falling in love with me."

Luke sat back in his seat. There was nothing he could do about that. He wasn't sure what he was expecting anyway. He knew she was going back, and he knew she would probably meet someone there eventually. If he would have thought about it, he would have been surprised that she hadn't already. Surely she was dating. But this guy sounded like someone she was serious about.

He lowered his gaze to his drink. "That's great," he said, and then looked back up at her. "Congratulations on that."

She let out a nervous laugh. She wasn't sure it was something that a person should congratulate her on. But it was clear he didn't know what to say any more than she did.

"Hey, I'm sorry if I'm the one to blame for everything that happened with us while you were here. I didn't know…"

There was a fire inside of her when her eyes met his. Sorry? Blame?

"I think what happened with us was beautiful."

He shook his head. He shouldn't have kissed her that night on the patio. Shouldn't have followed her to her hotel room. Shouldn't have talked to her about all those things he never talked to anyone about. Should have just kept her at a safe distance like he managed to do with every other girl since Scarlett.

But that's not what he did. He had let her in, and the whole time she had her sights set on some other guy.

"Mila, we could have slept together if I wouldn't have made the decision not to. I mean, you were there. You weren't the one who was stopping it from happening. And there was another guy the whole time?"

Her heart sank. It was one of those moments where you could see a person changing the way they feel about you. She had to fix this. She had to make him understand.

"We're not together," she said. "I'm not with him."

"He told you he was in love with you. And you said you see a future with him."

"He didn't say he was in love with me. He said he thought he was in love with me." As soon as the words were out of her mouth, she realized how stupid they sounded. She looked down shamefully.

213

"OK. Well, you know what? I think I should go. Mind if we take a rain check on lunch?"

No. She couldn't let the afternoon go like this. She watched as he stood, a part of her unable to believe the way he was reacting to Gabe. He threw money down on the table to cover the drinks they ordered and turned to walk out the door without looking at her. He was going to have to drive her home. After that, he wasn't going to see her again.

She followed him out the door and got into his truck. He started down the street toward his house.

"I didn't know that was going to upset you like this," she said quietly.

"I'm not upset."

"What do you mean you're not upset? You just walked out of a restaurant, and we didn't even get to order our meals yet."

"That's because this isn't a good idea. You and me. Not a good idea."

"We were just having lunch together."

He nodded, and the look on his face told her that she had just said exactly the wrong thing. She sat back in her seat and looked out the window. They drove in silence the rest of the way to his house. He pulled into the driveway and turned off the truck. Mila looked over at her car. He would expect her to get in and drive away, and that would be the end of it.

"I'm sorry," she said softly. "I'm not with him. I'm not..."

"You're not the person I thought you were." He looked at her. "That's all."

"What's that supposed to mean?"

He shrugged. "I just... I didn't think you would be the kind of girl who would have a meaningless fling with someone when you had another guy on the line. I don't know. I didn't think about it. I just assumed that you were single when you took me to your hotel room with obvious intentions." He looked out the windshield. When he spoke again, there was no harshness in his voice. He was just quiet and resigned. "It's no big deal, really. It's not like I haven't been around girls like that before. I just didn't think you were one of them."

Tears invaded her eyes. "Stop saying that. It wasn't some meaningless fling."

He looked at her. He would like to have been unaffected by her tears. He had seen enough woman use tears as their primary means of manipulation, but he didn't think she was doing that. He knew his words were unkind. He knew that they probably cut through her and went straight to her heart.

"What do you want me to say?" he asked quietly.

"I'm not with him, and I'm not with you. You take women home all the time, and it doesn't mean anything to you. How are you going to sit there and judge me when you're ten times worse than I'll ever be?"

He turned toward her, and his calmness in the heat of the argument would have been scary if she didn't know better. "I'm not about to sit here and defend myself to you." He said it quietly, but with finality, opened the door and got out of the truck, then turned away and closed it behind him. It was so cold, the way he moved, the way the door slammed.

Mila got out of the truck and caught up with him on the porch. "I'm sorry," she said. "I'm sorry I didn't tell you about him sooner. This thing that happened between us, it just happened. That first night when you kissed me… I tried to stay away from you after that, but I couldn't. I just wanted to be with you. Maybe it was selfish of me, but I couldn't stop myself. I tried." She stood before him, reached out and touched his arm and waited for him to look at her. "I'm sorry."

"I think you should go."

"I don't want you to think that this didn't mean anything to me. It did. It meant a lot to me. *You* mean a lot to me."

"Mila, please. Let's not make it into something that it's not, OK? When it comes down to it, you're just another pretty girl who happened to be there."

"That's not true. You know it isn't."

She was right, of course. If she had been just another girl he wouldn't have treated her any differently than other girls. He certainly wouldn't have told her the things he did about Scarlett and the day she died, and she never would have inspired him to go talk to Jay. But he had to squash this, the sooner the better.

"You can believe whatever you want. But I meant what I said in the truck. You and me are not a good idea. I don't want to see you again after today. Have a safe trip back to London. And have a great life over there."

"Stop talking to me like that. Stop dismissing me like I'm nothing to you."

He shrugged. "Mila, you *are* nothing to me. You're Colt's little sister. That's what you are. That's all you are."

She wanted to slam her fists into his chest and force him to admit all the good that came from their time together. All she could think about was the way he looked at her that day he stopped by Colt's house after he had seen Ava. It wasn't nothing. She knew it and she knew that he did, too.

Those memories and the way he was looking at her now made her eyes swell with tears. They spilled over onto her cheeks, and she turned away. There was no point in arguing with him, and she wasn't going to stand on his porch and cry.

She walked to the car and opened the door, then turned to him. "If that's the way you want it, goodbye then." She sucked in a breath and wiped away more tears before she got into her car and drove off.

Dammit. He needed to go after her. She was in no shape to drive like that and if anything happened to her…

His heart raced as he jumped into his truck, swearing to himself under his breath. What was he doing talking to her like that? How could he have taken the one person who meant more to him than anyone through this whole disaster and made her feel like she was nothing more than a bother to him? He ran through a stop sign to catch up with her. He couldn't see her yet, but he knew she wasn't that far ahead of him.

He was trying to figure out a way to make her pull over when he found her, but it turned out that wasn't necessary. She was already pulled into an abandoned parking lot and he could see that she had her head in her hands and she was crying.

Nice job, Luke. You should have just left her alone to begin with.

He pulled up beside her and she waved him off, but he got out of his truck and walked to her car anyway. He could have asked her to open the window, but he needed more than that. He walked to the passenger side and opened the door and slid inside, the sound of her crying destroying what was left of his heart.

216

"I didn't mean any of that," he said softly. "I didn't want to think about you with someone else. That's the truth."

She inhaled in a way that sounded almost like a hiccup, trying to calm herself down, embarrassed beyond reason that he was seeing her like this.

"You mean so much to me. Even if I never see you again after today, you will still mean so much to me for the rest of my life. You are the first person, the only person, I have ever talked to about that day. You are the reason I'm going to be able to see Ava again. You are the reason that I believe I can take this heart and love again." He looked into her eyes. "You are all those things. You will always be all those things."

She stared at him, too overcome with emotion for words. If she would have spoken, she was afraid that the only words that would come out of her mouth would be *I love you*. She swallowed and remained silent.

He moved closer. "I'm sorry. So sorry I said those things. So incredibly sorry that I did anything to make you so upset. It's breaking my heart to see you like this and know it's because of me when you're the one who saved me. In so many ways, you're the one who saved me."

She couldn't get to him quickly enough. Tears were still streaming down her cheeks as she climbed onto his lap, crumbling into his arms and letting him hold her as she cried. He whispered that he was sorry over and over again as he held her to him, stroking her hair softly. When she finally pulled herself together, she sat back and looked into his eyes. There was a trace of tears in his own eyes as he reached up and wiped the tears from her face.

She sat mesmerized by the beautiful mess before her. She loved him. She knew it in that moment. Without words, she moved closer to him, ever so slowly touching her lips to his. She kissed him softly, knowing that the emotion behind her kiss was obvious.

"Come back home with me?" He touched her hair. "Please."

She nodded, and he pulled her out of the car with him, locking the door and holding her to his side as he walked her the short distance to his truck. Mila slid across the seat to lean against him as he drove back to his house. She couldn't get close enough.

They reached the house and he held her hand as they walked to the front door. He pushed it open and pulled her inside, lifting her so she could wrap herself around him and carrying her to the bedroom. He lowered them both to the bed without removing his lips from hers.

His kiss was hungry, so fervent. It was so much more than he had given her any other time they kissed. She laid her head back against the mattress and arched herself against him as he pulled off her shirt and lowered his lips to her cleavage.

Never had he wanted to claim someone so badly in his life. Not Scarlett, not anyone. He wanted her to be his, right now tonight, even if it wasn't going to last more than a few more days. Even if she was going back to some other guy in London.

"Amelia," he murmured against her ear, his breath hot on her earlobe, his hands like fire on her body. "My beautiful, beautiful girl."

She closed her eyes and smiled. She loved everything about this moment. The way he touched her. The way he kissed her. The way he whispered her name. The way he called her his.

He kissed her again and she tugged at his shirt so he would pull it off. As he slid his shirt over his head, she reached for his belt and unbuckled it. Quickly, he pulled her to him and rolled them both over so that she was on top of him.

"Mila." He looked up into her eyes. His voice was low and sounded deeper than normal. She loved seeing him like this, his cheeks flushed and his pupils huge. He reached up and touched her hair, looking at her lovingly. She had never seen that look in his eyes before.

She lowered her head and separated his lips with her tongue as she settled over top of him, her knees falling to either side as she took in the feel of his body beneath hers.

His head fell against the mattress and a soft moan escaped him as she kissed him on the neck. "Do you want this?" he whispered, and felt her nod against him. He reached around her back and held her tight so she couldn't move. "Are you sure?"

She didn't know what there was to think about. And she wasn't sure how he expected her to think at a moment like this anyway. "*Luke.*"

He squeezed her even closer. "I just need to know that you're sure."

"I'm sure." She felt his grip on her slowly loosen. What was this woman doing to him? He was aching for her in every way possible as he felt her hands slide down to his waist again. The girl meant more to him than he could admit, even to himself. He couldn't deny that, and he couldn't deny this any longer. There would be plenty of time to deal with the consequences after she was gone.

***

Colt and Alaina had just gotten back from dinner at a restaurant she'd affectionately described as shabby chic. The only thing he liked about his dinner was the company. He didn't understand half of what was on the menu without looking at the description and when he got his entrée he felt sure it must have been an appetizer based on the size of the portion. He had ordered a pork and rice dish, and he was expecting something similar to what he got at home. But what was placed before him, with a smile from the waitress, was six slices of pork over a miniscule portion of rice with several pieces of asparagus sticking out at random. The whole thing was covered in some substance that looked a lot like spit.

Alaina had gone on about what a great opportunity this was to experience something different, but she wasn't fooling him for a second. He would never get used to food that looked more like leftovers to be thrown in the trash.

Back at the apartment, Alaina poured herself a glass of water and opened a beer for Colt. They sat down at the table and Alaina started talking about museums and restaurants she wanted to take him to. Some of them actually sounded interesting, which was good, because he needed something positive to focus on after that dinner they had tonight.

"We need to figure out a time to go visit my mom," she said. "Oh, and I want you to meet my friend Raye. Do you remember me talking about Raye? She's the one who beat cancer and runs the Boston Marathon every year."

He smiled. "I would love to meet Raye. And I would love to see your mom." It had been a long time since he met her mother. It was six months into their relationship, the first time he was in New York with her. At that time, he had loved every aspect of her life almost as much as he loved her. He wasn't sure why he wasn't able to capture that same feeling now.

She got up and sat down on his lap, and he put his arms around her.

She gazed out the window and he turned to look at the scene, buildings everywhere you looked, lights as far as you could see, traffic all over the place. Off in the distance a car horn blared. There was some yelling on the street, not the fighting kind, just the New York City kind. The people up here were coronaries waiting to happen. This place didn't know the meaning of the word relax.

He took a deep breath, turned back to Alaina and pulled her closer, planting a kiss on her shoulder and inhaling the sweet scent of her. He was just about to lose himself in her, forget about every awful thing that surrounded him outside of the two of them, when her phone rang.

"Don't get that," he murmured.

She stiffened. "It might be my agent." She crossed the floor and looked down at her phone and smiled. "Oh, it's Neema." She looked at Colt. "I'll just be a second." She turned away from him and answered the call.

Neema. That had to be another model. They always had the most exotic names to go along with their personas. He took a sip of his drink and waited while she talked, not quite feeling comfortable enough at the apartment to do anything else. She didn't have a TV, so it wasn't like he could even kick back and put on a game.

After a few minutes, Alaina came walking back to the table. "Neema's at the Ritz-Carlton, and she said Ariana Skye just walked in and sat down at the bar."

He nodded, trying to figure out why that was news that was worthy of a phone call. They were in New York City. Surely famous actresses could be spotted every day of the week.

Alaina continued. "She's starting a new clothing line. Everyone's trying to model for her. It would be huge. *Huge*."

"So, you want to go to the Ritz-Carlton and see if you can talk to Ariana Skye?"

Alaina moved closer to him, shaking her head. "No. I told her to go on without me. I'm not looking for more work right now. All I really want to do is spend the evening with you."

She sat back down on his lap, and he saw the look of pure happiness all over her face. It was this look on this woman's face that made him want to try so hard to make this work.

"I love you, Laney." He pulled her to him and buried his head against her neck, far more thankful than he'd let on that she opted for an evening in with him tonight instead of making him go out into the city again. He needed a break. He needed – her. That was all he needed. He almost had himself convinced of that as he wrapped his arms around her and held her tight.

Chapter 25

Mila laid next to Luke and watched him while he slept. He was on his back with the covers shoved down to his waist, his seductive naked chest exposed, and his head turned to the side. It was a peaceful moment, a moment where that hint of unrest he carried with him all the time seemed to have disappeared. She thought about everything that happened the night before, the things he said and the things he did. There were no words of love spoken between them, but there didn't have to be. She felt it, and she knew he felt it, too.

Quietly she slid out of bed, pulling on the blue and white cotton flannel shirt that had been so carelessly discarded to the floor last night. She buttoned a few of the buttons and went into the bathroom to freshen up. There was no evidence of all the tears she had shed the night before. She stood before the mirror brushing her teeth, her natural self staring back at her. No make-up, her morning hair falling a bit flatter than she liked around her face. This was her. Unlike the way she felt the morning after with other men, she loved that he would see her like this. Wanted it even. It was her authentic self, and she wanted to share it with him.

She walked back into the bedroom and climbed onto the bed, moving over top of him and straddling him over the covers. He opened his eyes and smiled. Such a soft smile. Such a happy look.

"Good morning," she said seductively and playfully all at the same time.

"You're wearing my shirt."

She nodded. "Did you notice that's just about all I'm wearing?"

He was fully aware, but he didn't think those words were necessary. He reached up and touched her face so gently that she closed her eyes and leaned into his touch.

He wanted to take the time to savor it, to memorize the way she looked and the way she felt in that moment. But that wasn't going to be possible for long. He could barely keep himself still as she unbuttoned each of the three buttons she had closed on his shirt, then moved to allow it to fall open. His throat went dry. She was breathtaking. His eyes traveled down her flat tummy to her lacy pink panties and back up again.

He reached up and put his hands on her arms, moving her off of him and laying her down on the bed beside him. "You could get a guy into a lot of trouble looking like that," he said softly.

She looked up at him with innocent eyes. "Do you think I'm trouble?"

He smiled and nodded, a wave of affection crashing through him. "Trouble like I've never seen before."

She smiled and wrapped herself around him as he lowered his lips to her neck.

***

Later that morning, Mila stood in the parking lot with Luke where she left her car the night before. She needed to get moving so she could spend the day shopping with Peyton like she had planned. She would never admit how hard it was to leave him for the day and couldn't even bring herself to think about what it would be like when she had to go back to England.

"Is it weird to say I'll miss you today?" She looked into his eyes, searching for that hint of suffering that was always subtly present. For the life of her, she couldn't find it.

An easy smile crossed his lips. "I'll miss you, too." He pulled her into a hug and gave her a kiss on the cheek, then stepped back, his hands on her arms. "Have a good day today. Give me a call when you're done shopping."

She nodded. "I will. See you in a little while."

He waved as she backed up her car, and she took a moment to enjoy the look of him before she drove away. This morning was pure bliss. She wanted to live inside this bubble forever.

Luke dropped his head and looked down at the ground as soon as she was out of sight. What he did last night was probably reckless, and it was only going to lead to more heartache in the end. But it was too late to think about that now. He had tried. But he was playing with fire, something that he knew all along.

It was never going to work, for so many reasons. He thought about trying to downplay his feelings for her for the rest of her time here but quickly decided that he didn't want to do that. She would see right through it anyway. He would just let it be whatever it was for the next few days and find a way to move on after she left.

They would both be OK when this was over. And he didn't think he would regret a second of their time together after she was gone. He got back into his truck and started the drive back to his house. It would feel lonely without her there. It felt lonely without her there already. He shook his head and tried to think of anything other than her.

***

Peyton sat in the passenger seat of Dylan's car and stole a glance. The bruise around his eye, that ever-present reminder of that day she would rather forget, was almost gone. He pulled out his wallet. They were behind at least eight cars at the drive-thru where they stopped after the basketball game earlier that night.

Dylan was benched due to an injury that lingered from football season, but he went to all the games anyway, dressed in plain clothes and sitting with the team and coaches. He drove home afterward instead of taking the bus, which was only allowed because he was listed as inactive on the team.

"Did I tell you I like that shirt you have on today?" He smiled. He knew he had already told her several times about the shirt.

"I got it when I was shopping with my Aunt Mila." She looked at him coyly. They had spent several hours that morning hitting every department store around looking for sales. By the time they were finished, Peyton discovered that she loved Mila's kind of shopping. "Know what else I got?"

"What?"

"She took me to get my first pedi. If you're nice, I'll show it to you later."

He tapped the steering wheel with his fingers, looking out the windshield. "What do I have to do for you to think that I'm nice? Buy your food? Does that count?"

"That would most definitely count, but you don't have to buy my food."

He inched the car forward. "You could show me now. We're not going anywhere anytime soon."

Her eyes lingered on him for a moment and then she bent to slip off her shoes. As she tugged at her sock, she started to feel silly. What was he going to care about her toenails being painted? It wasn't a thing guys cared about, was it? Trevor wouldn't have. He probably wouldn't have even pretended to. For that reason, she never would have thought to show him to begin with.

She pulled off her socks and lifted her feet to the seat between them. Dylan looked down, then pulled her feet onto his lap. Perfect toes on perfect feet.

He lifted one foot up to get a closer look. "Beautiful," he said.

She pulled her foot away. "All right. I know it's silly."

He looked at her. "It's not silly. Your feet look beautiful. And now you've made me want to suck your toes."

She burst out laughing, pulling both feet closer to her. It was incredible the way she looked, the way she sounded when she laughed.

"I was only half kidding about that," he said, glancing at her and moving the car forward. "Bring those feet back over here." She relaxed them on his lap again and he picked one up. "Are you ticklish?"

"No," she said, laughing again.

He tickled her foot, and she squirmed away from him. "You just said you weren't ticklish."

"I just said that so you wouldn't tickle me."

He laughed. "Why don't you bring the rest of you over here?" She complied with his request without giving it a second thought. As soon as she reached him, he pulled her to him and started tickling her all over, holding her tight so she couldn't escape.

"Hey," she protested between giggles. "Stop that!"

"Are you ticklish all over?" he asked playfully.

"Yes, now stop it!"

He pulled her onto his lap, looking up at her. "OK," he said softly. Then he kissed her. There was a part of her that was aware that she should have felt silly kissing a boy in a drive-thru lane, but that part was convincingly overruled by the rest of her.

She slid off his lap and moved to his side, leaning against him. Dylan's hands remained on hers to stop her from retaliating with her own exploration of seeing where he was ticklish. He pulled up to the window and ordered their food, never taking his hands from hers. Moments later, they had their meals, and he drove them to the back of a grocery store parking lot.

He cut the lights, and she started opening the bag to get their food out. "How hungry are you?" she asked.

"Starving," he said and leaned in to kiss her again. It only took her a moment to forget all about the food. God help her, she was really starting to fall for him.

***

Luke pulled up to the street beside Lily Ann's apartment building and looked around. The neighborhood was kind of rough. Not that things like that bothered Lily Ann, as evidenced by the fact that she was working at Cobra's.

He turned off his truck and sat there, staring at the building and remembering the last time he talked to her. In more ways than he had ever known possible, he was a mess. It wasn't long after Scarlett had died, and he drank himself into oblivion that night. When he went to leave the bar, Lily Ann took his keys and insisted he couldn't drive. She took him outside, and a huge argument ensued. He didn't even know what he said to her, but he knew she offered him a ride home, and he insisted on walking. He walked the five miles to his house and crashed on the couch as soon as he got in the door. The next day, she stopped by with his keys, thinking everything would be OK. But he was unforgiving. He told her to stop interfering with his life and asked her to leave. He barely noticed the devastation in her eyes, he was so immersed in his own struggle.

But today, he remembered. Somewhere deep in his mind was that look of hurt she wore the day she walked out of his life. He took a deep breath and let it out, then got out of the truck and walked down the sidewalk, opening the door to the building. His heart was pounding when he found apartment number 7.

He thought about leaving. Stopping by unannounced was probably a bad idea. But he needed to see her. He raised his hand to the door and hesitated just a second longer before his knuckles fell lightly against it.

He heard footsteps. Then Lily Ann opened the door, looking up at him with surprise, and he exhaled a breath he had been holding.

"Lily Ann," he said softly.

Her brows wrinkled in confusion. "What are you doing here?"

He licked his lips. He would have liked for her to invite him in, but he wasn't going to ask. "I just um…" He looked down, then looked up at her again. "I'm sorry. I'm a little nervous."

He saw her mouth tip up in what might have been a hint of a smile. Then again, it might have been a scowl.

"I saw you at Cobra's the other night," he said. "And Colt told me you picked up a job there for some extra money and…Lily Ann, I'm so sorry. I'm so sorry about how I acted toward you. I was out of my mind." He shook his head. "I didn't care if I lived or died that night. As a matter of fact, I would have rather died than lived."

Her eyes softened.

"You did the right thing, obviously." She nodded, wrapping her arms around herself and looking down at the ground.

"I don't want years to go by not knowing who you are. I don't want to not be there when things happen in your life. I want things back the way they used to be before I screwed everything up."

Her eyes were shining with tears when she looked back up at him.

"Please," he said. "I am so sorry. I should have told you that the next day. I don't know why I didn't."

She opened up her arms and moved forward to pull him into a hug. "It's OK," she whispered, allowing herself to be swallowed up in the warmth of his arms. Tears spilled down her cheeks. She never thought she would see the day that he would come back.

He released her. "I was out of my mind," he said again.

She touched his face. "How are you doing now?"

"Some days, I'm still out of my mind," he said, then smiled. "But mostly, I'm not. I'm getting better. Every day. Going in the right direction." He reached up and rubbed his jaw. "What about you? What happened with you and Steve?"

She shook her head, wiping the tears from the brims of her eyes. "It's a long story."

He nodded, sliding his hands into the pockets of his jeans and rocking back on his feet, expecting her to dismiss him.

"Do you want to come in and talk? I have hot chocolate."

He couldn't hold back the smile that quirked up his lips. Lily Ann made the best hot chocolate. He had forgotten all about it until now. "Hot chocolate? Your hot chocolate?" His eyes lit up like a child's.

She laughed. "Yes. My hot chocolate. Your favorite."

"How could *anyone* turn that down?"

She laughed and stood aside, holding the door open so he could come in.

***

Colt looked into the eyes of Alaina's mother. Something felt off, but he didn't know what it was. They had taken the subway and caught a cab to get to her place for dinner. It was a nice change of pace since her mother lived on the outskirts of the city and away from the constant activity. It was also the first home-cooked meal he had in days, which was another welcome change. The evening had been quite enjoyable, except for the feeling he was getting every time he focused attention on Camille.

It was something in the way she looked at him. She was making him feel like he was the person she had been waiting for to come rescue Alaina. He understood to an extent. He knew that Camille felt like she had let Alaina down because she didn't choose a good father for her, and she wanted nothing more than for her to settle down with a good husband.

They were sitting in the living room of a reasonably sized house, and Colt was just happy to be in a place where he didn't feel like the walls were closing in on him.

"So, Colt, now that you're going to be staying in New York and getting a place with my daughter, I assume you two are talking about getting married." There was nothing warm or motherly about

228

the way she said it. She was more like a shrewd businesswoman who was used to telling it like it is and getting her way.

Beside him, Alaina squeezed his hand reassuringly. He cleared his throat and gave her the same smile that had charmed her daughter when they first met. "Um, well, we haven't really talked about that."

Camille nodded. "You've been together for two years. Surely you must know if you want to get married by now?"

"Mom!" Alaina scolded. "This move is a big adjustment for us. He's giving up everything to be with me. I think he's committed."

Her mother smiled, and he could see her softening. "I'm sorry. It's just that I don't want Alaina living with you for years on end without getting married. Maybe I'm being old fashioned. I apologize."

She wasn't sorry. He could see that. She was just backing down because she had made her point and didn't see the need to draw it out. Suddenly, the size of the house didn't feel so comfortable anymore. He felt the walls closing in on him even as Alaina reassured her that they would be getting engaged sometime soon.

He knew she was just trying to appease her mother, but still he felt like a noose was tightening around his neck, not at all how he should feel about marrying the woman that he loved. Maybe it was just too much to think of right now with everything else that was going on.

The next few hours were something akin to torture for him. He had to fake his way through a nice evening with Alaina and her mother, and faking was not something Colt had ever done well. There was never any need to as far as he was concerned. Telling the truth, no matter how hard it could be sometimes, was just his way. Always had been.

But he couldn't do it here. He just had to wait it out, which was what he did until Alaina finally told her mother they needed to get going. They couldn't say their goodbyes quickly enough as far as he was concerned. Her mother drove them to the subway station, and he had never felt more eager to get back to a place he didn't even want to be at.

Alaina held his hand as they walked back to her apartment, didn't say a word about anything that happened at her mom's. He was beginning to wonder if she hadn't noticed at all how uncomfortable he was, but when they got inside, she closed the door and stood before him, her back to the door.

"I'm sorry she got so overbearing tonight," she began, and then gave him an apologetic smile. "She's just so used to looking out for me. Not that you're someone that needs to be on her radar. Not at all."

"I just...I'm not thinking about marriage right now. I know you're ready for us to get engaged, and it's not that I don't love you, but I want to get used to New York first. I've barely spent any time with you here, and you have all these new things going on with your career. I just need things to settle down a little before I can think about..."

She took a step closer. "It's OK." She touched his neck with her fingertips.

Was it? He felt like she wasn't listening to a word he was saying. But he wasn't about to make the same mistake twice. So when she leaned in and kissed him, he pulled her into his arms and kissed her back.

***

Mila took a glass of wine from Luke and crossed the living room floor to sit down on the couch with him. After she went shopping with Peyton, she had dinner with her family, barely able to contain herself long enough to have a nice visit with them. She needed to see Luke again. She had been counting the hours all day long.

"How was your day?" he asked as she got comfortable, leaning against the arm of the couch and turning toward him to engage.

"It was good. I was thinking a lot about how much I'm going to miss my family and the girls and how different it's going to be with Colt not here." Her eyes met his. "And I was thinking about us."

"What about us?"

"I can't stop thinking about us."

He looked down to the ground, then back to her. "There is no us, Mila." He shook his head. "There's you, and there's London,

230

and there's me, and there's this big thing that I'm dealing with. I wish it would go away, but until it does I'm not sure that I'm ready for any kind of us."

She put her hand on his knee. "I understand that," she said softly. "I think we could work through it."

"While you're in London?"

She shook her head. "I mean if I stayed."

"No. You can't stay. Not for me."

"Why?"

"Because I can't promise you anything."

"I'm not asking for any promises," she said. "And I know you, Luke. I know that you wouldn't just break my heart."

He leaned forward and ran a hand over his face. "You can't trust me with your..." He stared at her as it dawned on him that maybe it was too late for that. "Mila, no."

Dammit. He should have stuck to his guns. Never should have slept with her. He knew it was going to change everything, and it did. "I'm sorry. I'm not ready for all this. You can't stay here for me. It's one thing if you stay for your family. And for what it's worth, I think they need you here. But don't do it for me."

"So you want me to go back to London?"

"I want you to do whatever it is you want to do, but I don't want you to make a decision based on us. I just don't..."

Slowly, she nodded. "It's OK. I understand. You don't have to say it." He had already explained it once, that night at the hotel room. He was a mess, and he needed to stay away from her. But then he didn't. And now she was pretty sure she was in love with him.

"It's not that I don't like you, because I do. You know I do. It's just that it's a big decision for you. And I don't want to be the reason you're not living the life you always wanted in London."

"What if I decided to stay for my family? What would happen with us then?"

"I don't know."

"Would you want to keep seeing me?"

"Don't do that."

She raised her brows innocently, and he suspected she knew exactly what she was doing.

"You're trying to make me paint a picture of what it would be like if you stayed. And if I told you that I would want to keep seeing you, you would weigh that into your decision. I don't want to be any part of that decision."

"You already are."

He shook his head. She moved closer. He looked at her with irresistibly defenseless eyes. "I don't want to let you down. I don't want to let your family down. Your family means more to me than my own family."

She touched him tenderly, leaning closer to him, and crooked a finger at him. "Come here, cutie," she said softly. It was a reference to the day he said the same thing to her on this couch, and he smiled when she said it, visibly relaxing.

She kissed him gently. "I only have a few more days," she said. "Let's not waste them worrying about things we can't predict in the future. OK?"

"Yeah, OK." He nodded.

She slid onto his lap, leaning forward to kiss him more passionately, a kiss that consumed him in a matter of minutes. They had already come this far. He would hold onto her until the moment came he had to let her go.

Chapter 26

Colt was looking out the window at Alaina's apartment, watching a brazen older woman yell out her window at the trash collector. He had to admit he admired her spunk.

"You're a trash collector!" she hollered in that bold New York accent that he found kind of endearing at times. "That means you collect the trash, not scatter pieces all over the street!"

"Hey, you want this job? If I'm so bad at it, why don't you come down here and do it better?"

"Why would I do that? I'm not the trash collector. You are."

Colt smiled as the man made a gesture to her and then waved her off, returning the can to the alley and jumping on the back of his truck. He could be entertained for hours by the locals around here. The way they acted was kind of charming in a weird way.

Alaina was going to be tied up with a photo shoot for most of the day. When she left, she told him she didn't know when she would be back and gave him a few suggestions of places to explore while she was out. They were thoughtful suggestions, but he wasn't interested in any of them. He just wanted some downtime. Time to think about whatever it was that was bothering him so much.

His phone rang. He thought it might be Alaina calling to tell him when she would be done with the shoot, but when looked down he saw that it was Lizzy. He stared at the phone for a minute, then took the call. "Hello?"

"Colt, it's Lizzy. I know you're in New York City, but I thought you would want to know. My grandmother had a stroke this morning."

He straightened. "What? How bad was it?"

"Pretty bad," Lizzy said, and he could hear that she was crying. "I stopped over on my way to work to drop off a few groceries for her and…"

"And what?"

"She was on the living room floor." Lizzy sniffed. "She couldn't talk. She was just looking up at me with these helpless eyes. Those eyes, Colt. I can't get it out of my head."

He gripped the phone. "Where are you now?"

"I'm at the hospital. Waiting for test results."

"Is anyone with you?"

"No."

"Can you call anyone to come sit with you?"

"I called my mom," she said. "But I don't know if she's coming or not."

Dammit, he wished there were something he could do. "I'll be home tomorrow," he told her. "What hospital are you at?"

"Mercy."

"OK. I'll check in with you tomorrow. If anything changes, call me."

"OK," Lizzy said tearfully. "Thank you, Colt."

He ended the call and stood up, sliding the phone into the back pocket of his jeans and running a hand through his hair. There had to be something he could do. Maybe he could get Luke to check in with her. It was a thought, but right now there were too many thoughts spinning around in his head. He needed a way to sort through them. He grabbed his jacket and headed out the door, no idea where he was going or how long he would be gone.

***

He was sitting in the living area when Alaina got home. The grave look on his face was a sharp contrast to the smile she had been wearing the whole way home, anticipating the apartment shopping they would be doing together in the coming weeks. Her smile faded quickly as she stared at him. He looked completely unsettled, like something bad had just happened, or was about to happen. Her heart sank. She had a feeling she knew what was coming.

She took a breath. "Colt, are you OK?"

He didn't answer her immediately, just stared at her and gave the tiniest shake of his head to indicate that no, he was not OK.

"What is it?" She was afraid to ask. She felt the blood drain from her face as she waited for his response.

His eyes met hers, and they were so weary, so tired looking. He looked like he had aged ten years since she left him at her apartment this morning. "Alaina, I'm sorry. So, so sorry."

She let out a breath and tried to brace herself for what was coming.

"I…" He closed his eyes. He didn't want this moment to become their reality, but he knew it had to happen. Everything had become clear to him after he got that call from Lizzy a few hours ago. "I can't stay here with you." He said it with conviction, in a way that she would know he was sure about this.

She licked her lips. All hope was not necessarily lost. Not being ready to stay in New York didn't mean their relationship had to end. They could work through that. "You don't like the city. We can compromise on that. I don't need to be here."

He stared at her for a long moment, the look of torture in his eyes unmistakable. "It's not that." He shook his head. "It's not New York, it's not your mom, it's not your contract and it's not you."

"What is it then?" she asked, and the innocence in her voice, the way she trusted him, the hope that maybe they could still fix this, just about killed him.

"There's someone else," he said quietly.

Her spine stiffened. "What?" she asked, as if she couldn't have possibly heard him correctly.

He looked down at the floor and then back to her, forcing himself to look into her eyes. She deserved that much. And she deserved the truth, no matter how hard this was.

"I wanted to make this work," he said. "I was going to leave everything I know and love to try to make this work with you."

"Who is she?" Her voice was quivering with emotion. She watched as he looked down at the ground and rubbed his forehead. "Look at me." He looked up and saw the hurt and disbelief in her eyes. "Who is she?"

"It's Lizzy."

"How did this happen?" Her voice was a whisper of disbelief.

"I don't know. She needed help with that house and it was just silly for me not to help her. And then...I don't know how it happened. I don't know. I wish I would have handled it differently, but I can't go back and change it now."

"Are you in love with her?"

Slowly, he nodded.

Her brows knit together and tears started to form in her eyes. "Were you cheating on me?" The very thought of that was devastating to her.

"No." He was flirty with her, he knew. He took her out to dinner once. But he never touched her, never gave her any indication that there was a chance for anything to happen with them. He didn't think what he did was cheating, and he didn't want to get into those kinds of details unless she specifically asked about it. "We were friends. That's all."

That wasn't exactly all. He knew she liked him and still he didn't stay away from her. Alaina nodded, and he could have left it at that. He didn't want to say anything that was going to hurt her even more, but he wanted to be honest with her, too.

"I could have been more guarded, obviously. I could have done better for you."

"I don't understand." Tears flowed freely from her eyes, and she wiped them away. "How could you let this happen? Why would you tell me you wanted to make this work and come here like this knowing that you were in love with someone else?"

He didn't know. That was the thing. But no kind of explanation like that was going to help. Nothing was going to help. He knew that when he looked at her and saw a woman he barely recognized. She was devastated, far beyond what he thought she would be.

"I wanted this to work," he said quietly. "I did. I'm so sorry."

She blinked, looking upwards to avert her gaze from his. "I can't keep playing these games with you, Colt. If you're leaving now and you're choosing her, that decision is final."

He nodded in a way that told her he was sure of his decision, and she broke down all over again. He closed his eyes, knowing that the sound of her heartbreak was something he would never forget.

She needed to get a hold of herself. This was happening. It was really happening, and there was going to be no way to work it out. Not with another woman in the picture. She stood and crossed the floor to get a tissue. And that was when she saw his suitcase and all his things, neatly piled and ready to go. Ready to leave, to walk out of her life for good.

She wiped her tears and turned to him. He was watching her, waiting for her to say something more. "Does she know how you feel about her?"

He shook his head, turning away from her slightly. He wanted to tell her that he didn't even know until today, until he had gotten that call. He knew he liked her. He was obviously attracted to her. But it was when she called him in distress and he knew he had to find a way to be there for her that it finally came together for him. The picture Luke was trying to paint. It was all there. In bright, vivid, undeniable colors.

"She doesn't know any of this," he said. "She doesn't even know that we were having problems." Problems that he created because of how he felt about Lizzy. He knew that now, too.

Alaina sniffed, nodding her head. For now, the tears had stopped. He saw the struggle for determination begin to emerge, saw her trying to get a handle on herself. That was good. He knew she would be OK eventually, and he knew that she knew it, too.

"Alaina, I know it doesn't make a difference to you right now, but I never meant to hurt you. I loved you. I really did. I still do. And I wanted this to work."

She looked at him, saw the sincerity in his eyes, and she knew he was telling the truth about everything. More tears started to fall, and he stood and walked over to her. She put her head in her hands and wiped away more tears, and then she felt his arms close around her, those strong arms that had made her feel so safe and protected, so loved for so long.

And she realized that nothing he could do right now was going to help her. Slowly she pulled away from him, her hands still clutching his arms, and looked into his eyes.

"I think you should go," she said quietly, and he nodded. She let go of him, and he took a step back. The devastation on that beautiful face. His fault. Every last piece of it.

He turned and walked into the bedroom to get his suitcase, then slipped on his jacket. Alaina was leaning against the wall outside the bedroom, staring down at the ground and trying to keep it together. He was leaving. And he wasn't coming back. She would probably never hear from him again.

He walked back out of the bedroom, pausing as he stood before her once again. How could this be goodbye?

"Laney…" he began, and she put up a hand.

"Don't," she whispered. "Please, just don't."

He nodded and took a step back. The only thing left to say was goodbye.

"I guess this is it," she said. "This is goodbye."

That wasn't what he wanted, but now was not the time to talk to her about keeping in touch someday after this was all over. He had to let her go completely, give them both the time they needed to get over this.

"Goodbye," he said, and she could tell there was so much more he wanted to say.

"Goodbye, Colt."

He waited another minute and then turned and walked out the door.

The fresh air out on the street didn't make him feel any better. He hailed a cab and got inside quickly. The faster he was out of here, the better off everyone was going to be.

"Where to?" asked the cabbie.

"Just take me to a car rental place, man," Colt said. To hell with catching a flight and being in Tennessee tomorrow. Lizzy needed him now. He would be there.

***

It was 3:30 in the morning when Colt arrived at the hospital, breaking the speed limit the whole way to Tennessee. He parked his rental in the garage and walked quickly to the elevators, punching the button for the ICU, his best guess to where her grandmother

238

would be. He walked down the hallway past a waiting room and stopped in his tracks when he saw her, all curled up into a little ball, her big orange hat on the table in front of her.

He walked into the waiting room, kneeled down before her and touched her arm. Her eyes fluttered open. Then he saw the confusion set in. "What are you doing here?" She glanced around the otherwise empty room. "What time is it?"

He looked at the clock on the wall. "3:30."

She sat up and blinked. "What are you doing here?" she asked him again.

"I was worried about you."

"You were worried about me, so you drove all the way from New York?"

He looked up into her fretful eyes. "No. I drove all the way from New York because I didn't want you to be alone." He wanted to tell her he loved her, but it didn't seem like the right time.

"I don't understand."

His eyes remained on hers. "I couldn't stay in New York while you were here like this worried sick about your grandmother." He reached up to touch her face, and her eyes filled with tears. "I wanted to be with you. I *had* to be with you."

The confusion on her face remained. "Didn't Alaina have a problem with that?"

He smiled wearily. "It's over with us."

"*What?*"

"It had to be. I can't be with her when I feel the way I do about you."

She stared at him, unable to believe her eyes or her ears. She closed her eyes. Surely she was dreaming. But when she opened them again, he was still there, smiling up at her. Those beautiful brown eyes. That gorgeous smile.

She reached out and touched his face, felt the hardness of his cheekbones against her fingertips. He bent his neck and kissed her hand. "I'm sorry it took me so long," he whispered. "But I'm here now, and I'm not going anywhere."

Her eyes filled with fresh tears. "This can't really be happening."

He stood and sat down next to her, pulling her into his arms. She crumbled against him, and he felt the tension release from her body.

"Colt," she whispered softly, and he tightened his grip on her. "I would have waited forever for you."

He smiled and kissed her on the top of the head. For the first time since he'd met her, his heart felt right. She snuggled in closer to him, and together they fell asleep in the waiting room.

***

Colt opened his eyes as day broke outside of the window. He looked at the clock. It was just barely after 6. Next to him, Lizzy stirred. She fit so snugly in the crook of his arm, her head on his chest as she slept against him. He rubbed his hand gently on her arm and she opened her eyes. Staring up at him, she smiled.

"You're really here," she said softly.

"Of course I am." He smiled down at her, no longer feeling like he needed to hide how very much he adored this girl.

"But I don't understand what happened. Last we talked you were moving to New York City to start your lives together."

It was a long story, and he could see that she was as exhausted as he was. "I will tell you anything you want to know about it when we get back to my place, or back to your place, or wherever we go after we talk to the doctors." It occurred to him that he didn't care where they were going as long as he was with her. Exactly the way he wanted to feel about Alaina, but never did.

For the life of her she couldn't understand why anyone, let alone someone as incredible as Colt, would walk away from a beautiful model with a million dollar contract to be with her. She didn't want to ask too many questions. She was half afraid that if she did, he would end up talking himself out of his decision.

A nurse appeared in the doorway. "Family of Hazel Montgomery."

Lizzy sat up straight. "That's my grandmother."

The nurse looked at her. "Her doctor would like to talk with you."

Lizzy took a deep breath. Colt grabbed her hand and together they walked down the hallway toward her grandmother's room.

***

Luke sat across the table from Mila at her mom and dad's house for what might have been the last time. He was going to miss her. He had a feeling that he hadn't even begun to realize how much.

She turned from her conversation with Peyton to take a sip of her iced tea and caught his gaze. He quickly looked down at his empty plate. Damn, he hadn't wanted her to catch him looking at her, didn't want her to know the things that were going on in his head.

He needed to get out of there, get some fresh air. He was just about to excuse himself when the front door opened. In the doorway he saw Colt...and right behind him was Lizzy.

"Mom, Dad, everyone, this is Lizzy."

Lizzy stepped out from behind him to say hello to everyone. Colt's dad scratched his head. "When did you get back?"

"Last night. Long story and I'll tell you all about it sometime but right now, we're starving and we were hoping you had two more spots at the table."

"Yes, of course," Mary Beth said, getting up to get two extra settings. Mila and Peyton moved down to make room for Colt and Lizzy to sit next to one another, but not before Mila shot an inquisitive look at Luke. He gave a subtle shrug, then grinned. She smiled back at him, lowering her face so neither Colt nor Lizzy would see.

As Colt walked past his father, he placed a hand on his shoulder and leaned down to whisper in his ear. "I'm staying, Dad."

John raised his brows, turning to look at him. "What?"

"I'm not going to New York," he said loud enough for everyone to hear. He looked around the table, then at Lizzy. "I'm staying."

From the kitchen, his mother wiped away tears. Mila looked up at Lizzy. "Happy to have you with us tonight," she said. "Welcome to our world."

Lizzy smiled. She had such a warm smile, Mila thought. Also, she was adorable. And when she watched Colt sit down next to her at the table, something felt very right about it.

***

Shortly after dinner was over, Colt announced they had to go. "Her grandmother's at the hospital," he said. "We need to get back and see her. Thanks for dinner." He looked at his mom. "Thanks for everything." He looked at his dad. "See you at work tomorrow."

He pushed his chair out and stood behind Lizzy's chair until she got out.

"It was nice meeting everyone," she said with a smile.

As soon as they were out the door, John threw his napkin on the table in front of him. "Thank you, Lord," he said, looking up toward heaven.

Mila's heart sank. She wondered if they were heartbroken when she left but just didn't let on because they didn't want to hold her back from doing what she wanted. She pushed out her chair. "I should get going, too," she said. "I have a few things I need to take care of before tomorrow."

Luke stood. "Me, too. Thanks for inviting me over," he said to Mila's mom.

"You're always welcome here," she said. "You know that."

Mila was on the porch when he walked out.

"Hey," he said.

She turned to him and smiled. "He's staying. I'm so happy that he's staying."

He studied her, his brows wrinkling in confusion. "You don't look happy. You look like something's bothering you."

She nodded, the faraway look in her eyes only serving to intrigue him further. "Would you mind stopping off at Drunken Lizard's for a drink before you go home tonight?"

He nodded, placing his hand on her back and escorting her off the porch to her car. "See you there," he said, taking a step back as she got into her car.

He followed her to the Drunken Lizard, trying to dismiss the feeling of impending doom as he drove. She would be gone from his life all too soon, and he would have to let her go.

He pulled in beside her at the bar, met her at her car and took her hand, walking her across the parking lot and opening the door for her. Once inside, their drinks in front of them, she started talking.

"Were you around my family much when I left for North Carolina?"

"I was always around your family," he said.

"Were they as upset when I left as they were relieved that Colt's staying?"

"When you went to college? They seemed OK to me."

"Oh." She had to admit she was a little disappointed to hear that.

"But when you left for London…"

She looked at him intently. "Yes?"

"They were devastated."

"Devastated?"

He nodded. "I imagine they will be devastated all over again when you go back."

She sat back in her seat. "Why didn't anyone tell me?"

"Because, Mila. You have to live your life. If you want your life to be in London, it shouldn't matter how much the people who love you want you to be here. They loved you enough to let you go. And they'll keep doing that as many times as you want to go."

She wanted to ask if that included him, but she knew that would be crossing the line.

"I was just thinking about Lizzy," she said. "And the fact that Colt's probably going to fall in love with her while I'm over there. I'm not even going to know the girl. What if they get married and have kids and they won't even know their aunt?"

"I think you're getting a little ahead of yourself."

"Today it sounds like that," she agreed. "But a year from now, he could be getting married. And I'll be honest with you, I wish I would have known Alaina. I thought I would have all kinds of time to get closer with her, and then he almost moved to New York and now we're never going to see her again." She took a sip of her drink. "Life keeps happening while I'm over there. It keeps happening, and I keep missing it."

"Maybe you should make a list of pros and cons."

She sat back and looked around the bar. "I just don't know if it comes down to a list anymore. I think…" She paused and looked at him with intention. "I think it comes down to what's in my heart."

He nodded. "You're the only one who can answer that."

He was right. She needed to figure out her heart. It would be one of the hardest decisions she would ever have to make.

***

Colt and Lizzy left the hospital late in the evening, completely exhausted. Lizzy climbed into the passenger side of his truck while he held the door for her. She could get used to this. She smiled as she watched him walk around the front of the truck and get inside. "Do you want to go home or do you want to come to my place?"

She looked over at him, still not able to believe what happened in the past 24 hours. She had wanted him from the first time she saw him, but she never thought she had a chance. Especially not after what she did at Cobra's that night. She smiled at him.

"What?" he asked, smiling back at her in a way that looked kind of shy. Up until this moment, she couldn't imagine this man ever looking shy about anything. It was adorable.

"I just can't believe you're here…asking me if I want to come back to your place."

"Do you?" he asked.

She nodded. "I do. I appreciate this. I appreciate you so much. I could really use the company tonight. Thank you."

He put his hand over hers on her leg. "Anything you need," he said quietly.

She blinked back the tears. She needed him, she realized. Not just today, but for her whole life. She had never gotten into much talk about her family, how both her parents were free-spirited hippies that she had a hard time relating to. She had always felt like the adult in her relationship with her parents, and even with her grandmother, Lizzy was the one looking out for her. No one ever looked out for Lizzy. She never thought about what this would feel like. Not until now, when it was so clear that Colt was there for her and so committed to taking care of her.

"She's going to be OK," he told her. "I have a feeling."

Lizzy smiled. "Me, too." She lowered her gaze and casually wiped away a tiny tear that spilled over the rim of her eye.

When they got to his house, he poured them both a glass of sweet tea, thankful maybe for the first time that Mila had stocked the refrigerator full of something other than cold pizza and a six-pack. He sat down next to her on the couch, handing her the drink and putting his on the coffee table in front of them.

"You OK?" he asked, turning toward her. The hardest part about situations like this was that you see someone you care about suffering and there is absolutely nothing you can do to make it better. Nothing, other than make sure the person isn't going through it alone.

Again, she found herself blinking back tears. "I'm OK," she said, taking a sip of her tea and then putting it on the table. "I'm just a little overwhelmed right now."

He nodded and pulled her to him, kissing her on top of her head. He loved the way she felt next to him. Next to him was where she was meant to be.

"Thank you for everything," she said softly.

"You're going to have to quit doing that."

"Doing what?"

"Thanking me for being here. I'm going to be here. We're going to get through this together. You don't have to thank me."

Tears flowed freely down her cheeks, and she nodded. "I'm sorry. I'm just not used to this, and I'm so overwhelmed by so many things…"

"Lizzy…" He watched as he wiped away her tears, wishing he could do something to bring back that warm smile of hers.

"I know she's going to be OK," Lizzy said, settling against him again, her head on his chest. "I just…I've never had anyone like you in my life."

He pulled her closer. "Do you know how many times you melt my heart?" His fingertips danced lightly against her side. "I swear you don't even know you're doing it."

She wiped more tears away and looked up at him. "But it's true."

"Do you know what else is true?"

She shook her head, and even though the moment was serious, and her feelings were not to be trivialized, his heart swelled beyond his control. "You are the most precious, adorable thing I have ever laid eyes on. More adorable than puppies."

Her eyes lit up. "Than puppies? No way."

He smiled and dropped his head against the back of the couch out of sheer exhaustion. "Puppies and kittens and fawns and penguins and baby giraffes…"

She smacked him on the chest. "Baby giraffes."

He picked his head up and focused on her again. "Have you ever seen a picture of a baby giraffe? Do you know how cute they are?" He shook his head. "It doesn't matter. You're cuter."

She laughed and settled against him again, drinking in the feeling of his warm body next to her and his arm at her side, pulling her close to him.

"Bunnies and ducklings and baby hedgehogs…" She smacked him again and he smiled. "Baby monkeys…"

"Baby monkeys are *not* cute," she protested.

He chuckled and gave her a squeeze. Within minutes, both of them were sound asleep.

***

It was hours later when he stirred to a warm feeling in his heart and Lizzy by his side. He squinted to see the time and rubbed his hand on Lizzy's arm until her eyes opened and she smiled.

"Hey," he said softly, smiling back. "Let's go to bed."

She nodded, and he led her down the hallway and into his bedroom, where they both slid into bed and he pulled her close.

Lizzy laid her head on his chest and listened to his heart beat. "This is amazing," she murmured.

She didn't need to explain what she meant. He thought it was pretty amazing too. He stroked her hair until they both drifted off to sleep again.

Chapter 27

Mila grinned as she walked past Colt's bedroom door. She knew they were sleeping on the couch when she got in last night, both of them so exhausted they didn't even move as she quietly closed the door and tiptoed down the hallway. Her brother looked so content, so peaceful, holding onto Lizzy even as he slept.

This morning she was making breakfast. She started out making bacon and eggs, but then decided to add blueberry pancakes to the mix. While the bacon was sizzling, Colt appeared in the kitchen.

"Good morning, sleepyhead," she all but sang to him. She smiled at him over her coffee mug. "Breakfast?"

He scratched his head. "I don't suppose you could eat this all by yourself. It looks like you've cooked enough for ten people." He poured himself a glass of juice.

"So tell me about Lizzy. I don't even know how this happened. One day you were in New York with Alaina, and the next, you're back here with her. What happened with Alaina?"

He looked to the ground. What happened between him and Alaina bothered him, and he was sure that it would for a long time. "It just…wasn't going to work out. But not for the reasons I thought."

"It was because of Lizzy."

He nodded, unable to stop the smile that appeared on his face at the mention of her name.

Mila stared at him. "I've never seen you like this before."

He took a sip of his juice. "I've never felt like this before."

Her eyes narrowed. That was an extremely forthcoming statement for Colt, and if she didn't already know this was something special by seeing them together, there was no mistaking the way he looked when he was around her and now the way he talked about her. It was the real thing, and she couldn't be happier for him.

"Good morning, everyone." Mila turned to see Lizzy standing at the end of the hallway and smiled at her. "Breakfast smells wonderful."

"Good," Mila said. "I hope you're hungry."

Lizzy smiled. "I am."

Colt patted the seat next to him, and she crossed the room and sat down. Mila smiled to herself as she tended to the bacon and eggs.

"Do you want anything to drink?" Colt asked. "Coffee? Grape juice?"

She shook her head. "Actually, a toothbrush would be fantastic."

"Sure," Colt said, and they disappeared down the hallway while Mila started getting plates ready.

***

After breakfast, Mila went to her mom and dad's to make more cookies. This time they weren't going to a bake sale but rather for the house, mostly for Hallie, who had requested her own cookie day. The four of them – Mary Beth, Mila, Peyton and Hallie had been in the kitchen for the past hour making a variety of favorites.

"You need more ovens in here," Mila said, looking around at all the cookie trays filled with raw ingredients around the kitchen.

"I've been trying to tell your dad that for years," her mother said. "Never got my double oven. What can I say?"

Mila smiled. "I guess we'll just have to make some drinks and wait it out."

It took several hours to get all the cookies done, and several stern warnings to get Hallie to stop eating all the chocolate chip cookies. It was difficult to be stern with a child who had gooey chocolate all over her face, though. When Mary Beth took her to get cleaned up, it was just Mila and Peyton at the table.

"Have you talked to your dad yet?" Mila asked. Hallie had taken the phone several times to tell her daddy hi when he called the house, but Peyton hadn't talked to him since the day he was hauled away.

She rolled her eyes. "He's been trying to call me. I just let it go to voicemail."

"You should talk to him."

"He ruined my life," Peyton said.

Mila took a sip of her drink, buying a moment to think. "He made a mistake. A really, really big mistake. And maybe even more than that. He quite possibly ruined *his* life," she said. "And I know it's had a great effect on your life, but Peyton, I wouldn't have changed our time together for anything. And you know what? If it hadn't been for that mistake your father made, you would probably still be with that slime ball Trevor." Mila leaned closer, conspiratorially. "And you never would have met Dylan," she said quietly. "What's going on with you and Dylan anyway?"

Peyton grinned, blushing slightly. "I don't know. We're hanging out."

"Now *that* kid's a good kid," Mila said. "Sometimes a doctor's kid can be a real brat, but that one…"

"I know, I know," Peyton said, allowing herself another smile.

Mila knew the words that were unspoken between them, that Peyton just assumed Dylan's affection toward her was only temporary and he would someday leave just like everyone else had…just like she herself was about to do.

"You know you can call me anytime in London," Mila said. "Day or night."

Peyton nodded. It was hard to miss the sadness in her eyes.

"And I'll be back sometime," she continued. "I won't let two years go by again before I come back. Hey, maybe I can come back in the summer when you're on vacation and we can do a girls' weekend together."

"Sure," Peyton said, and Mila saw that she wasn't buying it for a second. She must have sounded a lot like Peyton's mother, making promises that she never intended to keep. But Mila was different. She *would* keep her promises. Peyton would just have to see that in time.

***

It was late afternoon, approaching dinner time, when Mila left her mom and dad's house to go see Luke. She stepped out of the car, pulled her coat around her a little more closely and stole a glance at the barn. A smile crossed her lips as she remembered the night in the pent house.

She stepped onto his porch and knocked on the door. Momentarily, he was standing before her, the beautiful man that she knew she would be thinking about for weeks to come.

His hair was adorably out of place. He had exchanged the usual plaid for a dark blue zip-up with a white zipper. She looked him up and down, trying to freeze this image of him in her head so she could take it with her to London.

"Luke, I'm leaving tomorrow morning," she said. "And I wanted to spend my last night here with you."

He grinned. "I was hoping you'd stop by."

***

It was dark outside. They were in the loft of the barn, doors wide open, eating Chinese take-out by candlelight. And freezing, but she didn't care. A bottle of wine waited in the cool evening air.

She looked across their food at Luke. His nose was red from the cold, and somehow that made him even cuter than he was before they made this silly but wonderfully romantic decision to have dinner in the loft tonight.

"What?" he asked, smiling at her.

"You look cold," she said.

He rubbed his hands together. "I am cold. Aren't you cold?"

She nodded. "Freezing," she said quietly, and took another bite of her meal.

Luke set his plastic fork down and moved to her, pulling her into his arms. She put down her fork and leaned into him, feeling the warmth immediately that she had been longing for all evening. Being in his arms felt like a novelty every time. She didn't think it would ever lose its shine.

"Did you know that the word barn comes from the English term bere, meaning grain, and the English term aern, meaning

250

storage place? They literally combined the two words and came up with the word barn."

"No. Of course I didn't know that." He pulled her closer. "But for some reason I don't quite understand, I love that you know that."

She smiled, wishing things could be less complicated between them. If she knew he was ready to fall in love again, that he wouldn't push her away, it would be an easy decision. It wasn't just his proximity. What she felt for Luke greatly diminished her feelings for Gabe. There was really no comparison. If she thought it would work, she would choose Luke. She would choose her life in Tennessee.

"We need to look at our fortune cookies," she said with an excitement that made his heart smile.

He let go of her so she could crawl over to the take-out bag. She pulled out both cookies and held them up, frowning. "How do we know which one is for you and which one is for me?"

He smiled. "I think we'll know when we open them."

She moved closer. "Pick one."

He went to pull the one in her left hand, but she held onto it. "Are you sure this is the one you want?"

He nodded. "I'm sure."

She exhaled a breath. "OK." She let him take it.

"You open yours first." He sat forward, his legs pretzeled in front of him, eagerly waiting to see what her fortune would say.

Mila opened the wrapper and stole a glance at him before she broke open the cookie that held all the answers. The cookie cracked and she pulled out the fortune, reading, then rereading it, then making a face.

"What does it say?" Luke asked.

"Ugh." Mila read it one more time.

"What?"

"It says… *your shoes will make you happy today.* That's it. My shoes will make me happy. What kind of wisdom is that?"

"That's no kind of wisdom."

She looked down at her feet. "Although…I do have an unreasonable attachment to these particular shoes…."

Luke laughed and she looked at him, her eyes warm. "Open yours. It's *got* to be better than mine."

He cracked his cookie and set it on his plate, then pulled out the fortune from inside and read it out loud. "The time to be happy is right now."

She wrinkled her nose. "That's not a fortune, either." She sighed. "How are either one of those predictions of the future?"

"Maybe the point is that we make our own future."

Mila scowled. "The whole point of a fortune cookie is that it's supposed to tell you your fortune. It's not supposed to make vague statements about shoes and happiness. Ugh. I hate fortune cookies."

Luke had backed up to the bale of hay behind them again and Mila leaned up against him, snuggling once again into the warmth of his arms.

"I definitely think we got the right cookies," he said. "I've never owned a pair of shoes that I've gotten excited about. Maybe when you go back to London you'll find a perfect pair of shoes at the perfect price and while you're standing in line to buy them, you'll remember what your fortune said. It could happen."

She shook her head, not buying it for a second.

"And if my time to be happy is right now...I think that's a pretty good statement about the future. I'm ready for more happiness in my life."

She smiled at the thought. It was all she wanted for him. She was about to tell him that when he lowered his head and buried his nose in her neck. She shivered.

"You don't like that?"

"Your nose is freezing. Of course I don't like that."

He laughed, throwing his head back.

"Maybe we should open the wine." Mila poured them each a glass and handed Luke his. They moved to the open doors of the loft, each of them sitting against either side of the opening.

"I'll never forget these nights," she said, looking out into the stars. "When I'm feeling homesick in London, I'm going to close my eyes and remember these stars." She looked at him. "And you."

He smiled. Tonight was like magic to her. It was the best evening she could have asked for as her last day in Tennessee.

"Do you think we'll stay in touch after I go back?" she asked.

He looked at her. "Sure."

"I mean, I'll be thinking of you. I'll probably be worried about you."

"I don't want you to worry about me. I'm fine."

"Oh, and I'll want to know how things are going with Ava. As a matter of fact, I want you to send me pictures of you and her every time you're together. And you can tell me where you are and what you're doing."

He smiled. "OK."

"And if you're taking her shopping, just think of me as your shopping consultant. Like if you need to know what bag to get her with what coat."

"She just turned four," he said. "Her bag doesn't need to match her coat. She doesn't even need a bag. What's a four-year-old going to carry around in a bag?"

"Goldfish, maybe?" she said. "The point is that she'll get older. And she's going to want the bag that matches the coat. And the shoes. We can't have her going around in shoes that don't make her happy."

He laughed. "Right. I'll make sure she has shoes that make her happy."

She sat back and looked out into the night again. "Excellent," she said, taking another sip of her wine.

***

The hours of the night were ticking away. They had long since abandoned the barn and come inside to warm up by the fire. Mila was snuggled against him on the couch as they watched the final scenes of a romantic movie she had picked out. Modern romances were nothing compared to the old-fashioned movies Mila fell in love with a long time ago. But she knew it was a stretch to get him to watch a modern romantic comedy, and she wasn't going to push her luck.

Contemporary romance movies didn't have the same sense of charm as the old movies, but they still moved her to tears almost every time. In the story they had been watching for almost two hours, the female lead was finally confessing her feelings for the man she loved. Tears spilled down Mila's cheeks and she sniffed, pushing away from Luke to get a tissue from the box at the end table. He looked at her with an adoring grin as she wiped her eyes.

"You OK?" He knew that she was of course. The question was mostly just to acknowledge the state she had worked herself into over this movie.

"Why do guys never cry at romantic movies?"

He shrugged. "Because we're guys."

She gestured to the TV. "What she said was beautiful."

"Actually, what she said got boring." He looked at her. "No offense. This stuff was just written for women. If a guy had something to say, he could say it in three words or less."

She looked at him incredulously. "You can't cover everything she just said in three words or less."

"Sure you can. As a matter of fact, anything that a person has to say of great importance can be said in three words or less. *I love you. I need you. I'm sorry. It's over. I forgive you.*"

"It's not the same." She crumpled up her tissue and moved toward him again, and he raised his arm so she could snuggle back in as the credits to the movie started rolling. She looked up at him. "I want to…" She smiled.

"You want to what?"

"Hmm…wouldn't you like to know? But I can't finish my sentence because I already used up my three words."

He blinked slowly, a lazy smile curving into his lips. "Kiss me."

OK, maybe he had a point. She reached up and touched the back of his neck, pressing her lips against his. When she moved onto his lap, he wrapped his arms around her and stood, taking her to the bedroom. She would contemplate an argument to his point later. For now, it was forgotten along with everything else in the world outside of him and her.

Chapter 28

It was early in the morning when Mila's cell phone rang. She groped for her purse on the floor by the bed, pulling out her phone and whispering an apology to Luke.

"Hello?"

"Where are you?" Colt asked.

"I'm uh…"

"Yeah. I know where you are. When are you going to be here?"

She looked at the clock. It wasn't even seven o'clock yet. "Half an hour?" she squeaked.

"See you then." She ended the call and looked at Luke.

"I guess this is it."

He nodded. "Yeah. This is it."

She looked him up and down, regretting with everything inside of her how bad their timing was. She pulled the covers away and grabbed her clothes from the day before. "I'll just be a second." She didn't wait for a reply and slipped out of the room before he could see the tears welling up in her eyes. In the bathroom, she brushed her teeth one last time with the toothbrush he had kept there for her. She wanted to take the toothbrush. Wanted to take a part of him, a part of this, with her.

She chased those thoughts out of her head as she pulled on her clothes, but she couldn't escape the ominous feeling that lingered. She wanted to go back to the night of the wedding and relive it all over again. Every single second.

She knew she couldn't spend too much time trying to hide the tears. She didn't have much time left. She stepped back into the bedroom to see that Luke had pulled on a pair of jeans and a long sleeved tee shirt. She tried to take a moment to appreciate every aspect of him one last time.

"I'll just be out there," she said finally, picking up her purse to walk down the hallway and wait for him.

She sat down on the couch, the couch they had shared so many stories about the past and hopes about the future on. The couch where they ate the peach pies. The couch where he had touched her and kissed her so softly, made her feel like she was something rare and special.

He walked out and sat down next to her, turning to her. "I'll miss you." he said, looking her up and down. He smiled and looked into her eyes.

She was crying.

He pulled her into his arms, and for a moment, she felt safe, as if maybe everything was going to be OK.

A million things came to her mind, but she knew that if she started talking it would just end up in a formless pile of babble, so she just let him hold her and tried to stop the tears.

Eventually he released her. "You OK?" he asked, and she nodded.

"We'll be in touch," she said, but it was no consolation. Being in touch with Luke wasn't what she wanted. She wanted to be in love with him. She wanted to start a life together. And there was no way she could do that if she was in London.

He walked her to the front porch and stood beside her as she looked out over the farm land one last time. Then she turned to him. "I never thought I was too good for this place," she said. "I love this place. I just want you to know that."

He smiled. "I know."

"And also…" There were no words. So she just closed the gap between them and kissed him. So many emotions swirled through her body as she kissed him, elated and devastated at the

256

same time. She felt his hands on her face and wanted those hands to hold onto her forever.

He broke away, looking into her eyes. "Mila, I was wrong."

"Wrong about what?"

"I was wrong about all those things I said that night. When I told you that you and me, that we weren't a good enough reason for you to think about staying. Because right now I can't think of a better reason."

"What are you saying?" she breathed.

He reached out and touched her chin, tipping her face to his. "I'm saying that if you feel strongly enough about us.... I know it's too late to have this conversation. And I know you have to go back, but if you get back to London, and you realize you want to be here and not there, if you want to give us a chance, I want that, too."

She reached up and touched his face, staring into his eyes. "I don't know what to say," she whispered after a moment.

"You don't have to say anything. I just wanted you to know. Because what I said that night was wrong. It was all wrong."

She stared at him a moment longer and then stepped back. "Thank you," she said, and he nodded. She pointed over her shoulder. "I have to go. Colt's going to be waiting for me."

"Right." He let out a breath, his eyes downcast to try to shield her from the disappointment that he felt. He walked her to her car, then opened the door for her, and she hugged him one last time, memorizing the feel of his strong body against hers.

After a moment, she pulled back and got into the car, unable to bear the sadness of their goodbye any longer. She started the car and put down the window. "Take care of yourself, Luke."

He took a step back. "You, too. Safe travels."

She refused to say goodbye, so she just put on a fake smile and drove away. There would be plenty of time for crying when she got back to London.

***

The goodbye with her family was sad, but not nearly as dramatic. She had been in the truck with Colt for the past hour and a half, trying to find a way to feel the excitement she used to feel when she thought about London. It was where her home was now. Her life, the life she'd built over the past two years. But somewhere along the way, she had become disenchanted with it.

"You don't have to keep up the act," Colt said. "I know when you're not happy."

"I'll be fine," she said quickly. "I just need some time to adjust."

"Right," Colt said. "That's the same thing I kept trying to tell myself. But you know what finally made me happy? Listening to my heart. That's what you have to do, Mila."

She looked out the window. "I have to go back to London. My life is there. Everything is there."

"Not everything," Colt said, and Mila closed her eyes, then wiped away more tears. "Why are you crying?"

"It's just…it's an adjustment that's all." She looked at him, trying to pull herself together. "Listen, I need you to look after Peyton. Make sure she's OK. I know she acts like she doesn't like you, but she really needs you right now, Colt."

He nodded. "Sure."

"And make sure you spend some time with Luke." She wiped more tears from her cheeks. "I just want him to be happy again."

"Yeah," Colt said vaguely, and she knew he was stopping short of saying that he'd never seen him as happy as he was in the last couple of weeks when he was with her. Her heart broke all over again.

"Look, this isn't easy." She looked out the window. "But the right path isn't always the easy path."

"Agreed." He turned down the road that would lead them to the airport and wondered if she had any idea how difficult his break-up with Alaina had been. He guessed that she didn't. No one really did. All they saw was that he was happy with Lizzy now. But that didn't come without a price. He wished he could explain that to her in a way she would understand, but this was Mila he was thinking about here. She wasn't going to listen to a word he said.

"I can't not live my life," she continued. "I can't just exist to make everyone else's life better. I have to do what I was meant to do with my life."

"You do."

Her heart pounded when she saw the planes coming and going from the airport. It took her a moment to realize she was filled with dread. She closed her eyes again as Colt pulled into a parking space. It would just take time. That was all.

Colt looked across the seat at her. "Ready?"

She nodded. He got out of the truck and got her luggage out for her, then walked with her to check her bags. Once her bags were checked, she turned and hugged him.

"Thanks for the room and board," she said. "Thanks for the ride." She pulled away from him, starting to feel slightly more at ease with her decision to go back to London. "Good luck with Lizzy."

"Thanks. She said to tell you safe travels."

She smiled, remembering her short time with Lizzy fondly. "See you sometime this summer."

He nodded. "See you in the summer." He watched as she walked away, wondering how long it would take her to realize her life was here now.

***

If the flight to New York was bad, the flight to London was killer. Luckily she was able to sleep most of the way, both physically and mentally exhausted from the past few days in Tennessee. She would be happy to get back into the normal routine, away from all the drama.

Luke would be just fine. Perhaps their time together was all he needed to realize that his heart hadn't died along with Scarlett that day. That someday he could fall in love again. She sighed. She hoped it would be with the kind of woman he deserved.

Landing at the London City airport, with all the familiar surroundings of the place she now called home, made her feel a lot better. Grabbing her bags and walking out the door into the fresh air gave her hope. Hope that she would quickly return to her life in London and still be able to keep her family close in her heart.

She was so close to seeing Gabe again she could almost feel it. She smiled as she remembered the way it felt to be wrapped up in his arms, his kisses falling softly on her lips. Today, they would finally be able to pick up where they left off. It had been such a long time coming, something she had longed for on so many lonely nights. She was sure all her feelings for him would come flooding back as soon as she saw him.

She hailed a cab, and the cabbie helped her load her suitcases into the back.

"Where to, Love?"

"The 300 block of Portobello Road," she said, trying to find some kind of enthusiasm in her heart for her return to her old flat.

The cabbie nodded. "Welcome to London. Are you visiting or do you live here?"

"I moved here from America two years ago. I was just visiting my family."

He looked into his rearview mirror. "America. Always wanted to go there. What part of America were you in, Love?"

"In the southern part. Tennessee, to be exact."

"You're a long way from home. I admire that kind of courage. But if you don't mind me saying, you look awfully sad."

Her eyes met his in the mirror, and she said nothing.

"I'm sorry," he said. "Didn't mean to pry. It's just a beautiful young lady looking so sad, seems a shame."

"It's OK," she murmured, and looked down at her cell phone to a picture of her and Luke that she had snapped the night before, an attempt at showing him how to properly take the kind of picture she would be expecting from him and Ava.

She had seen sadness in his eyes last night, but in the picture, she only saw happiness. A happiness that he was just beginning to find again, and she was taking it away from him. A tear fell onto her lap and she wiped her cheeks dry.

"I think I fell in love over there," she murmured before she could stop herself.

"Fell in love?" the cabbie repeated. "No wonder you look so sad."

She looked up at him in the mirror again. "It will pass."

He smiled amicably. "Why in the world would you want love to pass you by?"

She looked out the window, watching the cars go by, the buildings, the familiar setting of these streets. She thought about Gabe and everything that was waiting for her at home. Her friends, her job...

"Stop the car," she demanded.

"Pardon me?"

"Take me back," she said. "I want to go back to the airport. I want to go home."

The cabbie grinned widely as Mila's eyes filled with tears again. "At your service." He pulled into a nearby parking lot and turned the car around.

***

Luke zipped up his jacket. He had just pulled up to Scarlett's tombstone on this bright, sunny morning. By now, Mila was probably back in London. He knew he had to let her go. They were a long shot anyway. He still wasn't in a good place. It just felt like everything was getting better after she showed up. In a matter of a few weeks, he had managed to convince Jay to let him see Ava again and taken steps toward repairing a relationship with one of his best friends. He wouldn't have done either of those things without her. He was sure she didn't believe that, but it was the truth.

He got out of the truck and walked to her plot. *Scarlett Rayne – Forever in our Hearts.*

"Hey, Scarlett," he said, feeling kind of foolish like he always did when he first started talking to her. "If you can hear me…"

He looked around. It struck him that he was the only person in the entire graveyard. But at the same time, it helped him relax. "Scarlett, did you know that if we would have ever gotten our acts together and made that trip to England or France or Italy, I was going to ask you to marry me? I always wondered if you knew that and you kept postponing the trip because you were afraid. Always wondered if there was a part of you that wanted to leave the door open so you could get back with Jay and be a family again."

He looked out across the broad expanse of tombstones, then back at hers again. "I guess things weren't perfect between us. But I loved you. There's a part of me that will always love you." He lowered his head reverently, then lifted it back up again. "I'm going to start seeing more of Ava pretty soon. I'm going to do the best I can with her. I mean, not just being around her and spending time with her, but also being the best person I can be. I want her to know that we loved each other. I want her to know that we were happy. And I want her to know that losing you was the worst thing that could have happened to me and to her, but it doesn't have to destroy the rest of our lives. I know you wouldn't have wanted it that way."

He paused, his eyes scanning over the dates on her tombstone. "That means I have to move on. I have to stop hanging on to this fear, or this anger, or whatever it is I'm hanging on to. I want something good again. Something like what we had." He smiled. "And I know what you're thinking, that this is about Mila. I guess in a lot of ways it is. She helped me see what life could be like if I move on." He lowered his eyes to the ground. "So I have to move on." He looked at her headstone again. "It just...it doesn't mean I didn't love you, Scarlett." He nodded, satisfied that he said everything he needed to say, stood by her tomb for a minute longer, and then got back into the truck.

Today the future looked dismal without Mila. But he still felt hope in his heart, and for the first time in a long time, he knew that his life was going to be different. It may take a while, but life was going to be good again.

***

Back at the house, Luke walked into his bedroom and picked up a picture of him and Scarlett, one she had framed and placed on the nightstand on her side of the bed. He moved it to his side after he lost her, stared at it all night long some nights. He was sure Mila had noticed it, but she never said anything about it. He held the silver frame in his hands, studying the smile that lit up her face one more time. It was nothing like the way she looked the last time he saw her, all swollen and bruised from the accident. The picture had been impossible to look at in the beginning, but today, he felt a sense of freedom as he looked into her face. There was a love that would always be there, captured right there in that photo, a love he would never forget.

But it was time to move on. He told her at the cemetery today, and he wanted to follow through with it. It was kind of scary putting himself out there for whatever the future would hold. As long as he remained closed off, nobody could hurt him. But he couldn't sustain that forever. Not if he wanted to live.

He put the picture in a box and placed it on the shelf in his closet. It would be there if he wanted to look at it, but the decision would be intentional. No longer would he fall asleep every night with a beautiful and cruel reminder of the time they had together.

He closed the closet door and the doorbell buzzed. He had no idea who it could be, but found himself hoping it wasn't Alicia or one of the girls from the bar.

He took a breath and put his hand on the doorknob, bracing himself for whomever it was on the other side. *Please be Colt*, he thought, almost frantically, closing his eyes as if it would make his wish come true and then swinging the door open.

He opened his eyes and his heart swelled. It wasn't Colt who stood before him on his front porch. It was either a vision or it was Mila, in her designer coat and boots, a bushel of peaches on her hip.

"What are you doing here?" He couldn't bring himself to think that she was forsaking her life in London so she could be here, with the rest of her family, and with him.

"I choose us."

He stared at her, waiting for her to say something more.

"That's all," she finally said. "The most important thing I could say to you, in three words or less."

He blinked, and when he opened his eyes again, she was still standing there with those damn peaches, and it was the most beautiful thing he had ever seen.

He pulled her into his arms, several peaches falling to the floor around them. "I can't believe you're here." His lips found hers, and if there was any doubt left in her heart, in that moment, she knew she had made the right decision.

She looked up at him and saw his eyes shining like she had never seen them shine before. "I love you, Mila."

Her heart stopped. "What?"

"I said I love you, Mila."

"I didn't think you were ready for that."

He blinked. "Do you know what makes you so special? Besides a million other things, I mean. The fact that you didn't know, but you came back anyway. You came back, even if in the end it wasn't going to work out. You left your life in London, and you came back."

She swallowed a lump in her throat and stepped back to set the basket of peaches on the porch floor, then stood to face him again.

"Whatever happens between us, I just want you to know it was worth it." He nodded, humbled by this beautiful woman and just a little too overwhelmed to speak. "And I love you, too."

He pulled her into his arms, holding onto her like he was never going to let go. It would be fine with her if he never did.

All of her things were in London. She had no job, no place to stay, no mode of transportation. But none of that mattered. Nothing in this world mattered more than love. The love of her friends, the love of her family, and the love of her life, who stood before her now.

The future, come what may, was theirs. She wouldn't want it any other way.

Like this book? Be sure to check out more books by Kelly Killian!

Love, Emily – A Love Story from the Files of Jessica Summer
Breaking up is never easy. But when your new ex-boyfriend is also your landlord who occupies the other side of the duplex you're living in, things can get out of hand pretty quickly. This is the situation Emily Bryant finds herself in quite suddenly after Matt, her boyfriend of three years, decides he's not really ready for a commitment like the one they have. From the files of Jessica Summer, an advice columnist who counsels people in matters of the heart, comes the story of a young woman who has a lot to learn about love, trust, relationships...and determining what things in life are worth holding onto.

Love, Rachel – A Love Story from the Files of Jessica Summer
Rachel White's love life was going just fine. She had been dating Ben, an ambitious, brilliant man that she once thought was out of her league, for more than two years now. Their future together was promising, and as far as she was concerned, he was the man her dreams. So when her high school sweetheart walks back into her life seven years after he dumped her, she wants nothing to do with him. And why should she? He was, after all, the man who broke her heart – and her trust – when he recklessly canceled his plans to go to college with her and instead opted to move to Colorado for no apparent reason. Keeping him at arms' length was her only option, and it worked...for a little while. But when Ben goes out of town indefinitely on business and Jason lands a job working at the same place as Rachel, it's not long before she becomes torn between the man she loves now and the man she once loved. From the files of Jessica Summer, an advice columnist who helps people in matters of the heart, comes the story of a young woman who has a lot to learn about love, honesty and forgiveness as she struggles to choose her path to happiness.

Love, Amber – A Christmas Love Story from the Files of Jessica Summer
Amber Scott's story of unrequited love just took a turn. Whether it's for the better or worse remains to be seen. But when Jake Reznik, the man she's had a crush on since puberty, begins to show an interest in her, she cautiously decides to take her chances. Against the advice of her cynical roommate, Erik; her well-meaning best friend, Candi; and her protective father, Amber puts her heart on the line for a man who is well known as a ladies' man by the entire population of the small town they live in. She is already uncertain of the future of their relationship when Jake's beautiful ex-fiancée comes to town and shows a renewed interest in working things out with Jake. Love, Amber, A Christmas love story set in the fictional town of Angel, Colorado, is sure to warm your heart and lift your holiday

spirit as you follow the adventures of a girl who still believes in Christmas miracles.

Love, Lauren – A Love Story from the Files of Jessica Summer
Lauren Kinsey wasn't looking to complicate her life. She already had more than enough going on from running her own event planning business to illegally housing a dog that would be cause for eviction if the landlord caught her. The last thing she was thinking about was adding tall, dark and mysterious Joe Costa into the mix. As their relationship unfolds, Lauren finds that he may just be the most complicated –and worthwhile—man she has ever tried to pursue.

ABOUT THE AUTHOR

Kelly Killian was born and raised in Johnstown, Pennsylvania, a town most historically noted for a devastating flood in 1889 and known by those who live there for the steel mill industry and the grounded, humble, friendly attitudes of their neighbors. Kelly is a graduate of Conemaugh Valley High School and Indiana University of Pennsylvania, where she earned a degree in Journalism with a concentration in  Public Relations. After graduation from college, Kelly's first professional job took her to Hollidaysburg, Pennsylvania, where she resided until 2014 when she moved to Nashville with her husband. Kelly currently resides in Mt. Juliet, a suburb of Nashville, with her husband, her dog and two cats.

Please share what you thought about "Tennessee Peaches" with the rest of Amazon's reading community. Post a review to have your opinion heard!

ACKNOWLEDGMENTS:

Erin Wilson, Keli Fisher, Bev Boock, Aurora Ressler, Virginia Fisher and Debi Tibbles – Thank you all for your valuable input. I could not have done this without you!

Brian Cherry – Thank you for your input and your never-ending support and encouragement. I could not have married a better man or found a better match for me than you!

Bert & Virginia Fisher, Jim & Carol Cherry, Dave & Melissa Meckley, Chris & Michelle Cherry – Thank you all for your support!

Cari Kollman – Thank you for expanding my fan base in several different parts of the country!

Diane Harris – Your words of praise and support in my writing endeavors mean so much to me. I appreciate the fact that you read all my books and support me like you do. Thank you so much.

Jana Selfridge – I can't thank you enough for encouraging your clients to read my books. I am forever grateful to you!

Conemaugh Valley High School – I want to thank you for your enthusiasm for this Conemaugh Valley graduate. I am proud to call myself a CV graduate and forever grateful that you've embraced me and my work the way you have. Thank you!

To every single person who has read my books and encouraged me along the way, from the bottom of my heart, thank you!